A YEAR

IN THE LIFE OF

LEAH BRAND

LUCINDA E CLARKE

A YEAR IN THE LIFE OF LEAH BRAND

Copyright © 2020 Lucinda E Clarke
ISBN 9788409205332
Copyright © 2019 Lucinda E Clarke
ISBN B07W3RRQX2
Umhlanga Press
All Rights Reserved

This book may not be reproduced, transmitted, or stored in whole or in part by any means, including graphic, electronic, or mechanical without the express written consent of the publisher except in the cases of brief quotations embodied in critical articles and reviews.

All characters, locations and events in this publication are fictitious and any resemblance to real persons living or dead is purely coincidental.

Cover art and design by Sharon Brownlie
https://aspirebookcovers.com/
Editors: Prof Richard Butler – Andrew Holloway

Compiled by: Rod Craig

Dedicated to the daughters I love
with all my heart

Also by Lucinda E Clarke

FICTION
The Amie series:-
Amie – an African Adventure
Amie Stolen Future
Amie Cut for Life
Amie Savage Safari
Samantha (Amie backstories)
Ben (Amie backstories)

Psychological Thriller series:
A Year in the Life of Leah Brand
A Year in the Life of Andrea Coe

MEMOIRS
Walking over Eggshells
Truth, Lies and Propaganda
More Truth, Lies and Propaganda
The very Worst riding School in the World

HUMOUR
Unhappily Ever After

CONTENTS

JANUARY

The nightmare began on the day the dog died.

It was New Year's Eve and, while Mason and I were out celebrating, my nemesis passed on to the big kennel in the sky. By the time we struggled out of the taxi, neither of us was in a fit state to notice the dog, dead or alive. Mason had to grab my arm as I caught my foot in the door jamb on the way out of the Uber. It was just as well the price of the fare would be billed automatically on the credit card; Mason was not sober enough to find the right notes to pay the driver.

We weaved our way up the path, arms linked, concentrating hard trying not to fall. It felt a long, long way to the front door. Mason propped me against the wall and then looked at me.

"Keys," he barked.

"I don't have them." Despite the pain above my left knee I couldn't stop myself from giggling. "Look in your pockets."

"I gave them to you." The fluorescent light from the lamp post on the street near the gate illuminated the scowl on Mason's face.

"No, you didn't," I replied, but to placate him I fumbled with the clasp on my dinky evening bag as if to check. The problem was I needed both hands to undo the clasp and I swayed from side to side desperately trying to keep my balance. I didn't remember drinking all that much, but I couldn't even stand straight and I knew before I peered into my purse it only contained a small wad of paper hankies and a lipstick.

"I don't have them," I repeated.

Mason glared at me and began digging into the pockets of his dinner suit. He cursed loudly.

"Hush, you'll wake the neighbours!" Apart from Andrea we didn't know any of them all that well, but I often got the uncomfortable feeling they did not approve of us. Well maybe that was a bit harsh, but I'd tried to get to know them and had little luck.

"To hell with the neighbours," Mason shouted louder. "Happy New Year," he screamed. "Stuffy lot, in bed already? Night to celebrate! It's a brand New Year."

I grabbed his arm, as much to steady myself as to quieten him down. The pains continued to shoot up and down the leg that was no longer there as I made a valiant attempt to stay upright. I had a moment of clarity. "The spare key, it's under the middle flowerpot, over there." I pointed to the row of them arranged next to the step under the lounge window.

Mason staggered back, bent down and put his hand out as his legs gave way and he promptly fell over. He looked so comical lying there. The well-respected owner and head of the biggest law firm in town sprawled on the grass. Then I really got a fit of the giggles and laughed until the tears ran down my face.

One look at Mason's face helped sober me up. He did not appreciate anyone making fun of him. He took his dignity and his professional standing in the community very seriously. He turned his attention back to the flowerpots, lifting each in turn until he found the key.

"Yes!" He slipped the ring over his finger and twirled it around and I watched in horror as it flew off and landed in the holly bush halfway down the path.

The holly bush fought back, tearing at Mason's hands as he fumbled among the leaves to retrieve it. There were several futile attempts to insert it in the lock after which we both tumbled into the hall. Next hurdle was to navigate the stairs, fling open the bedroom door and collapse on the bed.

It took me a while to orientate myself as the ceiling revolved above me. Good heavens, how much wine had I drunk? I manoeuvred my way towards our bathroom by clinging onto the furniture. I tore off my black evening gown and my prosthesis, and hopped into the shower. I leaned against the wall and let the steaming water pour over me before I realised I was still wearing my bra and panties. But I was past caring. I think, if I remember correctly, I was beginning to sober up and questioning why I was this far out of it after less than half a bottle of wine. I don't drink all that often; I'd got out of the habit while taking the cocktail of drugs they poured into me after the accident. Everyone knows medicine and alcohol can be lethal. Now, I was down to a few daily tablets but I'd not taken any for a couple of days beforehand. I knew there would be plenty of booze at the party but maybe even the modest amount I had was enough to make me really drunk.

I clutched the shower door, grabbed a towel, sat on the loo and rubbed myself hard all over. My head was pounding but the biggest pain was in my leg, the one that wasn't there. How could my brain be so stupid? Consciously I knew the surgeons who saved my life had no option but to remove a limb crushed beyond repair. Five years later some of those complicated synapses told me it was still there and throbbing. I should take some of my pills but they were downstairs and I would never make it in my condition. I hopped back into the bedroom where Mason was comatose, spread corner to corner across the bed, arms akimbo, his dinner jacket crumpled and stained and his shoes covered in mud. He was out for the count.

I sighed. I knew that nothing short of a nuclear explosion would wake him, so I sank onto the bed, removed his shoes and rolled him over to his side. I pulled out my nightie from under the pillow and slipped it over my head, crawled under the duvet and, despite the pain, I remembered no more.

Loud, piercing shrieks coming from downstairs woke me. I flung myself out of bed, and tumbled onto the floor. In moments of stress I still forgot I can't walk. Swearing under my breath I rubbed my eyes and grabbed my false leg. Strapping it on, I dragged on my dressing gown and opened the bedroom door. It was no use trying to wake Mason; he was still dead to the world and not even the cries from below would wake him. I hurried down the stairs as quickly as I could. I knew who was screaming but

I didn't know why.

Belinda was standing in the kitchen, still shrieking, when I shuffled in.

"What's the problem? Stop it. Calm down." A quick glance showed everything looked normal. The back door was still closed, the window panes intact, the counter tops as clean and tidy as I'd left them before going out last night. Everything in place, if you ignored the spilled cereal all over the floor where Belinda had dropped the corn flakes. They crunched under my feet as I went to hold her but she stepped quickly out of reach and backed up against the pantry door. She looked petrified.

"Look. Look. He's dead, isn't he?"

I shuffled forward, rubbing the sleep out of my eyes. My head felt fuzzy, the little hammers still banging away inside, and Belinda's intermittent shrieks were going straight through me. There was a strange smell wafting into the kitchen. I followed Belinda's finger which pointed through to the breakfast room.

There on the carpet lay the dog.

Mason's dog.

The love of his life.

It was stone dead.

An enormous sense of relief washed over me. At last, after two years of slobbering, sniffling, piddling and dropping hairs all over the furniture I had so carefully and lovingly acquired for the first house I'd ever furnished brand new, he was gone. I had to work hard to stop the smile from spreading across my face.

There had never been any love lost between us. Zeus

had sized me up very quickly on my arrival. Now don't get me wrong, I love dogs, and cats and all animals, I really do, but there is always the exception. Despite Mason insisting that Zeus had a pedigree as long as his arm – a pedigree incidentally I had never seen – I could not tell you what breed he was supposed to be. My husband had insisted he'd paid a shedload of money for the puppy which developed into what appeared to be a cross between a mastiff, a bull terrier, a Rhodesian Ridgeback and one of those dogs that have been banned in the UK – what were they? Yes, pit bulls. Zeus would not remember his parents, but I doubt they had any pedigree status at all. My husband the lawyer would need to own a very expensive and rare breed as befitted his status. I remember Mason getting quite het up when I questioned his choice of dog, asking him to tell me precisely what breed it was. He became very aggressive and I backed off and did my very best to get on with the animal. After all, it was his house, he'd been there long before I'd arrived and wasn't there some saying about not coming between a man and his dog?

I looked over to my arch enemy. He'd attempted to take a chunk out of me on more than one occasion, something Mason had refused to believe, even when I pointed out the teeth marks on my false leg. This morning, or probably last night, he'd left me his final present. His bowels had relaxed in death and he lay there in his own excrement, front paws dug into the sofa cushion, his rear end on the carpet. Had he suffered a fatal heart attack? Do animals have heart attacks? I wondered.

"Yeuk. Get rid of it. Now. I can't bear to look. It's

disgusting. Leah, take it away!"

"It's only a dead dog," I said. "We all die eventually." I stood and stared almost mesmerised by the sight of the carcass, mentally weighing up whether I had any large black dustbin bags left in the drawer. I think I'd run out.

"I think your father should see to it… him," I added hastily. "He was after all a member of the family."

"My family, not yours," Belinda snapped back at me. She had slid behind the island in the kitchen with her back to the scene in the breakfast room and was busy with the coffee machine. Out of the corner of my eye I noticed she only took one mug out of the cupboard. Well I guess it would be too much to expect her to make a drink for me as well.

When I'd first been introduced to Mason, he'd talked a lot about Belinda. We would get on like a house on fire. She was such a sweet girl, kind, helpful, friendly and outgoing. As far as I was concerned the only outgoing thing about her was her wish that I was outgoing – out of the front door and out of her life.

I had tried, really tried. I explained I had no intentions of taking the place of her mother, who'd run off to Brazil with a man barely old enough to date her fifteen-year-old daughter.

The children from my previous marriage have gone. I lost the husband I adored and my two angels who were fast asleep in the back of the car on that fateful night. I could only pray they never woke before death took them. I have no desire to replace them. Nothing ever could.

On our first date, Mason had grilled me about children. "Did I want any?" Before I had a chance to answer he informed me he'd had a vasectomy so there was no possibility of my getting pregnant any time in the future. So, if I had hopes of becoming a mother…"

"No." I'd hastily assured him at the time.

I don't think he even bothered to listen to my response. He was already the father of two beautiful children; Leo, who was twenty-two and over in Australia, and thirteen-year-old Belinda who still lived at home.

I was fast approaching forty. I only had one leg, and the prospect of pregnancy was not something I would find easy, nor did I want another child. It had taken me a long time to learn how to use my artificial limb and, even several years later, I was not totally comfortable on the dance floor, or on the beach. I felt ninety as I carefully navigated stairs and escalators.

The hospital staff were kind and thoughtful, but I must have been one of their worst patients ever. I was angry at myself, at the drivers of both cars, and the cruel act which had destroyed my cosy, happy world.

At first I'd hidden away, lost in a sea of self-pity. I snarled at the re-run broadcasts of the Paralympics and the bright young athletes who refused to let a missing limb or two get them down. I had never been athletic or shown any aptitude for sport, or, in fact, any outstanding ability in anything particular.

There were too many bad memories for me up north, so I sold up the family home which was mortgaged to the hilt, and fled south. I found myself a flat to rent on the outskirts of London and reverted to my maiden name. It was only an alarming and diminishing bank balance that forced me back out into the workplace.

It wasn't easy finding employment if you were not disabled; it was even harder if you were. I couldn't move quickly, walk too far, or drive long distances.

Many of the HR officers were sympathetic but I could see from the look in their eyes they were worried about employing anyone who might be in a position to sue them as the result of an accident or similar. I began to see why the government had introduced a quota system for taking on all ethnicities and disabilities. Few firms seemed willing to do it without legislation.

While I was still wallowing in my sea of despair I ran into Mason, or rather he ran into me in, of all places, the local supermarket. He'd come racing down the aisle, using the shopping cart like a battering ram, desperate to get to the front of the queue. He misjudged the distance and sent me flying.

Mason could not have been more caring as he abandoned the trolley and came to help me up, horrified at what he'd done. He insisted on paying for my groceries and demanded that I allow him to take me home.

I protested loud and long, but he ignored me and swept me off to his Lexus, even going so far as to gently lift me into the front passenger seat. He was tall, handsome, divorced, amusing and self-confident. It was impossible to find fault with him.

Life moved into the fast lane. Dinner dates, trips to the theatre, walks in the park, a weekend away in a luxury hotel where he actually booked two rooms and slept in one of them.

I was bowled over. I admired his lovely house and briefly met his daughter who simply nodded before disappearing into her bedroom. Mason assured me I could decorate the place to my taste as he had never bothered since his wife had moved out. He even went so far as to show me his divorce papers just in case I worried he was not a free agent.

After so many months of depression it seemed the gods were at last smiling on me. Mason ran his own law firm, was a respected member of the community, a member of the Chamber of Commerce and the local Round Table. What more could an unemployed, disabled widow with an almost empty bank account ask for?

A small, quiet wedding in the local registry office, two glorious weeks on the French Riviera, and life was heaven.

That was over two years ago and life wasn't heaven all the time. Zeus had dented my euphoria and I'd got no closer to Belinda despite my best efforts. But today, at least one of my problems had departed.

'Goodbye Zeus,' I chortled under my breath. 'Hope you find lots of things to bite to your heart's content in doggy heaven.'

I walked over to peer closely at the hair-shedding beast and reached out a hand to make sure the creature was stiff. It would be a terrible disappointment if Zeus suddenly woke up and lunged forward to take another chunk out of me.

"Eeew, don't touch it!" shrieked Belinda from the

other side of the kitchen island.

"Well someone has to. We can't let him lie there and rot, can we?"

"I'll get Daddy," she announced and, before I could stop her, she'd bounded up the stairs and I heard her race into our bedroom.

That was another problem I had with my stepdaughter. There were no locks on any of the doors, besides her room and the bathrooms, and she saw no reason to knock on our bedroom door at any time. I'd spoken to Mason about it and he told me not to be so paranoid, but I found it very difficult to relax at intimate times. It didn't appear to worry him, and I cringed whenever he cried out in passion.

There was a howl from upstairs, and Mason barrelled into the breakfast room. His hair was mussed, his suit creased and his shirt tails hung out, but I barely noticed that as I watched in amazement at his undiluted display of grief.

It was a dog, for heaven's sake, and yes he loved him, and he was part of the family, and I would expect a few tears and even a gentle sobbing. But Mason was in full wailing mode, louder than an African funeral. He shrieked, and howled and cried and made such a noise that I walked back into the kitchen.

I caught Belinda's eyes which she rolled to heaven and then shrugged her shoulders before turning back to the coffee machine.

Had we finally bonded?

I decided to ignore Mason in his grief and cooked bacon and eggs for breakfast after gulping down a couple of strong painkillers. The cacophony from the breakfast room was not helping my headache one bit.

Belinda grabbed three slices of bacon out of the pan before I had a chance to plate it and disappeared upstairs into her room, slamming the door. I can't say I blamed her; I would have been embarrassed to see my father behave like that, especially in front of my stepmother – if I ever had one.

I finished my breakfast and decided to go upstairs. There was nothing I could say or do that would ease Mason's pain, and quite frankly I didn't even want to try.

I was up in the bedroom tidying away the mess from last night when I heard the kitchen drawers slamming one after the other.

"Where are the bloody bin bags?" Mason hollered up the stairs.

I walked out and looked over the bannister.

"We're out of them, they're on the shopping list for tomorrow." My heart sank. I knew exactly what he was going to say and he didn't disappoint.

"I might have known," he sneered. "How many times have I told you to stock up as soon as anything runs low, but you never listen, do you?"

I've heard this all before. It used to upset me, but now I try and ignore it. It always hurts and there are days when I can understand why Caro left him and ran off with that youngster.

Then I rationalised and thought of the alternative. I didn't want to be on my own again, and I could put up with his moods. I refused to let his moaning and complaining get to me and I tried to ignore it. It didn't do much for my self-esteem, but then I had Andrea, my best friend, and she helped keep me on the level.

I tidied up the bed, got dressed and decided to leave Mason to his grief. Nothing I could say or do would help right now. I hoped that Andrea was in, she usually was on a public holiday. Not that she worked, she was a woman of independent means, courtesy of a huge life insurance policy from her late husband.

Strange really, he was only a minor clerk at the local council, not the kind of high-flyer to have insurance amounting to a couple of million pounds. Maybe the company never expected to pay out. That was before that spectacular plane crash over the Pyrenees where no one had survived.

Andrea had never fully explained why he was on the plane at all. If it wasn't for business then why was he taking a holiday by himself? I did ask a few tentative questions but she obviously didn't want to talk about it. Bless her, she was always more interested in what I was doing.

I crept down the stairs as quietly as I could, remembering to take my mobile and house keys, and gently closed the front door behind me.

Andrea lived next door but one. The house between us had been for sale ever since I moved in and not once had I seen an estate agent bring anyone round.

Every house in our cul-de-sac was different. They were all large and well appointed. It was a far cry from the new-build, modern estate where I was brought up; rows and rows of identical boxes only distinguishable by the numbers on the walls and the colour of the paintwork.

As I turned out of our driveway and walked past the overgrown, neglected property that divides us, I felt a shudder run down my back. Irrational I know but I had the feeling that unseen, malevolent eyes were watching me. I hurried on past and turned into Andrea's immaculate property. Gardeners tended the perfect lawns and flower beds twice a week and there was not a leaf or a blade of grass out of place. Before I even reached the front door, it was flung wide open and Andrea greeted me with open arms.

"You look as if you've seen a ghost!" she cried as she crushed me against her pink, cashmere sweater which went so nicely with her tailored grey trousers and matching pink ballet shoes. Not once had I ever seen Andrea in a dressing gown, or old, baggy clothes. She was always immaculate and I don't know how she did it. She put me to shame.

I hugged her back and I found myself giggling again.

"I'm not the ghost, but Zeus is."

My friend's eyes sparkled. "Then this calls for a celebration. A New Year and a new start without the vicious hound. Champagne?"

"No." I put my hand out to grab her arm. "I had far too much to drink last night. I'm swearing off alcohol for life."

Andrea laughed. "We'll see about that! But I'll go gentle on you today. A coffee it is then."

She made for the kitchen, all steel and glass and, like everything else, immaculate. I often wished I could be as organised as Andrea; she just had that knack.

I wriggled onto a bar stool at her central kitchen unit

and watched as she put a pod into the coffee machine. At my place we used coffee mugs. Andrea offered large bone china, gold-rimmed cups and real silver teaspoons.

Looking back now, despite her wealth and class, I never felt as if Andrea looked down at me. We were friends, mates even and we agreed on nearly everything. In fact, I could tell her anything, and I did, and trusted her to keep it to herself. She was always there for me. I only hoped I was as good to her. Never before had I felt so close to another girlfriend, and to think we had only met two years earlier. The moment we smiled, both reaching for the same historical fiction book off the just-returned trolley in the library, we'd clicked.

As we sat and sipped our coffee, I told her about the night before. Andrea was eager to hear all the details. She'd spent the evening alone, watching Big Ben strike midnight on the television before taking herself to bed. That didn't seem to bother her though. She was bright and optimistic about the new year ahead.

"So tell me," she said spooning sugar into her coffee and pushing the milk jug towards me, "how has he taken it? Upset?"

"Upset isn't the word for it. Totally distraught. I couldn't stand it a moment longer. I'm so glad you were in. I couldn't escape fast enough. He was weeping and wailing loud enough to be heard in the centre of town."

"Bloody hell. I knew he was fond of the dog but… he was really that upset?"

"Yes, believe me. Horrendous performance. You'd think he was auditioning for some soap on the television!"

We both began to giggle. "And, to top it all," I continued, "I've run out of black plastic bin bags. He was furious about that too."

"Oh, you wicked, wicked woman!" Tears ran down Andrea's face as she rocked on her stool. "Priceless. I wish I could have seen that."

"Oh no you don't; it was not a pretty sight. He'll be in a bad mood for days."

We both stopped laughing. Andrea knew me well enough to understand that it was time for the silent treatment. Mason would refuse to talk to me, though he always managed to keep an even keel with Belinda.

At the beginning I would try everything in the book to help him snap out of a mood when things went wrong for him. A hug, which he shook off. Commiseration which he ignored. Teasing which caused him to blow up and shout at me or walk out, slamming the door. Two years had taught me to keep my distance, preferably take refuge like today with Andrea, and wait until it all blew over. I wasn't too hopeful that the death of his beloved dog would blow over too quickly.

"I wonder," I mused, "if I went to the dog pound and found another dog?"

"Oh no, you mustn't do that!" Andrea was shocked. "It would be far too soon."

"Yeah, you're probably right, but in a couple of weeks maybe, a month?"

Andrea shook her head. "No, that's the last thing, the very last thing. And you wouldn't choose a dog like Zeus, would you?"

"Hell no. I'd adopt a cute fluffy little mutt, one that

will sit on my lap in the evenings."

Andrea shook her head again. "Not Mason's type of dog at all."

I sighed. One Zeus was bad enough, I'd be crazy to introduce another into the family.

I stayed at Andrea's until way past lunch time. We chatted about this and that, she showed me the fabrics and paint colours for the new en-suite upstairs, and we made plans to go shopping that week.

As I walked back home, I wondered why Andrea stayed in such a large house all by herself. I'd broached the subject once, but she mumbled something about not liking to move. She was a creature of habit and liked the space.

It wasn't as if she had any children to come and stay and use that new en-suite bathroom, and I couldn't understand why she was spending so much time and energy, not to mention money, on it. Ah well, if she wanted to tell me she would. There were times though when I noticed we chatted mostly about me and what I had been up to. If I mentioned this Andrea only laughed and said my life was far more interesting.

I didn't agree. I'd been on my own for almost four years before Mason bumped into me and, on the one or two dates I'd tried previously, I found I had nothing at all to talk about.

I was right about Mason's mood following Zeus's departure. He barely even spoke to Belinda who made herself scarce at every possible opportunity. He blundered around the house slamming doors, kicking furniture and was thoroughly unpleasant.

I'd had the sense to borrow a roll of bin bags from Andrea which I was going to use as an excuse for leaving him to his grief. But he'd found some green garden refuse bags in the shed, which were larger and, by the time I'd returned, the dog was wrapped in plastic and Mason was digging a hole at the end of the garden. I didn't feel too comfortable at the thought of a carcass rotting away next to the compost heap. I would have taken Zeus to the local vet and asked for him to be incinerated. I don't like burials, even for humans.

Still I knew better than to say anything. It was left to me to remove Zeus' final offering and give the carpet and the sofa a thorough scrub.

Life settled back to normal. I've never been a natural housewife. Some women are born to it, aren't they? I do it because I have to, not because I want to. I knew that Mason liked a clean, tidy house, and a full meal in the evening and I did my best.

My first husband was easy going and never noticed inch-thick dust on the top shelves or an overflowing laundry basket. I spent most of the day playing with the children, believing that was more important than a spotless house and a regimented life. Looking back on those days I was so happy then. We had our worries; money was always tight, we never took holidays, and I haunted the charity shops for clothes. Christmas was low key, a couple of presents each at most, and Santa's offerings were very practical. Yet we were happy.

We met when I was nursing. James had left school the moment the law allowed, fed up with sitting studying subjects he could see no use for. He took a string of jobs, none of which paid much and were all dead-end.

Then he was mugged in the street by a gang of thugs, knifed, and left bleeding on the pavement. They rushed him to hospital, the first time he'd ever attended one, and that's what changed his life.

I was the nurse on his ward.

I'll never forget the first words he said to me. "I'm wasting my life. I'm going to be a doctor."

"Ah, right. Takes years you know. What do you do now?" I whipped the empty bag off his drip stand and replaced it with a full one.

"This and that. But I mean it, whatever it takes."

James was true to his word. We dated from then on, he studied online to get his A levels and, on his second attempt, was accepted to train as a doctor. We put off having children; it could wait until he was qualified and, in the meantime, my salary would supplement his student loan. I worked extra shifts to put food on the table and pay the rent.

It was a long, hard, nine years until James was a fully qualified hospital doctor. He talked about specialising, but the inevitable happened – I became pregnant. It was not planned, just one of those things, a bout of sickness and vomiting and the first little bundle was on the way.

In one respect I was glad, I'd already turned thirty and my biological clock was ticking.

Brandon was a healthy, cheerful baby and a year later

Henrietta was sharing the nursery. Maybe it was a fluke, but neither gave us any problems. They reminded me of the children in that rather creepy film where the little people were almost perfect. No colic, minimal fuss teething, sharing toys, even the temper tantrums were low key. We couldn't believe our luck.

Despite the chaos in the house, we planned out our lives with thought and care. I'd be a stay-at-home mum until Henrietta was in school full-time, and then go back to nursing. Maybe then James might look at specialising; he was very keen on paediatrics. We had paid back part of his student loan and clambered onto the lowest rung of the property ladder, mortgaged up to the hilt, but it was ours.

All that was before the accident.

I was in hospital for months.

They told me later I was in an induced coma. It took further weeks of rehabilitation, during which time the household bills mounted. Life went on as normal outside the hospital for everyone else. But not for me. Never again.

It was difficult not to sink into depression. I went to stay with my mother for a short while but that did not work out well. From the day my father had his last and final heart attack she had been going downhill, even though she was only in her mid-sixties. She was querulous and demanding, often forgetting she'd asked for chicken for supper and then complaining when I cooked it for her.

Her dependence on me was too much. I needed to have someone care for me. I was still struggling to cope with the prosthesis which I hated and I was not pleased when my sister and brother, one in Australia and the other in Canada, Skyped and said they were so glad I was there to look after Mother. It was such a relief they didn't have to worry about her.

Yes, I could guess it salved their conscience but they didn't have to put up with it twenty-four seven.

Then my mother became quite violent towards me. The information I got from the Internet assured me it was nothing personal and all part of the onset of early dementia.

In the end, it got so bad it was impossible for me to live there. Even the sight of me was enough to evoke rage and viciousness. I have no idea what I had done to cause such anger, but I expect it's because she didn't see anyone else except the neighbours popping in from time to time.

At last everyone suggested it would only make things worse if I stayed. It broke my heart to be the brunt of my mother's fury and I didn't know whether to blame myself or believe she would have reacted in a similar way towards my siblings.

I packed my bags and left. The wonderful neighbours assured me they would keep an eye on her and let me know if they thought she couldn't cope.

I felt bad leaving her, but it was mixed with a lot of relief. Where to now?

That's when I decided on a fresh start at the other end of the country. I had a little spare cash to last a few months and then I would have to find a job.

Could I return to nursing? Not in the immediate future. I couldn't be put in charge of patients when I was still taking so many drugs. I was also nervous about losing my balance, or causing them further harm when I was supposed to be helping them heal. I needed more time. My mother's behaviour had eroded my confidence more than I cared to admit.

FEBRUARY

Life went on as before. I couldn't believe that the house seemed so empty without my nemesis Zeus. With Belinda at school all day and Mason out after breakfast and not returning until mid-evening, time hung heavy on my hands. In an effort to make a new start I began in the guest bedroom and worked my way through the house, room by room, scrubbing, polishing and scouring.

Andrea told me I was insane. "If you want to have the house perfectly clean, why not hire a professional company and save yourself all that angst and hard work?" She'd grabbed my hands and turned them over. "Look how rough your skin is and your cuticles are peeling. You need to look after yourself."

Her kindness almost reduced me to tears. Was she the only person in the world who cared about me? There I went again, feeling sorry for myself. I had a roof over my head, plenty to eat, clothes to wear and not a care in the world; so why was I so depressed?

A small voice niggled, telling me it was because no one loved me; but whose fault was that? And it wasn't true. Mason loved me, he told me that in his own way. Deep down he appreciated me, he just wasn't the slobbery kind. What was wrong with me?

Andrea was always cheerful, nothing got her down. She had no siblings that I knew about, no husband or boyfriend and she had never mentioned any children. She was truly alone, so if she could remain happy and content then so could I. I would model my behaviour on her and use her as an example of being grateful.

The rest of February passed with only one incident.

Against my better judgement I visited the local animal shelter and chose the cutest little dog. They assured me it was two years old and fully house-trained, but timid due to mistreatment in early puppyhood. I looked at his little button nose, the large liquid eyes and I was sold. I'd gone to find a dog similar to Zeus, and even took a photograph with me. The kennel maids stared at it and were no wiser guessing his possible pedigree.

As it happened there were very few large or Zeus-like dogs in there but I thought as a dog lover Mason would get attached to this one too.

I felt nervous as I trundled the carrier into the house. It got a reaction from Belinda at least. She was in the kitchen raiding the fridge. I said nothing as she grabbed two of the sausages I had earmarked for tonight's toad-in-the-hole.

"What's that? I hope it's not a cat. Dad hates cats," she smirked.

"No, it's a dog."

"What! You must be out of your tree. He'll fucking freak. I'd get rid of it before he sees it."

I opened the wire door and swept the bundle of brown fur into my arms.

"I love him. How could anyone not love him?" I smiled as a large pink tongue washed my face.

"Oh yeuk. Do you know how unhygienic that is? He's been sniffing all kinds of dirt and gross stuff and then you let him spread it all over your face. You could get all kinds of diseases…" She paused, perhaps reasoning that might not be such a bad idea. She turned, swept upstairs and slammed her bedroom door. Loud thumps reverberating from overhead signalled her kind of music, it wasn't mine and I prayed she wouldn't play it for too long.

Mason's reaction to the dog was much worse than I feared. He took one look at the cute mutt and shouted "OUT!!" He didn't wait for me to tell him I'd got the dog for me and I wanted to keep it. I needed something to love me in return. But I never got the chance.

Mason stormed round the kitchen, opened the fridge, took yet another sausage and drank from the juice bottle. He knows I hate that.

"When I get home tomorrow, I want that creature gone. Get it? Nothing on this planet could ever replace Zeus and I wouldn't even try." That said he went into the lounge and settled himself in front of the television and watched the news at full volume.

I felt miserable the next day as I returned to the shelter. I told them the truth, what else could I say? It was hard to hold back the tears as one of the maids tucked my furry bundle under one arm and disappeared towards the pens. In the few short hours I'd had him, he'd already wormed his way into my affections. As I watched him taken away his ears drooped and his tail stopped wagging. I had probably destroyed his faith in human nature for ever.

I climbed back into the car and sat and cried. What was happening to me? Why had a perfect life turned sour in the last few months? Mason was even more tetchy, Belinda more distant, my mother ignored all my letters and, to top all that, my sister's planned visit from Australia had been postponed. It seemed I had nothing to look forward to. Perhaps I should push harder and get a job, despite Mason wanting me to stay at home. I'd go back to nursing. I needed to do something if I wasn't going to go mad.

The weather turned really cold and Mason grumbled at the size of the electricity and the gas bills at the end of the month. I immediately felt guilty. I was the only one in the house all day and I turned the heating up. I feel the cold – I always have and the house is large and partly open-plan and expensive to keep warm.

The only other thing of note was Belinda's behaviour. She became more distant than ever. She never replied to a question or statement from me. She was better behaved with her father, at least she was polite to him. When I asked her what was wrong, was it something I said or did, she rolled her eyes and left the room. In the end I gave up. I hoped she would come around in her own good time.

I just couldn't imagine my little angels ever behaving like that, but maybe if they'd lived to be teenagers they'd have gone through the same phases.

I had nightmares about taking that little dog back. Several times I woke and my cheeks were wet. I must have been crying in my sleep. Twice I put on my coat to return to the animal shelter and rescue him before common sense kicked in. I didn't trust Mason to be kind to it – I hadn't given it a name and now I was glad. If my husband was in one of his moods, I wouldn't put it past him to kick it or be cruel to it – even Zeus got whacked a couple of times for misbehaving and Mason was besotted with him. I told myself he would find a new home where every member of the family loved him. Truth was, I'd done him a favour.

February has always been my least favourite month of the year. The clouds stretch from one side of the sky to the other. An unbroken blanket of grey hanging over my head.

I didn't realise until I was in my mid-twenties there really is a syndrome for people like me who suffer when the sun doesn't shine. The acronym is SAD but don't ask me what that stands for. I just know that it's the most dismal time of year when the trees are still leafless, the bulbs hidden, the wind whistles, and I need layers and layers of clothes to feel comfortable, even in the house.

I probably do more cleaning at this time. Sweeping, vacuuming, dusting and polishing helps keep me warm. I would much rather curl up under a blanket, hot coffee to hand, reading on my Kindle, but I knew how Mason would react if he caught me doing that.

Maybe the new dog incident began the change, but I was starting to feel rebellious. I was getting tired of worrying about what Mason would complain about next. Wasn't it about time I stood up for myself? Fought back, at least verbally? Was I being honest about this relationship? For over two years I'd seen it as a refuge from poverty, a sanctuary from a life struggling and alone. Could I return to that? Would I be happier?

Strange when you encounter a topic, it seems to come up again and again. Have you noticed that?

They were interviewing an author on the radio whose self-help book was all about weighing up your choices on relationships. He said that life was too short to waste a moment being trapped in a situation that made you unhappy. We all have two options. Change the relationship from inside, or walk away.

I paused, duster in one hand, polish in the other, dropped both and dived for a pen and paper. I sat waiting to write down the name of the book. This would be my starting point.

I booted up my laptop and was about to click the 'buy now' button when I paused. Even though it was my personal computer, Mason would often pick it up without asking and peruse my emails and the book lists in my Amazon account.

So, not a good idea if he saw I was buying a book on behavioural manipulation. I was hoping this was my gateway to becoming more assertive and, at the same time, defusing Mason.

The library? No. By now there would probably be a waiting list for it a mile long and a paperback would be hard to hide. I paced up and down the lounge mulling over the problem.

Get a grip Leah. You're being paranoid. Buy the bloody book and be done with it. If Mason gets nosy, you'll just have to think of some reason why you're reading it. Maybe it has tips on how to get on with teenage stepdaughters from hell? Perfect. That will be the reason

I'm getting it. He can't argue about that.

I pressed the 'buy now' button and breathlessly waited for it to download. Today would be the beginning of a whole new life.

Chapter One: *How to be Assertive without Confrontation.*

Oh yes, this was exactly what I needed. I began to read and it was only the banging of the front door that snapped me back into my real world. Belinda was home from school. I looked at my watch. She was late. Dare I ask her where she'd been until 5.30pm? Why not?

I followed her into the kitchen. "Hi there," I said brightly, reminding myself that tone of voice was as important as words – according to A J Cromptom, my new hero.

Belinda's reply was to turn her back on me and grunt.

I persevered. "Did you have hockey practice, or a rehearsal or something?"

She spun round and glared at me. "Are you checking up on me? Why so nosy? You're not my mother you know. You can't tell me what to do, so there!"

She yanked open the fridge and grabbed one of the avocados.

I took a deep breath. "No Belinda, I need those as starters for tonight's meal. Choose something else for now please." I smiled. There, I was being assertive and non-confrontational, just like the book suggested.

It didn't work.

She banged the avocado on the kitchen counter, cut it open and scooped out the pulp.

"This is my dad's house in case you haven't noticed.

He's the one who works and pays for everything. So, it all belongs to him and I can take what I like. I'm not listening to you. Get it?" She gave me what I think youngsters call a death stare and proceeded to plaster the whole fruit inches thick on one slice of bread and stalked out, leaving the counter top for me to clean up. Loud waves of laughter from the lounge told me she'd switched on the television at full volume.

I leaned against the wall and sighed. Didn't that go well? I hoped the book would tell me what to do when a conversation was hijacked. How would A J Cromptom react in this instance?

Round one to Belinda.

I could feel the cloud of depression settling over me as I cleared away and began making dinner. There would be no avocado for starters, so I needed to think of something else.

Dinner that night was a silent affair. Belinda refused to sit with us, even though her father bellowed at her to come to the table and be sociable. Instead she ignored him and stormed upstairs to her bedroom. For a moment I thought Mason was going up after her, but he turned his attention back to the report he was studying next to his plate. I was tempted to get my Kindle and learn a bit more from Doctor Cromptom, but didn't want to answer any questions on my choice of literature.

I sat in silence, only that didn't last too long before the thumping of an overeager drum player from upstairs made it impossible to think. It continued long enough for Mason to react and the resulting shouting match with my husband bellowing and banging on Belinda's bedroom door was drowned out by the music being turned up even louder.

There was no way I was getting involved. Stepmothers don't, if they have any sense. I lost my appetite, took my plate through to the kitchen and scraped the food into the bin. Catching sight of myself in the reflection on the back door I wondered what Mason had ever seen in me.

I've never been a beauty, though a friend did tell me once I resembled a pixie, a cute one she had added hastily. My hair is neither brown nor blond but a sort of in-between mouse colour and it suits me best short. Like many men Mason loves long hair on women so to please him I let it grow, but it hung in lank strings on either side of my face and did little for me. My green eyes are possibly my best feature but I have a suspicion I'll soon need to wear glasses as my eyesight is not what it was. I'm a medium height, with a reasonable figure but I'm no longer in one piece. That's the real down side. Not only did I lose a leg, I lost my confidence too.

We take walking, dancing, swimming, running and driving for granted, until we can no longer do them, not without hours and days of practice. I've never managed to move as smoothly as I could before the accident, now I'm perpetually clumsy and harbour a terrible fear of falling over.

I didn't like the image reflected back at me. I looked at least ten years older. I shrugged and began to stack the dishwasher.

I sneaked into the lounge, muted the television and continued to read and inwardly digest the pearls of wisdom that Dr A J Cromptom shares with the world. Sound advice? Yes. It all made sense, but I wasn't sure it was possible to put any of it into practice.

The following morning I got the household chores done in record time. Maybe it was because I knew Mason would not be at home that night, or tomorrow night either. Every few weeks he visited one or two of his important clients who lived some distance away and who expected their solicitor to come to them. On occasion he has been away for weekends on fishing or hunting trips up north.

Mason never discussed his work with me, but I suspected some of his wealthier clients were on the wrong side of the law and needed his advice before their cases came up for a hearing. Who else, apart from the landed gentry, could afford estates in Scotland or send chauffeur-driven cars to collect their pet lawyers? They have the money to choose the best legal firms in the country and Mason's company is one of the very best. He told me it was.

I've seen the smug look on his face when the news programmes show some of the better-known villains getting off scot-free and sounding off about their innocence on the court steps. I shouldn't complain – I guess it pays for his excellent standard of living.

I phoned Andrea to see if she was free for a coffee, but there was no reply on her house phone or mobile. I knew she hated carrying her phone, she said it deprived her of her privacy.

Perhaps my new me was emerging as I decided to go for a coffee by myself. I'd treat myself to a large latte and a custard cream slice. Why not?

I'm not sure what made me check my purse but, when I opened it, it was empty, not even one coin. I wondered if Mason had taken it for change before he left that morning, but he would have said something. There were no notes in my wallet either but to my relief the bank cards were still there. I would have to draw cash from the ATM in the square before going to the café.

I was just about to close the front door when the phone rang. Thinking it might be Andrea and she was free for coffee after all I hurried to answer it. A voice I didn't recognise asked if I was Mrs Brand. For a split moment I was tempted to ask who was calling, or who wanted to know, because society is getting so paranoid these days. Instead, I simply said "Yes."

"I'm sorry to bother you Mrs Brand, but is Belinda there?"

"Belinda? No. She's at school."

"No, she's not come in today and she didn't attend yesterday either. I'm June Cartwright, her year teacher, and I've been meaning to have a word with you and her father."

"I, I'm not her real mother… what I mean," I stuttered, "I'm only her stepmother and I've only known her for a couple of years, and to be honest we're not that close." I hated myself for making excuses. I would support Mason of course, but I wasn't up to liaising with his daughter's school.

There was a long silence on the phone and I rushed to fill the gap. "Her father is away for a couple of days but, as soon as he's back, I'll get him to phone and make an appointment to see you."

"If that's the best you can suggest." June Cartwright sounded disappointed. "To be honest Mrs Brand we are extremely worried about Belinda. She was one of our best students and her work has been going steadily downhill."

Along with her behaviour, I thought. She had never been friendly towards me but her hostility had increased.

"You do know that her mother…" I paused.

"Yes, we have it on record, but it was two years ago Mrs Brand. And her work was excellent until quite recently. I do feel it's important that we have a talk to both you and Mr Brand as soon as possible."

"Yes of course." I sank down on the chair next to the telephone table, and took a deep breath. Wasn't life difficult enough? The silence from the other end of the phone prompted me to say. "My husband will be home the day after tomorrow and I'll speak to him and we'll come and see you. That's if you think it is necessary for me to…"

June Cartwright interrupted. "Yes, most definitely both of you. In my experience women tend to notice little details. We are much sharper at seeing even the smallest of changes. I'll wait to hear from you then. Goodbye for now."

She hung up before I had a chance to ask her just how many days Belinda had missed school. Nor could I explain that I had little or no chance to notice anything. Belinda had made it quite clear the day I moved in that her room was out of bounds. I rescued her dirty laundry thrown onto the landing outside her door and left it washed, folded and ironed on the breakfast room table for her to retrieve. Once in a blue moon she disappeared dragging the vacuum behind her and reappeared with black plastic bags which she deposited in the bin outside. I'm not sure I have ever had more than a glimpse inside her room. That brief peep had shown a double bed, dressing table and stool in a pretty pink matching set with frills. The sheets and towels she put out for washing were also pink so, at one time, someone had furnished her bedroom and bathroom with love and care.

At the time I was forbidden entry I shrugged my shoulders and thought one less room to clean. Now, I was curious. Would the room hold any secrets to Belinda's deteriorating behaviour? I hovered at the base of the stairs for a few moments then decided not to risk it. Maybe after a glass or two of wine? Right now, I needed that coffee and to get away from a house where the walls felt as if they were closing in on me.

I was so preoccupied that I'd ordered my coffee and cake before I remembered I had no money on me. My stuttering explanation to the waitress was met with raised eyebrows as I abandoned my table and went in search of the cash machine. I was almost halfway there when I realised I could have paid using the debit card. I felt so foolish, I wasn't thinking straight. I needed to pull myself together. How many times had I heard my mother say that to my father? Did this lack of concentration run in the family?

Having drawn the cash, I returned to the café and clicked on my Kindle. What would my new guru have to say about a situation like this?

Chapter Two: *You are also Important.*

Well that was nice to know, but important to whom? Certainly not Belinda and not often to Mason either, unless he was persuading me to do something I didn't want to do. To Andrea? Yes of course, she told me every time we met that I was her best friend, but neither my brother in Canada nor my sister in Australia were close and I doubt if they thought of me often, if at all.

The book went on to suggest *joining clubs, developing a skill, meeting like-minded people who shared interests. All this would help to boost the ego of anyone with low self-esteem. We all need praise, validation and boosting each and every day to stay on track.*

I stared at the remaining custard slice crumbs on my plate. What was I good at? Did I have any skills?

"Excuse me, but have you finished?" The waitress was back, a pimply-faced teenager not much older than Belinda, with a scowl on her face. She was leaning forward on her toes and I could see the wet cloth in her right-hand dangling on the edge of the table, fingers twitching. It was obvious she was dying to clear away my empty cup and plate.

I glanced up to see a queue for vacant tables by the front door and gave up. I gathered my things together, paid at the counter and left.

Outside, an icy blast of wind nearly blew me over. Where could I take refuge? Somewhere warm, but I didn't want to go back to the house and I couldn't walk around the small mall for long; I was still a little unsteady on my feet. The answer was our local library. Perfect.

There were two large tables surrounded by seats, a

couple of sofas, three easy chairs, and a friendly, hushed interior. I grabbed a couple of novels off the shelves and settled down to continue my self-education. I didn't even mind when a party of school children arrived and were ushered through to the reading corner where one of the librarians waited to tell them a story.

I didn't know it then, but the library was to become my refuge – it was safe and comfortable plus I was surrounded by books. What more could I ask for?

It was a shock when I realised I'd been sitting there for hours and it was time to go home. I needed to feed myself and perhaps cook something for Belinda? As I picked my way carefully along the pavement, I mulled over whether to mention the phone call from school. I didn't think she would be very pleased but then nothing I said would please her beyond 'I'm moving out'.

I also wondered if I should mention the money that had disappeared from my bag. Could I ask her without being confrontational? I wasn't sure how. We both knew it would be wrong of her to take it. I decided to wait and check with Mason first.

In the end, I had no chance to say anything.

Belinda didn't return home before I went to bed. I tried her mobile number several times but I only heard her voice mail suggesting I leave a message and she'd get back to me. Now that would surprise me.

To begin with I waited up for her, dozing on and off on the couch. When the clock struck midnight, I gave in and climbed the stairs, too tired to stay up any longer.

Should I phone the police? I didn't think they would

help. There must be hundreds, if not thousands, of fifteen-year-olds staying out at night and wasn't there some rule about waiting forty-eight hours? Then, my brain reasoned, she was still a minor by ten months so perhaps I should report it. Damn, I'd left it too late to phone Mason. He was the one who should decide, it's his kid.

The next morning, I woke bleary eyed and, scrambling out of bed, I went immediately to Belinda's room and knocked on the door. I thumped and shouted as loudly as I could but there was no response. Turning the handle, I discovered the door was locked. Was she in there? I didn't get the sense, you know, that one you get when you just know there's someone close by? I tried for several minutes and then shuffled back to grab my mobile phone. It was definitely time to phone Mason.

He answered on the third ring. Just hearing his voice, I began to cry. I was giving him a garbled version of events, words falling out interrupted by sobs and gulps.

"Wait," said the voice on the other end. "Are you telling me that Belinda didn't come home last night?"

"Yes. I mean no she didn't, she wasn't here and I'm so worried. I didn't know whether to phone the police…"

"Calm down and pull yourself together." Mason did not sound reassuring nor comforting. "Did you forget completely?"

"Forget?" I dropped down on the bed. "Forget what?" I was angry my voice sounded so timid.

"I told you I was taking Belinda with me on this trip."

I gasped. "You did! Are you sure? I don't remember."

"Well you might if you concentrated more, and yes, I did tell you."

"Well you didn't tell them at school!" I snapped back.

"I asked you to inform the school. I suppose you don't remember that either?"

"No, no I don't. I searched my memory. There had never been any mention of taking Belinda on a work trip. What would she do while her father was meeting with clients? Wouldn't it look unprofessional to drag family members along? I didn't ask any of these questions, but simply enquired when they would be home.

I dropped the mobile on the duvet. How could I forget something like that? How could I not have informed the school? June Cartwright would think I was a complete idiot. I was not looking forward to explaining to Mason that Belinda's teacher phoned to say she was concerned about her work, behaviour and absence from school.

Another long day stretched in front of me. As I showered and dressed, I made up my mind I was going to be pro-active. That's what Dr A J Cromptom said and he was right. I had to stretch my imagination and strive to do something right outside my comfort zone. *Even if,* the book said, *it is a high-flying goal beyond your own wildest dreams, such as studying to become a doctor, aim big. You can always tailor your end game when you have travelled some distance along the road. It's the travelling part that is most important. Take the road and begin your journey to self-awareness and self-improvement and self-confidence.*

I didn't have any of those but no one would hand them to me on a plate. The word doctor resonated with me as I went down to make myself some breakfast. I'd qualified years ago as a nurse; what more would I have to do to qualify as a doctor? I felt a small flutter of excitement in the pit of my stomach. I'd start researching right after my cornflakes and toast.

As I scrolled down the pages, according to Google my prospects didn't look too good. By lunchtime I was beginning to feel the depression again. I couldn't see me going to medical school full-time for four years. The shorter courses that were offered to qualified nurses with degrees didn't apply to me. When I trained it was for three years and, as I was supporting James through medical school, I didn't continue to specialise. And then the children arrived – before I knew it, life had moved on.

But there was nothing to stop me now – thirty-nine wasn't the end of life. Yes, I was going to give this a go. Why not? I wasn't stupid, and having a degree would give me lots of confidence. I'd aim first to get a degree, something in the health field. Mason had gone to university as he reminded me frequently. Now it was my turn. There was nothing to stop me from studying online. I smiled as I logged in to the Open University. Now, where did I start?

I was still hyped up hours later. This was going to be my secret. I would study during the day at home with no one to distract me and, when it came to practical stuff, I was sure I could find a good excuse to be away for a few days. It wasn't going to be easy.

Should I tell Andrea? I thought about this for a while and then decided I would wait a bit. I'd register and pay the initial fees from the little I had in my bank account and, from the end of the month, I would start raiding the housekeeping. One thing that was comfortable about

Mason, although he managed all the money, and to be quite honest I had no idea how much he was worth, he didn't ask me to account for every penny. If I blew £500 on a dress for a special occasion he wouldn't complain – though I never had – I wouldn't have a moment's peace wearing it. This was different, I would not be wasting money, not by educating myself. Goodness Leah, if this wasn't standing on your own feet and being assertive, I didn't know what was!

It was frustrating to have a whole evening to myself and not be able to start work immediately on my studies. I'd filled in all the online forms they asked for and now all I could do was sit and wait. As usual there was nothing worth watching on the television, and I couldn't get into the book I had borrowed from the library. The heroine with the unlikely name of Honeysuckle couldn't decide whether to jump into bed with the handsome but dangerous Dirk. Fair enough, but she'd been going on about it for a hundred pages. Too much.

The book landed on the floor, as a wave of pure energy swept over me. Usually I was exhausted at the end of the day, but tonight I couldn't sit still. I'd make a start on clearing out my clothes. I had far too many and the charity shop would be glad of them.

I clambered up the stairs clutching a wad of plastic bags and opened the top drawer in the chest. I blinked and took a step backwards. James used to tease me how retentive I was about the way I stored all my clothes. I could never just fling my panties into the cupboard, but folded each pair and placed them in piles of the same colour. The undies I was staring at now were still in piles but the colours were all mixed up, black next to red, beside white with my green pair in between the cream ones. I staggered back and collapsed on the bed. It was so weird. When had I done that? What motivated me to change the habit of a lifetime? I had always colour coded my clothes, it made it easier to find things and see what went with what.

The scary thing was I didn't remember doing it – just like I didn't remember Mason telling me he was taking Belinda away with him. I must have something wrong with me. A neurological disorder or something. Was I losing my mind? All my new-found energy and self-confidence trickled down my spine and left me feeling drained and fearful.

I squeezed my eyes tight as I climbed into bed that night. I was determined not to cry. I could cope with this once I made a plan. The first thing was to seek medical help and get diagnosed as quickly as possible. I'd seen too many cases where patients had denied and ignored symptoms until it was too late. I'd ring for an appointment first thing tomorrow.

Frustrated, I slammed down the receiver and went to make another cup of coffee. I'd forgotten that you no longer phone the surgery and ask for an appointment. The receptionist, or whoever answered, wanted to know what the problem was, how urgent it was, and then said she would phone back. What about the privacy rules everyone was screaming about? I'd now told a complete stranger I thought I was losing my mind. I'd probably have to repeat all that when they phoned back.

The surgery didn't call until after lunch – just as well I'd not been bleeding to death. I was interrogated by another faceless voice and given an appointment for early the following morning. I must have sounded quite frantic to get to see a doctor so quickly.

This was another secret I was going to keep to myself. No point in upsetting anyone until I had some sort of diagnosis. Thirty-nine was too young to have dementia, wasn't it?

A few more hours to myself, so I spent part of the day checking out all the other drawers and cupboards but I could find nothing out of the ordinary. The only signs of disharmony were the mixed-coloured piles of panties. It sounded so stupid now. I dreaded explaining that to the doctor face to face.

I phoned Andrea hoping a chat would take my mind off things, but there was no reply. Had she told me she was going somewhere? Had I forgotten that as well? I remembered some things, like phoning the doctor, how to prepare my breakfast and use the coffee maker. Did we lose our minds sporadically, and only about certain things? Worrying wouldn't help, but it was difficult keeping a blank mind, was that even possible?

By mid-afternoon I was stir crazy and went off to the library. I could bring my laptop here and study. Yes, this would be my refuge. I settled down in a comfortable chair and pulled my Kindle out of my bag. I was eager to see what else Dr A J Cromptom had to teach me, but I doubted he would mention forgetfulness and losing minds. His words of wisdom were all about moving forward. I got fed up with his pontificating and turned back to a novel I'd started days ago.

A slight cough made me look up to see the librarian peering at me.

"Excuse me."

"Yes? Oh, dear is there a problem? I'm sorry, I've been here for ages."

"That's no problem at all, only you'll need to leave now unless you don't mind being locked in for the night." He chuckled.

I looked at the windows and realised the sun had gone down and the streetlights were twinkling outside. I jumped to my feet.

"I'm so sorry, I didn't mean…"

He cut me off. "No need to explain, that's what we're here for. Anyone with a love of books is welcome to stay as long as they like, but only during opening hours." He paused as he changed over some of the books on the nearby table with new ones from the shelves. "I've seen you in here a couple of times and it's nice to have company. We don't get as many people in now, not like we used to." He smiled and I followed his gaze between two of the book stacks. "I remember, a long time ago we'd have to call out for quiet. 'Shush, the library is a quiet place.' But it's not like that now. Not many youngsters, only the older folk."

"I've always loved to read."

"Me too. But those," he stared at my hands, "have made a huge difference."

I glanced at the Kindle I was clutching and a wave of guilt washed over me. Even sitting here surrounded by books, real books, I had still chosen to read from the electronic device. I found the dictionary feature a blessing, loved the ability to enlarge or shrink the print and it was so much lighter and easier to carry.

"If they told us when we were nippers that, one day, we could carry six hundred books in our pockets we would have thought they were mental. Ready for the looney bin," he added.

We both laughed as I made my way to the door and waved him goodbye. As I walked carefully – I was always careful – along the rain-soaked streets, I wondered how old the librarian was and how long he had worked there.

I popped into the local deli and bakery and bought myself a few treats. This would be my last night of peace and quiet and I was going to make the most of it. I refused to feel guilty as I pointed to the sliced corned beef, a pork pie, a custard tart and a jam doughnut. I planned to pig out and eat the lot.

The house looked neglected and threatening as I walked up the front path. We usually left lights on if we planned to be out after dark. I didn't think I'd dozed off in the library, but while I was far away on a Hawaiian island following the adventures of a 17th Century galley, I'd lost all sense of time.

The phone began to ring as I put the key in the lock, and in my haste to open the door I fumbled and dropped the bags. Flinging my purse on the table I lunged to grab the receiver but the second I picked it up the ringing stopped and all I heard was the dial tone. I rescued my precious package of forbidden foods, glad that I wouldn't have to cook tonight.

I piled everything onto one large plate and settled down to watch a box set I'd been keeping for a special occasion.

The phone rang again. This time I reached it before it cut off, but there was no sound on the other end. I said 'Hello', several times but there was no response. I slammed the handset down and returned to the sofa. Probably some kids left alone making prank calls.

Five minutes later it rang again and, as I stumbled into the hallway, I began to get cross. The same thing happened, absolute silence. "If you phone again, I'm going to blow my whistle very hard, so stop making nuisance calls. I can get them to trace the call and then you'll be in real trouble." I slammed the receiver down so hard I thought for a moment I'd broken it. Almost immediately it rang again. I would have used the whistle but I had no idea if there was one in the house.

This time I reached down and pulled the cord out of the socket. Now they could try all they wanted and, if anything was urgent, they could call me on my mobile.

I decided on an early night; my doctor's appointment was possibly the first in the morning and I'd need to shower and wear something respectable. I turned off the lights downstairs and trundled up to the bedroom. I'd choose what I'd wear tomorrow and lay it all out to save time in the morning.

When I pulled out my underwear drawer, I went cold

and began to shake. All my panties were now back in their colour coded piles. All the black, all the white with smaller piles of red, green, cream and blue. I took a couple of steps backwards and grabbed at the bedside table as I sank down on the bed. I must be going mad. Had I imagined the colour mix up before? No one had been in the house except me and I would have noticed a broken window or a forced lock. No thief enters without stealing, they don't rearrange underwear and disappear. It didn't make sense. What was I going to say to the doctor in the morning? I felt so stupid.

My underwear might be colour coded now but as I walked into the alcove that served as my dressing room, I saw immediately that my sweaters and shirts had been mixed up. They were still neatly arranged on the shelves, a couple of sweaters and a cotton shirt, then another woolly and two more blouses. It was bizarre. I swayed, clutching the edge of the shelf, then went back downstairs and fetched my phone. I took several photos of the jumbled clothes. It was too late to record my panties in disarray but at least I had some proof. Even if the doctor didn't believe me, it was a record for myself. I was not deluded, I was not. Unless I'd had some sort of black out and did things I couldn't remember, but then I wasn't aware of losing time. I glanced at the time on my phone. I'd been out all afternoon and the clothes were in their normal places before I went to the library and I remembered looking at the kitchen clock when I got in. I'd poured a glass of wine, watched the television and apart from the prank phone calls I'd not moved all evening. I added up the time taken to watch three episodes of the series, plus minutes for a nature break and answering the phone, and I'd not lost any time at all. And how long would it take to rearrange a few clothes? Seconds rather than minutes, but I didn't remember even coming upstairs.

I grabbed a notebook from the bedside cabinet and wrote down all the timings and then calculated how long I'd been home just to reassure myself that I had not blacked out. The numbers added up. I gave myself a good shake. I would be honest with the doctor in the morning. If I could persuade him to let me have the tests then it would prove if I had one or more screws loose inside my head.

I didn't sleep well that night. While I was trying to be brave, my brain was not cooperating. I tossed and turned, checked the digital clock over and over again scared I would oversleep, and staggered out of bed feeling like a lump of lead.

With a sense of relief, I saw the clothes I had laid out the night before were still in place waiting for me. I prayed they wouldn't move while I had a shower.

The rain was teeming down yet again, and it made sense to take the car to the surgery, it wasn't far away but I'd get soaked if I walked or waited for a bus. For some reason our local transport company decided it was not necessary to provide shelter for those waiting for the buses. These arrived in their own good time at random intervals which bore no relation to the information on the signboards.

One of the best features in our house, or rather Mason's house, was the direct access to the garage from the laundry room. Before I left, I carefully checked that all the downstairs windows and the front door were firmly closed. I counted to see all the spare keys were still hanging in the kitchen cupboard, and I talked out loud as I went from room to room.

"I am now locking the laundry. I have also locked the back door and all the windows are closed. The house is secure." I reconnected the phone and switched on the answering machine. Would there be more prank calls this morning?

I gave myself a good shake and hobbled over to my car. You have to hand it to the National Health Service; despite the large number of people who complained, they had been wonderful in getting my automatic car adapted to make it easier for me to drive.

Another surprise. My car door was not locked. But I always locked it, even in the garage, didn't I?

I flung open the door and was about to slide into the car when I froze. Sitting behind the wheel was a stuffed blue rabbit. It was about twelve inches high with large, black, staring eyes that gave it a malevolent look. It wasn't mine. I'd never seen it before. Belinda's? I doubted it belonged to Mason.

I poked it with my finger and it toppled to one side. I jostled it again and it slipped down next to the gear selector. I took a deep breath and picked it up. It had scared me, but there was nothing threatening about it, just a small cuddly toy. I didn't want it in my car, it didn't belong there. I leaned over and hurled it to the other side of the garage where it bounced off the wall and landed upside down on Mason's work bench.

I brushed the seat before I got in, slammed the door,

locked it and pressed the fob to open the roller door.

The drive to the surgery went without incident, but I took it slowly. I was shaking. Another thing out of place. This time I was certain I had not gone out to the garage carrying a blue stuffed rabbit. I told myself not to be so stupid. Mason probably put it there, or even Belinda. Was it her way of saying sorry? I debated whether to mention it to the doctor as I reversed into a spot around the corner from the surgery – fate had been kind about something today.

I sat facing Dr Morton not sure how to begin. He studied the file that the nurse had left on his desk then lay back in his chair and smiled.

"So, Mrs Brand what seems to be the problem? I take it," he glanced at the notes, "you are worried about the onset of early dementia?"

"Yes. I'm not going to ask for tranquilisers or any medication but there are tests aren't there? I need to know if I'm losing my mind and if so, what I can do about it."

He steepled his fingers, the light glinting off his wristwatch, and waited for me to begin.

I told him everything I'd experienced in the last two days. I was as honest as I could be. I even told him about the stuffed rabbit and felt embarrassed when I saw one eyebrow shoot up.

"Okay, so that could have a natural explanation, but why would I rearrange my clothes? Or forget my stepdaughter was going away, or get jittery about prank phone calls. I don't know anyone who would want to hurt me."

I stared at Doctor Morton's checked shirt

remembering the days when the doctor wore a suit or a white coat. Everything was so casual now. When did doctors get so scruffy? My mind was wandering, I'd not heard a word he said but drifted off into my own world. I was just in time to hear him say he would arrange for tests, but I would need to be patient as the waiting list was quite long. I stood, thanked him, and hurried out of the surgery.

All I wanted to do was rush home, hole up like an injured animal and metaphorically lick my wounds. I didn't stop to do any shopping but took the fastest route back and breathed a sigh of relief as I pressed the fob to open the garage door.

Once inside, I looked around for the blue rabbit. I was curious to know if it belonged to Mason or Belinda and discover the reason it was in my car.

It was not on Mason's workbench where I'd thrown it. I searched the surrounding area, even backed the car out again and looked everywhere. No rabbit. A shiver ran down my spine. Why hadn't I taken a photo of it? Even if I'd tossed it there in a kind of fugue, when did I remove it?

Home did not feel the safe refuge I craved. Home is where I was hallucinating.

As I dumped my bag on the kitchen counter, I tossed up whether to have coffee or pour myself a good strong drink. No, I wasn't going to go down that path, it led to a dangerous, slippery slope. I turned on the coffee maker and popped a capsule into the holder. I opened the cutlery drawer and shivered.

Every knife, fork and spoon was now resting in the wrong place and they were all pointing the wrong way – all the handles were now facing the back of the drawer. It looked so weird that for several seconds I blinked, not quite believing what I was seeing. No one stored their cutlery that way, no one.

Had I turned them all around, and if so, when? I could feel the hairs on the back of my neck go up, my spine was tingling, every muscle was twitching. I spun around as fast as I could. Was someone watching me? I listened, my ears flaring as I concentrated but the only sounds were the ticking of the kitchen clock and the birds cheeping outside.

One by one I tiptoed from one room to another on the ground floor. I checked every window, the front door, and then paused at the bottom of the stairs. I would have to go up sooner or later. I gave myself a quick shake and I was half way up before I thought it might be a good idea to take some form of weapon. It was too late now. If an intruder lurked waiting to attack me then I'd fight back as best I could. My biggest enemy was probably my cowardice.

Back down in the kitchen, because of course there was no one hiding in the house, I poured my coffee and returned the cutlery to its proper orientation. The moment I'd finished I remembered that yet again I'd not taken a photo as proof. I was falling apart. No time for that Leah, there's a meal to prepare. I'd make a lasagne. I knew both Mason and Belinda loved pasta.

I spent the rest of the day pottering around the house, checking out the drawers and cupboards to see if anything else had removed itself. Everything was normal. I jumped at the jangling of the phone in the hallway and approached it cautiously. Damn. I'd still not looked for that whistle.

"Hello," my voice wobbled.

"Hi there, it's me. You sound strange."

I let go the breath I didn't even realise I was holding in. "Andrea! It's you!"

"Who did you think it might be?"

"Uh… a prank call?"

"Oh, have you been getting those too? Men making lewd suggestions?" She chuckled.

"Not as bad as that, just silence. I think that's more threatening."

"Just slam the receiver down, that's what I do. I'm seriously thinking of having my landline disconnected. If it's not crank calls, it's cold calling for double glazing or sun lounges."

"And you've already got both."

"Triple glazing."

I should have guessed. Andrea's place is always several degrees warmer than ours.

"I think you need cheering up," she continued, "so I have a treat in store for you."

"You have?"

"Yes. A whole day out at the Manor House Spa. How does that sound?"

"I couldn't Andrea, they charge a fortune."

"Yes they do, but it's worth every penny and it's my treat. I won't take no for an answer. Leah, you'll be doing me a favour. I hate going to those places on my own, it's not as much fun. You need a girlfriend there to giggle with. Come on, don't let me down."

"Well, if you put it that way." I stood there chewing

my lip. Of course, I could afford it and Mason wouldn't say no, but if I was to squirrel away the housekeeping to pay for my online university degree course, I'd have to make a few sacrifices.

"Good that's a date then. I'll phone and book us both in now." She put the phone down before I could ask her which day she had in mind. Not that it really mattered much, I was free most days; that was part of my problem and maybe that was why I was unconsciously making odd changes around the house.

Belinda and Mason arrived home in the early evening. I could hear them chattering as they parked up in the garage and then I heard Belinda complaining the door to the laundry room was locked. I hurried from the kitchen to open it for them.

Mason's brow furrowed. "Problem?"

"No," I replied hastily. "Just a bit of extra precaution when I'm home alone."

He grunted, gave me a quick peck on the cheek and made for the bathroom. Like all teenagers Belinda was already raiding the cupboards.

"Did your father starve you?" I kept my voice light and cheerful.

"No, course not. As if he would." She snatched a packet of crisps and marched out, knocking a bowl of salad off the counter.

I held back the tears as I bent down to rescue the greenery that was now decorating the kitchen floor. If I'd had more guts, I should have insisted she come back and pick it up, but somehow it wasn't worth it, more angst and I was already on edge. I bent over and scooped up the leaves and sliced tomatoes and peppers and ran them under the tap. Think positive, I reminded myself, visual images of Dr Cromptom swimming before my eyes – not being the retiring type he had a large picture of himself on the front cover of the book, and there were a few additional photos of him receiving several awards for this and that. No shrinking violet Dr Cromptom, but then he got rich from little people like me buying his book in the hope that one day… yeah right. What was positive about the salad? I'd not added the feta cheese or the dressing and I didn't have to worry about Zeus slinking around the corner slobbering over it all. I even managed a giggle.

"What's so funny?" Mason wanted to know as, freshly showered, he wandered into the kitchen and leaned over the central island.

"Nothing really. Just trying to be positive." I smiled, then my heart sank as I remembered the message I had to deliver. It could wait until after supper. For once I would procrastinate. I busied myself finishing the salad.

"Is it nearly ready? I'm starving." Mason began nibbling bits off the freshly washed lettuce.

"Yes, I just need to lay the table and we're all set." I bent over to open the oven door and removed the lasagne.

I paused as I put the dish on the island counter.

"Mason?" Damn. I sounded too hesitant.

"Yes?" He turned and gave me his full attention.

"Can you remember when you told me you were taking Belinda with you on this business trip?" I found myself holding my breath. How was he going to react?

He leaned over and began lifting small pieces of cheese off the edge of the dish with his fingernail. "You really don't remember, do you?"

"No, I don't and I'm so sorry." There I went apologising again, I'm sure Dr Cromptom wouldn't approve.

"Well to remind you, we were here, in this kitchen a week ago and you had just taken the toad-in-the-hole out of the oven and I told you the plans and I asked you to let them know at Belinda's school. She's never been to Scotland before and it's more educational than sitting in a stuffy classroom all day. I should probably take her away more often." He leaned closer to me invading my personal space and I took an involuntary step backwards. "Now do you remember?"

I searched my mind frantically. "No, no I don't." To hide my confusion, I turned to get the serving spoons out of the drawer. Then I had a flash of insight.

"Wait!" My words stopped Mason as he was walking out of the kitchen.

"What?"

"We've not had toad-in-the-hole for months. So, something's wrong."

"Really? You expect me to remember every dish we have every night? So, I was wrong about the menu, whatever it was we had that night. Though I remember the toad-in-the-hole quite clearly."

You couldn't have I thought. You both cannibalised the sausages I was planning to use. I know I'm right. I just know.

But Mason was no longer in the kitchen. He was

seated at the dining table waiting for me to bring the food through. He gave Belinda a shout and she eventually appeared and joined us.

"So, what did you think of Scotland?" I asked as I helped myself to salad.

"Alright, I s'pose. Nothing special."

"Most people rave about the scenery, the lochs and the heather and the towns and all the houses built of granite."

"I'm not most people," Belinda snapped.

I was hoping Mason would correct her rudeness, but he concentrated on his food.

I tried again. "What part of Scotland did you go to?"

Belinda shrugged as she tore off a piece of garlic bread and stuffed it in her mouth before replying. "I dunno."

"I prefer not to discuss the exact location of my clients' estates," Mason stated. "You must have heard of client confidentiality." The tone in his voice suggested that I was too ignorant to know about such things.

"Yes, of course, but I wasn't aware it extended to their residential addresses. Unless they're hiding assets from the taxman."

Mason banged his fork down on his plate making Belinda and me jump. "I've just said, did you not hear me? I do not discuss my clients with anyone."

Except you took Belinda with you when you went to meet with them, so she knows. I was tempted to reply, but held back. I still had the unpleasant news to share and now was as good a time as any.

"The school rang while you were away," I began.

"Unnecessary, if you had told them as I asked," Mason

snapped. "I suppose they thought she was playing truant."

"No, it wasn't only that. It was June Cartwright who phoned and she would like to see both of us as soon as possible."

"What the fuck for!" Mason slammed down his fork again.

"And why the fuck does she want to talk to you?" Belinda looked furious.

I was waiting for Mason to tell his daughter to clean up her language but he ignored her. "And when is this great consultation to take place?"

"She didn't give me a time and I had no idea what your schedule was. I said you would contact her."

"Thoughtful of you." Mason stood suddenly. "It's not as if you have much to do all day."

I ground my teeth in anger and dug my fingernails into my palms under the table. I wanted to explode but it would only lead to a slanging match. What would Dr C suggest? I wish I'd got further than Chapter 3.

Mason was being totally unreasonable and mean. I caught a glimpse of Belinda's face and was sure she was smirking. I doubted she would smirk in front of June Cartwright. Maybe they thought the meeting was to discuss her absence. I'd quite forgotten to mention her marks were slipping and how would she explain the other times she was not at school? And there was also the mention about her behaviour too. That would not please Mason, he was keen she did well and later qualify to work with him in the firm. You needed good marks to study law. It didn't make sense taking her out for three days just to gawp at some Scottish scenery. None of it added up.

Belinda leapt up out of her seat the moment her father disappeared from view and I began to clear the table. They might not have said a word about their favourite lasagne but there wasn't a scrap left. At least I'd done one thing right.

If I'd hoped that Mason would show some affection that night after his absence, I was to be disappointed. I cuddled up to him in bed and stroked his chest, walking my fingers up and down, inching lower and lower. After a few minutes he grabbed my wrist and placed my arm back on my side of the bed. His message was clear. He didn't need to say anything. A moment later he was snoring.

The arrival of the postman, long after Mason was in the office and Belinda supposedly in the classroom, cheered me up. I opened the door and grabbed the large brown packet. I could barely wait to see what was inside. They must have accepted me to have sent such a large envelope. My fingers were trembling as I tottered into the lounge and collapsed onto the sofa. I fumbled with the thick brown paper, hacking and tearing until a sheaf of documents fell out. There it was, my first assignment.

I would have to find a safe place to keep all the paperwork and maybe some reference books, there was probably stuff you couldn't find on Google. I couldn't wait to start and began reading when I was interrupted by the jangling from my mobile.

It was Mason instructing me to be at Belinda's school in an hour for the meeting with her teacher. He couldn't fathom why they wanted to talk to me as well, but for some weird reason they had insisted on seeing us both.

I sighed and, gathering all the paperwork, went upstairs to change and find a hiding place. I was not going to tell either of them I was studying. It would only run the risk of them sneering and laughing and my confidence was low enough as it was. I'd wait until I'd earned my first few credits. If I could keep it a secret for the next few years then I could casually invite them to the graduation ceremony. I sniggered to myself, it was a dream I could hug close to my heart.

Of course, parking was a nightmare near Belinda's school, near any school in the country; they have yellow lines stretching either side of the gates for miles. By the time I had wriggled into the smallest space between two huge SUV's it had begun to drizzle and I'd not brought my umbrella. I cursed as I hobbled as fast as I could along the pavement and then rang the bell at the gates. All this security was frightening, a reminder of how scared people were. If it wasn't a terrorist attack it was a lurking paedophile or an out-of-control child drugged-to-the-eyeballs – and there were plenty of those – racing out into the traffic. When had it all changed? When had it all gone wrong?

The gate buzzed and I pushed it open and walked across the playground. It dawned on me that they must have been watching me as I stood there. Of course, there were cameras everywhere. That's the only way they caught criminals, no one was brave enough to grass on anyone for fear of reprisals. At the same time the ordinary, law-abiding citizen had to resist adjusting wrinkled underwear, or scratching a personal body part since you never knew who was watching.

As I scurried into the front hallway, I could see Mason was already there, pacing up and down. He glanced up at me and nodded abruptly. I nodded back and looked around for somewhere to sit.

A voice from a doorway called us both in. Mason took my arm gently, smiled, and said "Come on, darling."

I nearly fell over at his chameleon behaviour. I couldn't remember the last time he called me 'darling'. It might have been on our wedding day. I forced myself to smile back and allowed him to steer me into an office and onto a chair across a desk where two women were sitting. One I guessed was June Cartwright and the other introduced herself as Ruth Lovall, head of year 11.

Ms Lovall smiled and welcomed us both and then her face became more serious. "We've asked you to come in for a chat about Belinda. The staff is worried about her performance, both her behaviour and the drop in her marks. Can you tell me if she is unhappy at home?"

Mason took one of my hands between both of his and turned to me. "Can you answer that darling? You see more of her at home than I do." He paused to look at the ladies on the other side of the table.

I managed to suppress a gasp. No matter what I said, it was not going to look good. I couldn't lie but I was about to dig myself into one big hole. I took a deep breath.

"Belinda and I have not formed a strong bond. I'm sure she misses her mother. I believe they were very close."

"We do find that parents separating does affect our

students." June Cartwright checked the notes on the file in front of her. "But in Belinda's case she appeared to adjust very quickly at the time and there were no problems until last October. Since coming back to school this year, the problems have got a lot worse."

"I wish I could shed some light on this." Mason's reply dripped with sincerity. He had concern written all over his face. "I can honestly say that her behaviour at home, as far as I can see, has not changed at all."

I fought to keep my expression neutral. How could he say that? Belinda wasn't as rude to him as she was to me, but she was hardly fun to live with. In fact, her behaviour was downright appalling. He saw it all the time. What was he thinking?

Ms Lovall was no fool. She picked up on my body language immediately. "So, neither of you have noticed any change whatsoever?" Her eyes were fixed on us waiting for a reaction.

I turned to Mason who looked at me with such love in his eyes that I nearly choked. I had to admire his performance, it was worth an academy award.

There was a long silence – one of those when you are desperate to say something to fill the void. I felt all eyes were on me.

"She doesn't say much to me. I mean, she's not confided in me at all. I really can't tell you if something is wrong." I paused. No one said a word so I stumbled on. "She is probably no better or worse than other teenagers, I've not had much experience with older children."

June Cartwright checked the file on the table in front

of her. "We are seriously concerned about Belinda's marks. Several of her assignments have not been completed or have been handed in late. She has not been concentrating in class, and she has stopped attending all her extra-curricular activities. She dropped out of the choir, the hockey team and the debating society."

"I don't like to hear that," Mason's voice echoed around the small room, he always talked loudly when he was upset. "Darling, you didn't tell me Belinda was coming home early?"

"She hasn't. Very often she doesn't come in much before you."

"Why wasn't I aware of this?"

I wanted to kick myself or, more honestly, kick Mason. I'd tried several times to voice my worries about his daughter's behaviour but each time he'd brushed me off. Now it looked as if I was getting the blame for his child who took more notice of the contents of the fridge than she did of me.

"I have mentioned it a few times." It was the best I could do. It was tempting to tell the truth but it would only start a row. In the end I would lose, I always did.

"I had no idea."

Did Mason really just say that?

"Maybe you can have a good talk with her when we get home, see if she will tell you what the problem is?" There, I'd bounced the ball right back into his court.

"That goes without saying, but I can't be there for her all the time like you are darling." He turned to address the teachers. "Like other single salaried households, I work very long hours. I will, of course, talk seriously to Belinda, but we've just spent three days together, an educational trip up north, and she was bright, and breezy and we chatted non-stop. And by the way, I do apologise for my wife's forgetting to tell you I was taking her out of school. No wonder you were worried."

It took all my self-control not to squirm in my chair or leap out of it and confront Mason. He'd never told me he was taking Belinda with him up north. I would have remembered.

I would, wouldn't I?

I tuned out as the conversation ebbed and flowed around me. I was not going to let myself get angry and I guessed this was the calm before the storm. The moment we were back outside and out of earshot I knew exactly who was going to get the blame for both my lack of behaviour and Belinda's bad behaviour.

I was wrong. Once outside the gate Mason turned and walked off to his car without so much as a goodbye. I stood staring at him before I set off in the opposite direction.

When I saw the parking ticket, thoughtfully encased in its little plastic sleeve, I wanted to scream. I dragged it out from under the windscreen wiper and threw myself into the driving seat. Violation, blah… blah… blah, rear wheels obstructing yellow lines in contravention of blah… blah; fine £150. I climbed out of the car and went to look. Sure enough, my back wheels were just touching the yellow paint that stretched from the school gates. The SUV behind me had gone and it must have been parked right over the lines. I was not obstructing any driveway or entrance and an inch was not going to hurt anyone. Yet some officious council employee had seen fit to deprive me of hard-earned cash.

I squeezed my eyes tight, determined not to cry in public. What else could go wrong? What would Doc C say? He'd probably laugh and put it down to experience. Most likely he had several million spare dollars in the bank, contributed by people like me buying his book to make us feel good. He wouldn't even miss wasting a few of those dollars on a parking ticket.

I drove home wondering what else could possibly go wrong, asking myself if I should confess my latest failure to Mason and invite his sneering and criticism or pay from my secret stash and hope he never found out.

MARCH

They say that March comes in like a lion and goes out like a lamb. That year I didn't notice any difference. The weather remained cold, wet and miserable. I slipped on the wet leaves on the front path and got nasty bruises on my hip and back. That was the day before Andrea announced we were having our spa day.

My best friend rang the front door bell just as I was packing the dishwasher with the breakfast dishes.

"Goodness, you're early," I exclaimed letting her in.

She was positively glowing. You would think she had just come from the spa. "Got to make the most of the day. Are you nearly ready?"

"Give me a moment to get my things together." I hobbled up the stairs.

"Don't forget your swim suit," she called up. "You're going to love their warm bath. They float oranges in it."

"Doesn't that make you all sticky?" I replied as I hunted frantically for my bathing costume.

"No, just refreshed. You can't help but float in the water. No idea what else they put in it but you feel a million dollars afterwards."

I raced through the drawers, flung open cupboard doors and rooted around on the shelves. No costume to be found anywhere. That's the problem with being neat and tidy, if something isn't where it should be you have no idea where to start looking for it.

"I can't find my swimming costume anywhere!"

"It can't be far," Andrea's voice in my ear made me jump, I'd not heard her follow me upstairs.

"It lives in this drawer. But it's not there now. I don't understand it. I can't remember the last time I wore it." I was beginning to shake – not another weird episode, please.

Andrea put her arms around me, the scent of her perfume filling my nostrils, the soft, white cashmere jersey caressing my cheeks as she gently rocked me back and forwards.

"There, there," she murmured. "It doesn't matter. I have several you can borrow. I'll pop back and grab a few and we'll have a fashion parade in the changing rooms."

Despite myself I couldn't help smiling.

She gave me an extra hug then stepped back and wagged her finger at me. "You grab your things and go wait in my car." She tossed me the keys. "I'll pop home and get them. Cheer up, it only gives you a good excuse to buy another one doesn't it?"

With a laugh she squeezed my arm gently then galloped down the stairs and out of the front door, slamming it behind her.

I did as I was told and, after carefully locking the house, I climbed into the passenger seat of her Lexus. I ran my finger over the leather upholstery, remembering happy times with James planning the day when the children were properly house trained, and we might consider leather seats. Until then plastic was a much better option in our old and battered Ford. Not that there was anything left of the car after the accident.

Stop it, I told myself sharply, stop looking back, remember what Doc Cromptom says – *that's the worst thing you can do. Look forward to a brighter future and focus on the weeks ahead.*

So, I would. This was going to be a great day out and I would ignore the bruises, which were still a bit painful, and wearing a borrowed costume which would not be as comfortable as my own – Andrea was a good deal slimmer than me – today was going to be a good day.

Andrea arrived a few minutes later a little out of breath. "I remembered I had an older costume from before I began dieting and thought it would be a better fit. Took some finding though." She flung herself into the car.

"No problem. I was thinking that you must be at least two sizes smaller than me now."

"It can't be easy getting enough exercise with a prosthetic leg." Andrea always understood.

"No, it's not. Even though there is a lot more acceptance in modern times I can't help feeling awkward. People do stare you know. They think they can hide it but I still notice."

"It's mostly curiosity. I'm sure they don't mean to be unkind." Andrea paused at the 'give way' sign and turned left.

We'd passed the string of local shops when I gasped and turned to stare. "I'm sure that was Belinda. Did you see her?"

Andrea turned her head to look, then jammed the

brakes on sharply as the car in front stopped dead at the traffic lights that had just turned red.

"Are you sure it was her?" Andrea asked as she wound down the window and gave two fingers to the driver she'd only just avoided. I hoped and prayed he didn't notice. A lot of people suffered from road rage and we didn't need a punch up on the High Street.

"Yes, I'm pretty sure it was. She's skipped school often enough so I shouldn't be surprised. I should go and…"

"Absolutely not." Andrea's voice was quite firm. "You've tried hard enough with that madam, and it's got you nowhere. She's not going to mess up our day out. We're going to have a ball and a lot of fun. So just you tell your overactive guilt feelings to shut up and put her right out of your mind. Frankly I don't think there is anything you can do to help her. She needs to do it for herself."

"I can't help but worry about her. I'm sure she's a sweet child underneath all that brash exterior. I'd love for us to be friends."

"Well it's not going to happen if she continues behaving the way she is. She's given you a really rough ride. And you can't say you've not tried."

"I feel I have, but maybe if I was her real mother…"

"Stop it, Leah. Face it! Her mother couldn't have cared a stuff about her – running off and leaving her like that. For a toy boy too! Most real mothers have this innate maternal instinct they can't get rid of no matter how badly their kids behave."

"Have you…?" I hesitated to ask, and it wasn't for the first time.

"I wasn't talking about myself." Andrea's voice softened. "We've all seen the wildlife programmes and that is the norm. Of course, there is always the exception, like Caro."

"Did you know her?" Strange, I'd never thought to ask Andrea that before. They were also neighbours.

"Not well." Andrea looked away to check the road was clear before she turned right onto the main bypass. "Our paths seldom crossed." She abruptly changed the subject. "Have you decided what colour you want your nails? I've ordered the whole package. Massages, manicure, pedicure, warm bath treatments and they've also opened a new hair salon so we're booked in there as well."

I gasped. This would cost a fortune. I knew the spa and it wasn't cheap, even for one treatment but, if it meant so much to Andrea to pay for me, I'd stop feeling guilty and lie back and enjoy. Tomorrow would take care of itself. I don't need to take on the cares of the world.

I can never make up my mind about spa treatments. Part of the day was delightful, relaxing in the warm water, sinking into the huge leather chairs while your hands and feet were soaked in water, soothed, beautified and coloured. The massages? Not so good, they hurt. As I lay there face down, gasping slightly as my nose clogged up, I tried to count my blessings and think of all the things I had to be thankful for. I was so ungrateful for the life I led. So many people had nothing, so many were starving, homeless, desperate or abused. What the hell had I to be miserable about?

Okay, so Mason snarled sometimes and constantly wanted his own way. Yes, he made me feel inadequate, stupid, clumsy and always on the defensive. He was a good provider though, and wasn't mean with his money.

It was up to me to be more assertive – there was that word again – yes, it was up to me. With Belinda I'm not sure I would have any success, but in time she would move out into her own place and the relationship would solve itself. She was almost sixteen with only two more years of school to go, I could hang on that long.

Thump. The masseur's hands landed heavily on my back squeezing the air out of my lungs. I grunted as she grabbed a wedge of flesh and rolled it between her fingers. It hurt, it really did. I had a brief flash where I saw Mason prosecuting them in court on my behalf. I lifted my head and made to roll over and ease the pressure on my nose, but the bully deftly flipped me back on my stomach and continued to pummel my bruised flesh.

I was tempted to chatter on about how I'd slipped on wet leaves and fallen over, but that would sound as if I was making excuses. I fretted the masseuse might think I'd been beaten up by my boyfriend or husband, how humiliating would that be?

In the end I said nothing. I'm not sure her English was that fluent either.

Despite all the pampering, I still found it difficult to relax. By the end of the day Andrea was totally chilled, waggling her recently manicured and polished nails in *Fireman Red.* She persuaded me to have the same colour. "It will make us soul sisters," she giggled. I enjoyed the foot massage and watched the girl paint my five remaining toenails bright red to match my fingers.

I always close my eyes when I have my hair done. Don't ask me why. I always have. When I looked in the mirror I was pleased with the result, the long lank look was gone and my mousy locks fell to my shoulders in gentle waves. I was convinced Mason would notice and approve.

I walked back into the house feeling a lot more confident. I knew I looked good and Andrea was right, the spa had helped me to relax.

To my surprise Belinda was home before me and already had her nose in the fridge. She looked up in alarm.

"Why do you always have to creep around?" she whined.

"I most certainly was not creeping anywhere." My reply was sharper than I intended.

She stood up, juice bottle in one hand and her eyes focused on my hands.

"Yeuk, bright red, that is sooooo last season. No one uses that colour anymore."

I put my bag down on the table and wriggled out of my coat.

"That's surprising since they had lots of bright nail varnishes at the spa. Maybe they use them for the older soon-to-be-wrinklies like me." I deliberately kept my voice light, although inside I could feel my confidence plummeting.

"When I'm really old I'll keep up with trends and not let myself go just because I managed to grab myself a man."

I gasped. I was tempted to lash out and slap her face, but I clamped both hands firmly on my coat as I went back into the hall to hang it up in the cupboard.

I was still trying to think of a clever put down in return, but I was too late. Belinda had already stormed up the stairs carrying the juice bottle in one hand and a plate of food in the other. Where did she put it all? She never put on an ounce of extra weight. I only had to look at food and the pounds piled on.

My heart gave a little flutter when I heard the interconnecting garage door open. I was busy beating up a pancake batter, we were going to have toad-in-the-hole tonight, and looked up with what I hoped was a welcoming smile. I needn't have bothered. Mason barely glanced at me but swept past with a nod and made for the study swinging his briefcase in one hand and clutching his coat in the other.

"Good day?" I called after him, but he only grunted in reply before slamming the door behind him.

My shoulders slumped and I fought back the tears. I would not let his behaviour get me down. I beat the life out of the mix before throwing it over the sausages.

The atmosphere was strained at the dinner table. To my surprise, Belinda came down the stairs at the first call, I usually have to shout several times, and Mason strode back in and sat down opposite me. Still no comment on my new hair style and very tasteful make up. The mirror told me I looked years younger, and even rather attractive, but it had no effect on my husband.

I had just served up when Belinda pushed an envelope across the table towards her father.

He stared at her. "What's this?"

"Letter from school." She concentrated on her dinner plate.

Mason put down his knife and fork and tore it open.

"Bloody brilliant. You've been excluded from school for three weeks, but I guess you knew that already?"

She didn't reply, but nodded as she crammed in another mouthful.

"I hope you're not expecting Leah to home school you?" It was almost a snarl.

"Of course I bloody don't."

Again, Mason ignored the swearing.

"Well I'm grounding you. You don't leave this house during the day. You stay in and study. No going down to the mall. No sneaking off with your friends."

"Dad. You can't expect me to stay cooped in here with her." She glared in my direction.

My hands shook slightly as I sliced through a piece of sausage. Surely Mason wasn't expecting me to be her jailor for the next three weeks. And how was I going to study privately with Belinda slinking around? I was itching to get on with my first assignment, I was really enjoying the work. I'd not done much yet but I had deadlines to meet.

The thought of Belinda at home all day was horrific. These few precious hours when I was in the house alone allowed me to regain my equilibrium before both husband and stepdaughter sent it crashing through the floor again.

"You will do as I tell you!" Mason's voice thundered across the table.

I noticed Belinda flinch and curl in on herself. She hunched over her plate, pushing the food round and round in small circles with her fork. I could almost touch the fury and rage that leapt across the table, but for once she did not reply.

After drawing a deep breath, Mason concentrated on shovelling the toad-in-the-hole into his mouth with almost indecent haste. The moment he'd cleared his plate he got up and began to walk out of the room.

"There's apple pie for dessert." I hated the way my voice sounded weak and tentative.

"I'll have it in the study," he flung over his shoulder, slamming the door behind him.

I sighed. I'd hoped he'd say something complimentary about me; the staff at the spa had worked wonders with my face and I was pleased with the new haircut. But no, I might as well be part of the furniture, though I guess I was a little more use.

"I'm sure the three weeks will pass quickly, maybe this might be a chance to bond with my stepdaughter."

"Yeah, sure," she snarled. "Be thrilling to have you hanging round my neck all day, every day."

"That's a nasty thing to say, Belinda!" I didn't mean to snap, but I had to draw the line somewhere. "Look, I've done my best to be friends. I've not tried to replace your mother. I've not bossed you around. I've fed you, washed and ironed your clothes and never pried into your personal life. Don't you think it's about time you gave me a break?"

I paused waiting for her response.

She stared at me for several seconds then rose to her feet. "Yeah well, we don't always have to like the people who are foisted on us, do we?"

Foisted on her? Is that how she saw me?

"I'm sorry you feel that way, I really am. But maybe if you gave me a chance you might discover something you like about me?"

"Don't think there's much chance of that." She leaned forward and pushed her half empty plate towards me, then turned and marched upstairs to her bedroom.

Well, I'd tried. I couldn't do any more. I stared at the food on my plate and realised that I didn't feel hungry. I'd feed Mason his dessert and curl up on the couch and watch television by myself. Who said you couldn't feel lonely in the midst of a family?

I don't remember Mason coming to bed. The sound of water running in the shower woke me the following morning. His side of our bed was undisturbed. I flung back the covers and went to peep into the guest room. There was no sign he'd slept in there either. Perhaps he'd fallen asleep at his desk. I decided not to mention it.

He was morose as usual at breakfast and, as he didn't appear to be in any hurry, I took a deep breath as I handed him his orange juice.

"Mason, is there a problem at work? Are you worried about something?"

He looked surprised. "No, of course not. Why should there be?"

"I've no idea, but you always seem so angry. The happy times are few and far between these days."

"And whose fault is that?" His tone was cold and dismissive.

"I… I don't feel I've changed. You're the one who is miserable all the time."

"Yes, I expected I'd get the blame. I was waiting for you to start whinging and whining."

I gasped. "I'm not. Not complaining that is. I'm simply asking you what reason you have to be so aggressive towards me. If I've done something wrong, then please tell me."

"There's no point. It's not going to change anything."

"So, there is something wrong?"

"Look," Mason slammed his juice glass on the table top and stood up, "I don't have time for all this drama. I have enough of it at work. I need peace and quiet when I come home. And you're certainly not helping."

I shrank back into my chair. There was no way I was ever going to get through to Mason, well not when he was in a mood. The problem was, one mood followed hard on the heels of the one before.

I watched him storm out of the room and grab his coat and briefcase. Then the door to the garage slammed shut, rattling the cleaning products on the shelf above the washing machine.

Life was so unfair. I'd not even burdened Mason with my fears, probably irrational fears, with clothes moving and knives jumping around. I'd kept all those worries to myself. I could hardly share them with Belinda either. If she wasn't the one shuffling my stuff then maybe I was hallucinating.

I dragged myself over to the sink and began to wash the dishes. Mason hated it when I did them by hand, but I couldn't bring myself to put the machine on for a few cups and plates, nor did I like to think of dirty dishes festering in the machine all day either.

"Why don't you use the dishwasher?" Belinda hissed in my ear.

"It doesn't seem worth it for a few dishes," I replied.

"Bit pointless having it then, isn't it?" She opened the fridge door and grabbed the orange juice and a glass.

"Maybe it will help to preserve the planet." I tried to keep my voice as light as possible. Now that the younger folk had woken up to the fact the world's resources were on their last legs, perhaps this would be a meeting point? Images of Belinda and me side by side holding placards while singing some protest song flashed in front of my eyes. This was swiftly dispelled by her next words.

"Well it's your generation which got us all into this mess, it's up to you lot to clean it all up. You'll have to un-fuck it won't you?"

Maybe I should accept the truth Belinda and I would never get on? It had taken me years to get over the death of James and the babies. Maybe I was still not over it. I'd moved on, you have to don't you? No amount of weeping and wailing would bring them back. Nor would it give me a new leg.

I'd been shocked when one of the physiotherapists told me that I was lucky to have had something to focus on after the accident. She'd explained further that learning to walk and cope with a prosthesis had occupied so much of my waking thoughts that I didn't have time to get too depressed and dwell on the death of my entire family. Little did she know; I was severely depressed and I'd been on enough medications to sink the Titanic.

By the time I met Mason I'd begun to wean myself off them and in the very early days I'd gone weeks without taking more than the odd Valium. Belinda hadn't been any friendlier but I'd been more optimistic in those days and hoped I'd win her around in time, as soon as she came to terms that I was her father's new wife.

But that had not happened and we'd already celebrated our two-year anniversary a few months ago. I wasn't hopeful another couple of years would make things any better.

I resisted turning around to see what Belinda was up to as she opened and closed drawers, slammed cupboard doors and banged dishes down on the counter top. I kept my eyes firmly focused on the soapy suds in the sink, admiring the colours reflected in each little bubble from the overhead neon light.

I didn't have long to wait until I heard her thump back up the stairs and slam her bedroom door. I'd run around with a duster and then set myself up in the study to work on my first assignment. I'd just ignore the fact Belinda was grounded and carry on as if she wasn't there.

By lunchtime I was pleased with my progress. Sure, I was rusty, it had been an age since I'd studied for anything, but it's like riding a bike isn't it? You can never unlearn. I have no idea how some of the knowledge I thought was long forgotten suddenly popped back into my head. They say you never forget a single thing, but as you get older it's more difficult to retrieve information. All those filing cabinets in your head now stuffed so full, it takes longer to rummage through. That's what I tell myself anyway.

I was so busy I worked right through lunch time and was startled to see it was late in the afternoon, the light already fading, and I'd not even planned anything for dinner that night.

I bustled around in the kitchen grabbing ingredients. Strange... the vegetable rack was not in its usual place next to the sink. I opened one cupboard after another but I couldn't find it anywhere. I knew I'd not moved it. I wouldn't have put it somewhere else, would I?

The telephone ringing jarred me into action and, as I rushed into the hall to answer it, I stumbled over the missing rack. It was standing in the middle of the hall and, as I fell over, it toppled to one side sending a variety of vegetables rolling all over the floor.

I lunged for the phone, but whether it cut off a moment before or after I picked up the receiver the only sound was the dial tone.

I looked up to see Belinda peering down at me over the bannister.

"Who was that?" she nodded towards the phone.

"I have no idea," I replied, trying to steady myself against the wall and scrambling to my feet. I bent down to reach some of the vegetables. "Can you come and give me a hand with these, please?" I called up to her.

She didn't move, but observed the mess. "Why did you throw vegetables all over the place?"

"I didn't, the rack was..." I didn't have the energy to explain. "Just give me a hand here."

"I'm busy!" Her door slammed shut and I was left as best as I could to clear up the mess. Bending over, even with two good legs, gets more difficult as you get older and, before long, I was hot and uncomfortable as the sweat trickled down into my eyes, making them sting.

I lugged the replenished vegetable rack back into the kitchen and pushed it into the cupboard by the sink. I just refused to even worry about how it found its way into the hallway. If I fretted, then I'd go mad, if I wasn't already halfway there.

I hurried to prepare the evening meal. If Mason had to wait then that would be another cause for complaint. It was all very well Dr Cromptom saying you should not run your life trying to please everyone else and putting them first. He was a man, wasn't he? I expect his cook or wife, or whoever, always had his meals waiting for him on time. He wouldn't have to spend a whole evening listening to a diatribe about how he had nothing else to do all day, how she worked her fingers to the bone and all she asked was a little cooperation. Was it too much to expect that… and on and on and on until he could scream?

I was busy taking the casserole out of the oven when Belinda walked behind me into the laundry and I heard the garage door bang.

Lord, please tell me she'd not gone out. There would be hell to pay if Mason found out she'd defied him.

I slid the Pyrex dish onto the wooden board and rushed out after her.

She'd left the garage door wide open and her bicycle was missing.

My shoulders drooped. There wasn't a thing I could do about it, but she'd left me to weather the storm.

I won't bore you with the details of the rest of that evening. It's enough to say that Mason was furious, I got the blame, and to avoid his ranting and raving I fled to our bedroom out of range of his vitriolic tirade.

As I sprawled on the bed, I became aware of a ticking sound. It wasn't the electric clock, that was silent. We had nothing in the room that ticked, the noise would have driven Mason mad. He demands total peace and quiet when he is trying to get to sleep.

I rubbed my ears hard. Maybe it was my imagination, but no, the sound refused to go away.

Tick. Tick. Tick.

I slid off the bed and began opening and closing drawers and cupboards. I checked in the dressing room and the en-suite bathroom but the noise didn't get louder or softer.

Tick. Tick. Tick.

Starting at one side of the door, I retraced my steps and worked my way round the room, peering everywhere. When I arrived back at the door on the other side, I'd still not found the source of the noise.

I stood and tried to rationalise where it could be coming from. Ah, the only place I'd not looked was under the bed. Slowly I eased my way down onto the floor, inched forward and lifted the valance. Two eyes stared at me, bright green, winking as they opened and closed.

For a second, I froze then shot out one arm and made a grab for it.

Pulling it towards me I stared at one of those metallised toy cats, the gold coloured ones made in China.

The left arm continued to move in time with the eyelids up and down, up and down.

Tick. Tick. Tick.

I resisted the urge to hurl it against the wall. Another object I'd never seen before outside the market and a couple of local shops. What the hell was it doing under our bed?

I scrambled to my feet and marched down the stairs with as much dignity as I could. I was still shaking, whether from anger or fear I couldn't tell you. I marched into the study disturbing Mason who was at his desk scribbling on some document. He immediately covered it up before I had a chance to see what it was.

"Do you know anything about this?" I banged the ticking cat on the polished desk.

"What? That? Good god, no. I wouldn't bring cheap tat like that into the house." His lips turned up in a sneer.

"Well it was under our bed. Ticking." Even as I said it, I realised how ridiculous I sounded.

"Don't be so bloody stupid. I don't believe you. If it was there you must have put it there."

"I did not!" I could feel my blood pressure rise. "Don't you dare say I'm making this up. The moment I walked in I heard the ticking."

The cat chose that minute to stop. The silence was almost deafening. I resisted the temptation to wrench its arm off.

"If you don't mind, I'm busy. Go and have your hallucinations somewhere else." He turned to his laptop and switched it on. "Go on, get out. You're losing it, obviously. Don't whine to me about your dementia." He turned his attention to the screen and tapped away on the keyboard.

Defeated, I walked out to the garage and dropped the cat in the rubbish bin. It would be collected the day after tomorrow and I hoped I'd never see it again. As I slammed the lid, I could see the bright, metallic green eyes glaring at me balefully.

I was still shaken. I felt violated. The safety and comfort of my personal and private space had been invaded and it had eroded my safety.

Three times now, someone had gone into my bedroom. Whoever was trying to scare me had moved things in the kitchen and there was the rabbit in the car.

I couldn't believe I had done those things myself. Had I? These silly little actions were all so petty. Not life threatening. Not dangerous, unless I counted the effect it was having on my nerves. I could almost feel them shredding. The nerve endings felt raw and irritated, my head ached, and my hands would not stop shaking.

When the phone rang again, I was tempted to ignore it. I wandered into the hall, and stood staring at the instrument as it screeched.

"Answer that damned phone!" screamed Mason from behind his study door.

Taking a deep breath, I lifted the receiver and said hello.

It was my mother's neighbour. Mother was sick. Would it be possible to come and care for her for a few days? They thought I should contact Social Services as she was not coping too well on her own.

I sighed and agreed. What else could I do? I told her I would be there the next day and she sounded more than a little relieved. As I replaced the receiver, I recalled that she had four school age children of her own and worked part time. Her life was busy and full, whereas mine? I had no excuse not to go. While I loved my mother, I could not say she loved me.

Ever since I can remember, I've been the disappointment in the family. I learned later they had a name for it. The Scapegoat Child. While my elder sister Daphne could do no wrong, and the sun, moon and stars shone out of my younger brother, they both escaped. Daphne went off to nurse in Australia and Martin got a job in a ski resort in Canada.

That left me as chief cook and bottle washer for a mother who was still grieving her widowhood years after the event. I escaped to some extent when I married James. We moved into our own house, but it was not far from my old family home and, in my nursing days, I would pop in several times a week.

When the babies came along, Mother made more of an effort to visit us, too often for my comfort. She fussed over the grandchildren and was not short on advice on how I should bring them up. Had they lived, I suspect she would have spoiled them rotten. She criticised everything. They were either too warmly dressed, or would freeze to death in their skimpy outfits. The food I gave them was too healthy with no fun treats, or fast food full of chemicals giving them diabetes or some other terrible disease before they reached their teens. They were too fat or too thin.

Her comments were way out of line, especially since the children were only two and three years old.

Then the miracle happened. Mother met a man and, in a whirlwind romance, they were married within three months.

I couldn't take to him. Not because he could never match up to the wonderful father I remembered, but I didn't like the way he dragged his eyes up and down my body. He made me feel very uncomfortable.

I was grateful to him though for taking the pressure off me.

Then, after the initial flurry of concern after the car accident, my mother weeping louder than anyone else at the funeral, they both left me to my own devices.

Had I really expected empathy, love and comfort when a bleak future stretched ahead? It never came. They popped in a couple of times, made awkward and critical conversation, cleaned me out of cake and biscuits and departed – much to my relief.

Then husband number two had a heart attack and once again I was back living at home for that short time as I attempted to mop up her tears.

It didn't work of course. Everything I did was wrong, and I was the cause of everything that had gone wrong in Mother's life. On one or two occasions she turned violent and I began to fear for my own safety.

I moved back to my own home and, as soon as I had recovered enough to be mobile after hours of agonising physio, I put the house on the market and fled south to the other end of the country. I wrote to her every week, but she never replied. The wedding invitation was ignored and occasionally I would phone her neighbour to update me on how she was. Nothing changed, but apparently Mother refused to contact the Social Services and would not even discuss moving into either assisted living or a care home.

Now this. I had no option but to travel north and do what I could. Mason would grumble and complain. He'd have to cook his own meals for a few weeks, but what about Belinda?

This time I knocked on his study door but I didn't wait for him to answer before I walked in. "That was Mum's neighbour, I'm needed to look after her and, hopefully, move her into a care home."

"And how long is that going to take? I thought Social Services made all those arrangements." Typical of Mason, always thinking of himself first.

"As far as I know, she's not registered or anything like that, so I'm not sure how to even get her on the list. Hopefully, I'll only be away a couple of weeks, but from what we see on the news, the whole system is over run with the 'flu epidemic as well. It's only right that families should help out if they can."

"Oh of course, even though you have a sister and a brother with healthy arms and legs who are even more capable."

I gasped. This was the first time Mason had ever referred to me as incomplete, broken, not a whole person. It hurt, and I could feel the tears threatening to spill down my cheeks.

I turned abruptly before he could see how much he had upset me and told him I would be leaving in the morning.

"And what about Belinda? What about your responsibility to her?"

I paused. For a moment I'd forgotten she couldn't be left alone. Not that fifteen-year olds couldn't cope, but under the circumstances it wouldn't be wise to leave her unsupervised. Like me, Mason must have suspected she was getting in with a bad crowd if she was skipping school.

I didn't know what to say. I stared hard at the patterned carpet on the floor in the hallway. Where did my loyalties lie? To a stepdaughter who hated me? Or a mother who had raised me and possibly hated me even more?

"Take her with you."

"What!"

I swung round to face Mason, too shocked to cry.

"I said, take her with you. She can't be left here all day and I can't take her to work."

Huh, you just did for three days, I thought. *When it suited you.*

"I don't think she's going to be too happy about that."

"I don't care what she bloody thinks. She'll do as she's told."

Mason turned back to his computer.

I plodded up the stairs and knocked on Belinda's door.

"What do you want?" came the muffled voice from inside.

"You need to pack, we're leaving tomorrow."

The door flew open. "What did you say?"

"I have to go care for my mother, and your father says you're to come with me."

"Like fuck I am. You can go. I'm not."

I sighed. "Well sort it out with your father. I'm only the messenger."

I left her and went to pick out what I needed to take.

That night Mason rolled over in bed and, grabbing me, made love. No, love is not the right description. While it was not exactly rape it was close to it. He didn't ask if I wanted it, he didn't wait until I was ready, but satisfied his needs without saying a word. Then he turned over and went to sleep. Was this a show of affection because I was going to be away for a while? Or his way of punishing me? I'd given up trying to second guess him.

It was the last day in March, would April be better?

APRIL

We left early the next morning. Belinda had a face like thunder and kept me waiting while she disappeared back into the house three times to grab something she needed. I didn't bother to enquire what was so urgent. I had yet to drop the bombshell that my mother did not subscribe to the Internet and she was going to be isolated from her friends for the next couple of weeks. At least having her with me gave me a cast iron excuse to stay only for two and a half weeks and I hoped that would put pressure on the authorities to get Mother settled somewhere safe.

Once we passed London and headed north up the M1, she relaxed a bit. She didn't go so far as to chat but I could feel a bit of the tension leave her as she put her phone down and looked at the scenery.

She was even quite gracious when we stopped at the motorway services for a coffee. I wasn't sure how to approach her, so I said the minimum.

We stopped a couple more times for lunch and a pit stop and it was dark long before I finally pulled into the familiar driveway.

"This it?" I could sense Belinda wrinkling her nose at the unkempt garden and the peeling paint on the garage door.

"Yes. Needs a lot of TLC now."

"There are no lights on," Belinda observed.

"Oh dear, I hope she's okay." I got out of the car as quickly as I could and fished the key out of my pocket as I rang the doorbell. I'm not sure what prompted me to hold onto the key I used for years as I was growing up. Nights out with friends – Mother never waited up for me – and sneaking in a boyfriend or two for a surreptitious cuddle on the sofa.

No one answered the door, so I pushed it open and peered into the darkened hallway.

"Mum. Mum, are you there? It's me, Leah. Leah, your daughter."

There was no reply. The darkness and silence bounced back at me and I jumped when I felt Belinda walk up behind me.

"I need the loo, urgent," she said, pushing past and peering into the first doorway on the left.

"It's over there in the corner." I pointed while I flicked the light switch. Nothing happened. I used the torch on my phone to check the main electric box in the hallway. At some point it had tripped. I pushed the lever and the downstairs was flooded with light.

I raced from room to room and found Mother fast asleep in her favourite chair opposite the television, which sprang into life showing some mindless game show with an over-enthusiastic audience. For a moment I thought she was dead as it took a lot of shaking and calling her name before she opened her eyes.

She squinted at me. "Leah? What are you doing here?"

Did I expect an ecstatic welcome? No.

"I'm here because your neighbour phoned me. She was worried about you."

"Nosy old bitch." Mother struggled to pull herself up out of the chair. "Well now you can see I'm fine, you can leave."

Oh, how I wished. I turned as Belinda walked in.

"And who is this?"

Belinda just stood and stared at her.

"It's Belinda, Mother. Mason's daughter. Remember?"

"No." She struggled to her feet, shaking off my helping hand. "And who are you? What do you think you're doing in my house! Get out! Get out at once or I'll call the police. Get out, d'you hear me?" She stepped up close shaking her fist.

"Bloody hell," Belinda spluttered. "She's mad."

I sighed. "She has dementia," I whispered. "Mother, why were you sitting here in the dark? Did you know the electricity had tripped?"

She ignored me, pushed past and tottered into the kitchen.

I followed with Belinda right behind me. She nudged me and handed over a huge pile of unopened envelopes.

"Where were these?" I asked her.

"On the floor, inside the front door."

I took them and shuffled through the pile. Several were from the hospital.

"Mum, you have post here. Do you think you should open it?" I held out the envelopes.

"Not interested." Mother was rooting around in the cupboards. There was little food to find. From the clothes she was wearing – an old, stained tracksuit and threadbare slippers – with her hair a mess and her hands shaking, she was not taking care of herself.

I turned to Belinda and handed her a local food delivery flyer tucked in between the unopened envelopes. "Phone them and choose anything you like but nothing hot or spicy for my mother."

"Pizza do?"

"Yes, enough for all of us."

"Cool." She wandered back into the sitting room fingers tapping away on her iPhone. She barged back a moment later, face like thunder.

"Bloody Internet doesn't work!"

"Ah, no. Lots of elderly people have not moved into the digital age, and my mother is one of them."

"And you knew that, before you dragged me up here?"

"Don't you have data on your phone? Can't you use 3G? Or 4 or 5G, whatever you have on there?"

She didn't answer me right away but kept tapping away. "The sodding battery is flat. So now I guess we starve."

"No, you can use the landline. It's in the hallway. I'm not asking you to use the Yellow Pages, you have the number on the flyer."

"Yellow what?"

I sighed and gave her a firm push back into the front hall, pointing to the phone. "You're a big girl now, sort it out."

I went back into the kitchen, sifting through the post. Mother took no notice of me, even when I mentioned there were several letters from the local hospital. She just shrugged her shoulders and continued to rummage mindlessly through the cupboards and drawers.

I opened the most recent letter from the National Health Services which stated that Mother had missed several appointments and if she did not attend the next one, they would be forced to reassign her, blah… blah… blah. I saw that she was scheduled for an appointment in the psychiatric department next morning.

I would make sure she'd be there. She must have been referred by her general practitioner who noticed signs of dementia or Alzheimer's.

The evening dragged on. We brought in the cases from the car, found sufficient sheets and duvets to make up the beds, and ate the takeaway in front of the television. The atmosphere was heavy, full of tension, and no one laughed at the stupid comedy show that played out on the screen.

Every now and again Mother would get up and wander round the room. Sometimes she mumbled, sometimes she shouted and asked questions neither of us could answer. She wanted to know where her husband was, often confusing the first one with the second.

Belinda ignored her, head bent over the phone, her fingers moving in a blur.

"Ah, you topped up your data?"

"Yeah. Had to."

"Belinda, I do understand the feeling of being cut off from the world. It seems strange not to be on line, even for an old wrinkly like me."

"Fuck me! No Internet. How uncool is that?"

"Most very elderly people don't have it."

"Duh. Dinosaur age."

I bristled. To a point she was right, but Mother was still only in her mid-sixties and there were plenty of grannies, great grannies and octogenarians Skyping and Facetiming and WhatsApping and chatting on Facebook.

"I'm going to bed," Belinda moaned. "It's bloody freezing in here."

She was right. I'd turned on the electric fire as the only form of heating I could find. All the radiators were stone cold and I had no idea if they ran on gas or oil. I'd have a good look tomorrow and I'd need to contact Social Services.

It took a while for me to get Mother up the stairs, undressed, and tucked into bed. She had calmed down and whimpered like a small child. I eyed the medications next to her bed, but didn't dare give her anything without knowing what she should take. I surreptitiously picked up the bottles and boxes and placed them in a top cupboard in the kitchen. It was grossly irresponsible leaving so many tablets within reach of a woman in her state of mind.

Next morning the skies were grey and brooding. It was an effort to drag myself out of bed. I'd barely slept a wink and the freezing cold bedroom tempted me to snuggle down and stay warm. It was already past eight and it would take time and patience to get Mother up, out, into the car and to the hospital for her eleven o'clock appointment.

To my surprise Belinda was not only less sullen, she

was also helpful. She made coffee and tea and put out the only packet of stale cereal she could find on the table. She offered to run to the corner shop for bread and a few other essentials. I handed her a fifty-pound note and went to rouse Mother and help her get washed and dressed.

One moment she cooperated, the next she resisted all my efforts. She threw the clothes I got out for her on the floor, and stamped her feet like a spoiled two-year-old.

With Belinda's help we finally got her fed and out of the front door. As I was easing her into the front seat Belinda announced she would stay in the house.

"Oh no you don't, you're coming too!" I didn't mean to snap but I was already exhausted and we'd not even left home.

Her face changed to the one I was used to, sullen and angry.

"Look," I closed the passenger door firmly after checking the childproof lock was on and turned to her, "I do appreciate your help this morning, I really do. And I'm not sure how I'm going to manage at the hospital. So please…?"

She grunted, flung open the back door, and plonked herself down before slamming it loudly.

As usual, I ended up having to park streets away from the hospital. Why can they never provide enough space for cars? When they do, the charges are exorbitant. I was regretting not calling for an Uber. At least the driver might have helped; Mother was a deadweight when she refused to cooperate.

"I hate hospitals," grumbled Belinda as between us we

steered Mother along one corridor after another looking for the right department. We left Belinda perched on a plastic chair outside the door when they finally called out Mother's name.

I thought the doctor lacked empathy. She was the brusque, no-nonsense type, battering Mother with one test after another, not even taking the time to reassure her or explain what she was doing.

Mother looked at me with hate in her eyes. "Take me home," she repeated over and over. "I want to go home. I don't like it here."

"It won't be long now." I tried to placate her. "I can't cope," I whispered to the doctor. "She needs to be in a home."

"I want to go home," Mother wailed again.

"Speak to Social Services," the doctor snapped and scribbled manically in Mother's file.

"Do they have a desk in the hospital? Is there information in her notes?"

The doctor sighed and shuffled through several sheets of paper. "Not as far as I can see. She's not listed on the register. You will have to visit them and they will assign you a case worker."

"I had no idea she was now so frail. Her neighbour called me and I've rushed up from London."

The doctor sighed again and picked up the phone. "We're all understaffed and run off our feet." She glared at me and sniffed.

"Yes, I understand that. But I can't stay with her indefinitely and she won't cooperate with me. She's too big to manage, I don't have the strength. I'm disabled myself."

The doctor's raised eyebrows told me she didn't believe me, until I pulled up my pants leg and showed her my prosthesis.

Unintentionally my mother came to my aid. She turned suddenly and began to scream. "What are you doing here? I don't want you. You've always been a disappointment to me. Not like Daphne. She was always the good daughter. She loved her mother. She would take care of me. But you young people, you're all the same. No care for those who gave you life, fed and clothed you, gave you a good education and then what did you do? Leave, yes, just selfishly run off to lead your own lives. Never a thought for your own mother."

"Mother, Daphne's in Australia, at least I'm here with you." My words fell on deaf ears.

"I'm also responsible for a stepdaughter, who has currently been excluded from school. So, you see, I can only stay up north a short time." I spoke directly to the disinterested white-coated medic.

The doctor sighed again and scribbled some more as the phone still rang unanswered at the other end.

"I can only write a referral and pass on the message," she said scribbling frantically.

My shoulders slumped. How was I going to get through the next few days? How long would all this take? I love my mother, well, as much as you can love the woman who gave birth to you and now hates everything about you.

At last we shuffled out of surgery to hostile looks from the long queue of waiting patients. I looked for Belinda but she was nowhere to be seen. I tried to leave Mother on a vacant chair while I searched for her, but she refused to be left, clinging to my coat sleeve like a limpet.

I walked both ways up and down the corridor, peering in all directions but there was no sign of Belinda. I took a deep breath. *Think, Leah, think.* I pulled out my mobile and dialled her number.

Mother tried to wrench it out of my hands. "I should have known you'd have one of those," she spat at me. "All this modern technology, where has that got us? Those things fry your brains."

I did my best to ignore her as Belinda's phone just rang and rang and then dropped into voicemail. She'd switched it off! Belinda never switched her phone off, she even took it into the bathroom with her. I groaned and then reasoned that she might have run out of airtime, or data or… I had no idea what package she was on. Maybe I was being unfair, but I'd told her to wait and she hadn't. I decided on a trip to the cafeteria for a strong cup of coffee. I doubted they would sell wine, or even something stronger, in a hospital.

I'd hoped to find Belinda grabbing a snack and a drink, she'd kept the change from the fifty pound note; but there was no sign of her among the crowds. I plonked Mother down in a chair and joined the queue. Twice I lost my place as I had to go back and put her back in her seat. She was refusing to sit still, so I steered her into the queue in front of me and kept a firm hold on her arm.

Once she had a drink, I was able to give her some of the medication I'd brought from the house. At least the doctor was able to list what she'd been prescribed, what it was for, and when to take it. I hoped the drugs would have a calming effect.

At one point she slid down in her chair and appeared to fall asleep. Dare I leave her and try to find Belinda? I didn't even know where to start. The hospital was a huge place and she could be anywhere. It was possible she was waiting by the car, I could only hope.

My hopes were dashed as I helped Mother along the pavement back to where I'd parked. No sign of Belinda. There was nothing I could do. She knew Mother's address, she'd dictated it to the pizza parlour last night, so maybe she had gone back to the house she'd not wanted to leave earlier.

By now Mother was half doped – those pills must be strong – as she allowed me to help her into the car and I drove her home.

I needed to phone in for a grocery delivery, go through the mail, sort out her overdue bills and pay the urgent ones to make sure they would not cut off vital services. Then I must contact the Social Services and plead with them to find new accommodation for her. I didn't even know where to start. Where was the nanny state when you needed help?

My hopes were dashed yet again when I parked up in the driveway. There was no sign of Belinda. I took the key out of the ignition and looked over at Mother. Her head was lolling to one side; she was not asleep, nor did she look fully awake.

I scrambled out and walked quickly round to the back door, in case my errant stepdaughter was waiting in the garden. I even rattled the chain on the shed, but it was firmly locked.

It took me several minutes to get Mother out of the car, into the house, and back into her favourite chair. She continued to grumble and throw accusations at me, but I did my best to ignore them. I think if Golden Girl Daphne had walked in at that moment, I'd have strangled her with my bare hands. I was sick of hearing how wonderful she was and what a disappointment I was.

It isn't a new phenomenon. Very often the child that does everything for the parent is the despised and berated offspring. I closed my ears to the moans, but Mother knew just how to attack where it hurt most.

As I went into the kitchen to put the kettle on and find paper and pencil to write out a grocery list, I could still hear the snide comments floating behind me.

"You'll never admit it, but your precious James was drunk that night, wasn't he? Dangerous driving caused that accident. And how did that end up? Two precious young lives wiped out before they even started and you left a useless cripple."

I held back the tears as I scribbled; bread, milk…

"Always said he was no good, that one."

… sausages… packs frozen vegetables… fruit, now what would Mother like best?

"But would you listen to me? Or your father? Oh no."

… chicken pieces… 3 steaks… bag pasta…

"Just because he was a doctor you decided he was a good catch."

… jars cook in sauces… potatoes… coffee…

"It's in the eyes you know. You can always tell. And James' eyes said it all."

… tea … sugar … jam … I was scribbling faster and faster, ignoring the tears that dripped off my face making the shopping list soggy. Wine… cases of it, and maybe a bottle of something stronger; I was going to need it. I was even tempted to add cigarettes to the list, even though I'd given up years ago. I'd have done anything for a puff right then.

As I scanned the list, I was sure I'd forgotten lots of things but it would have to do for now. I doubted Sainsbury's sold ear plugs, but they would go nicely with the brandy. I dialled the central number and read out my list, praying that my voice did not sound as tearful to them as it did to me. To my relief they promised delivery within the hour – as well they should since I was a regular customer and spent plenty with them.

I'd used the last of the coffee and found myself gravitating to the window, ready to pounce on the delivery man. An hour went by, then two, then three. I was beginning to wonder where the Sainsbury's van had got to when my mobile rang. It was Mason.

"What the hell did you have all this stuff delivered for? You know I don't like chicken! What am I supposed to do with all this food?"

My heart sank. So much for modern technology and centralised computing. How was the supermarket to know I was up north? Once they'd registered my mobile number, they'd automatically connected it to my bank account, my store account, and my home address. They'd ignored the fact that I'd given them Mother's address.

"I'm sorry," I stuttered as I tried to explain the error to Mason, but he wasn't listening. He was enjoying his rant and by now he was in full flow. He listed all the things I couldn't do; cook well, keep the house clean and tidy, organise a simple delivery, and on and on and on. I was about to cut him off when I took a deep breath and shouted back.

"While you're throwing a hissy fit about a few groceries delivered to the wrong house, your daughter has gone walkabout! I have no idea where she is. I left her waiting for us at the hospital…"

Mason shrieked down the phone. "What have you done to her? Is she hurt? Why was she at the hospital?"

I tried to butt in and explain my mother's appointment, but he wasn't listening. He continued to rant so I pressed the off switch. He had this address. It was his daughter. He was responsible for her and she was probably classed as an adult for most things as far as the law was concerned. Hell, you could even get married at sixteen and she only had a few weeks to go.

Of course I was worried about her, but I couldn't cope with everyone's problems. I was close to breaking point. I fished the crumpled shopping list out of the rubbish bin and dialled Sainsbury's again.

I'd always done my best to be polite to Mother. It's the way I was brought up, to respect your elders. But on this visit I was past caring. She was driving me to it. The sooner I could get her sorted the sooner I could return home. I was feeling less and less guilty by the moment.

My next task was to contact the right agency to get help. I began with the Citizen's Advice Bureau. I wandered out of earshot at the far end of the hallway, away from mother's whining complaints, and listened as the phone rang and rang and rang. I glanced at my watch and realised it was past four o'clock. They'd probably packed up and gone home.

The evening dragged on and on and on. The groceries were delivered, eventually, and I cooked us both a meal. I didn't bother to ask Mother what she fancied eating and I was beyond caring whether she ate it or not.

I had one of those lightbulb moments, when I realised that, while the government offices might be closed, the doctor's surgery would be open. I felt like a thief sifting through my mother's personal papers looking for the phone number which, I guessed, must be on some of the correspondence that had piled up on the floor inside the front door.

When I finally got through, the receptionist sounded friendly, and then doubtful when I explained that I wasn't the patient but speaking on behalf of my mother. She was however able to provide the correct number for me to contact in the morning.

Mother was persuaded to take her medication before I helped her upstairs and into bed. As she snuggled down under the duvet, I had a flash of compassion. She looked old and frail, her sparse, grey hair splaying out over the pillow.

She sat up, startling me. "What are you doing in my bedroom?" she snarled. Then shrieked "Get out of here, get out at once. If your father comes in…"

I fled before I heard any more. I'd read enough about dementia to know that lucidity came and went and there were good days and bad days. At least now I had an idea that her outbursts were not just her normal attitude towards me. My father had passed on years ago, so she was really confused.

I paced around downstairs worrying about Belinda. I tried her phone several times, but now it was dropping into her voice mail without ringing. The pictures dancing on the silent television in the corner showed police cars and that yellow tape they put up around crime scenes. I rushed over and turned up the sound.

Please don't let it be Belinda, I prayed. It was yet another knifing on an estate with a bad name on the other side of town, and the victim was male. I let out the breath I was not aware I'd been holding.

I tried home again, but this time Mason didn't answer and his mobile wasn't on. It was so frustrating. When had modern technology taught us to expect to get hold of anyone at any time?

Slumping down on the sofa I dialled Andrea's number. I needed to rant and cry, at least from a distance, on someone's shoulder. She didn't answer either. I couldn't remember feeling more alone.

I'd had a couple of close friends in this area; I'd grown up here, but two of them had moved away, one to Europe and the other to Australia. Those I had not been as close to avoided me after the accident. Were they ashamed they still had husbands and healthy children and were embarrassed to be cheerful in front of me? At the time I can't have been much fun, enveloped in my own misery, struggling to recover and then learning to walk again. I know I pushed them away and you know how it is when you lose touch. I couldn't bring myself to look them up when I would only dump more problems and misery into their lives.

I climbed the stairs, went to bed and fell asleep the moment my head touched the pillow.

Next morning I was up early and put the kettle on for the first coffee of the day. While the house was quiet, I tried contacting the Social Services office number, but this time I was too early. I crept back up the stairs to check if Belinda had somehow managed to sneak in. That was stupid really; she didn't have a key. As I suspected, her bed was empty, the sheets and duvet lying on the floor. Did I really think she would have made it yesterday morning?

Back downstairs I connected with the office at one minute past nine and I could almost hear the social worker taking her coat off as she answered the phone. She agreed that my mother's name had been flagged but they were so run off their feet that she wasn't sure whether she could get a case worker to come to the house today, or even tomorrow. I offered to bring Mother in but she didn't think that was a good idea. Then the doorbell rang.

I looked out of the front window and my heart jumped. "Don't go away, don't hang up," I pleaded, "the police are here."

"What?" she squawked down the phone.

I opened the door expecting a sullen faced Belinda but

was shocked to see my mother, still in her nightgown, no slippers or coat, standing between two policemen.

"Morning Ma'am. We found this lady down by the traffic lights on the High Street."

My mother wriggled in his grip. "Let go of me. Take your hands off. This is my house and I want to go in and get dressed. Why did you drag me out in this state?" She glared at me. "Cruel daughter, putting your own mother out of her own house!"

I stood there stunned. What was she saying?

She glanced down at her nightie, folded her arms across her chest and barged past me and into the house. I had to grab at the doorframe to stop myself from flying backwards.

I didn't know whether to talk to the police first or keep the lady from Social Services on the line. The policemen looked embarrassed, smiled, nodded and walked back down the path.

"Did you hear that?" I asked breathlessly down the phone. "The police have just returned my mother to the house. She was down the street disorientated and in her nightclothes." I forced back a sob. "I can't cope. Please, you have to help."

The friendly voice on the other end assured me they would liaise with the hospital and the doctor and send someone over today. I thanked her profusely before going to see what my mother was doing.

I found her standing in the kitchen attempting to open a packet of cereal. She was poking it and shaking it and banging it down on the counter.

"Here, let me." I put my hand out to take it from her but she whisked it away. I shrugged and spooned coffee and tea into mugs. I'd checked to see if Belinda was in bed but it had never occurred to me to check on Mother. I took a deep breath and focussed, trying to steady my hands. A squawk made me turn around to see cereal all over the floor. While I wasn't looking, she'd slashed the box open with a knife and the contents had cascaded onto the floor.

I was about to open my mouth and shout at her when she burst into tears. I crunched through the muesli and folded her in my arms. She was confused, she was helpless and she was my mother. It took a couple of seconds before she pulled away and shrieked at me.

"Now look at what you've done. You always were clumsy. A whole packet, wasted. Money doesn't grow on trees you know."

My sympathetic emotions drained away like quicksilver and the anger bubbled up inside me. At the same time a bolt of fear shot down my back. Mother wasn't safe here on her own, and I wasn't safe being with her either. There was no way I could see to lock the front door, there was only a Yale lock and a bolt. At any time, she could wander off and how could I watch her twenty-four seven? And the house wasn't exactly childproof either. Tools in the garage, knives and scissors in the drawers, and dozens of innocent objects could become lethal weapons.

I took her by the arm and firmly pushed her back into her favourite chair and turned on the television. Out of sight, I gathered some of the cereal into a container and swept the rest into the rubbish bin. I took her a bowl of muesli and a mug of tea and set it down next to her.

For a moment she stared at the fruit and flakes below the frosting of sugar and I thought she would remember it had been on the floor, but then she began to eat. I breathed a sigh of relief and to assuage my conscience helped myself to a bowl of the same.

As soon as I had cleared the dishes and made the beds, I tried again to contact Mason, Belinda and Andrea in that order, but all three phones rang before dropping into voice mail.

The clouds hung grey and heavy, the rain intermittent as the day dragged on. Mother sat happily in front of the television laughing hysterically at silly game shows, the news, and a documentary on crematoriums. Her comprehension was seriously affected and there was nothing I could do for her.

The doorbell rang mid-afternoon. Standing on the step was a harassed mid-twenty-year old clutching a briefcase and fighting to close her umbrella.

"Hi, I'm Eileen Markham, from the Social Services department." She indicated the lanyard round her neck.

"Bring it in," I nodded at the umbrella which was refusing to fold.

"Ah, some people, superstition and all that?"

"True, life could get worse, but my luck is all out at the moment. What's one more thing to worry about?" My laugh rang falsely even in my ears.

She bustled inside and between us we collapsed the umbrella and I helped her out of her coat. "Mother's inside. She may be lucid at times but it doesn't last for more than a few minutes. I've no idea how long she has been like this."

"Who you whispering to out there?" Mother shouted through the open door. Drat, I should have closed it before I let Ms Eileen Markham in. It was too late now.

"A lady to see you Mum," I called back. I clutched Eileen's sleeve. "Please… please… I can't cope with her. I don't have the strength and I'm not that steady on one leg."

She gave me a puzzled stare until I gave her a glimpse of my prosthesis. She nodded and went in to see Mother.

"Who are you?" she asked rudely.

"My name is Eileen Markham and I'm here to see how you are, Mrs Northam."

"I'm perfectly well today thank you. Would you like to stay for tea?" Mother gave her a dazzling smile. "Leah, go and make tea for our visitor. And bring those cakes I baked yesterday, the ones with the pink icing."

"Yes, Mother." I raised my eyebrows as I walked past Ms Markham as she said that she could not stay too long.

"No hurry," my mother insisted. "We've all the time in the world. Leah there doesn't have a job and I'm retired." Her voice floated out into the kitchen. I plugged in the kettle and slumped against the sink. Thoughts and words were whirling around in my head. I had to convince them not to leave Mother here in my care. I tried not to listen to the murmured voices from the other room. I'd leave the expert to chat to Mother and put my plea in before she left.

As I walked back in balancing a tray with the tea things, Mother rose to grab it from me. "Give it here," she snapped. "You know how clumsy you are." I risked a glance at Ms Markham and wondered how often she saw the browbeaten daughter left at home to cope with irascible relatives. The doormats who never got away.

I was pouring the tea when the social worker said the magic words.

"We would like you to spend a couple of nights in hospital, just to check you over. Would that be all right?"

"No, it bloody wouldn't," Mother snapped. "There's nothing wrong with me. I want to stay here."

"We think it would be in your best interest if we were able to give you a good check-up."

"There is absolutely nothing wrong with me. Poor Leah is oversensitive and worries about me. I'm quite happy here but she's come running up from London and decided I can't cope. It's all nonsense of course. Do I look ill or mad to you?"

I held my breath. She sounded so lucid, so normal, so healthy.

"Now my dear," Mother leaned forward to pat Ms Markham lightly on the knee, "I know you are all rushed off your feet, understaffed, and you don't need another old lady to cope with. You go back and tell them at the office that it was all a big mistake and I'm managing quite well here on my own in my own house. Will you do that dear?"

I could see Eileen Markham hesitating. It was tempting to lighten her case load and one look at the nervous, jittery daughter perched on the edge of the sofa and the laid back, relaxed, charming Mother with the beaming face and I know who I would have believed.

To my horror she began to gather her papers together

and stuff them back into her briefcase.

"You can't leave!" I gasped. "Remember I told your office Mother went walkabout in her nightie? The police brought her back. How can I cope?"

"Oh Leah, darling, you do exaggerate." Mother gave a tinkly laugh. "I only went out to check the post and the nice policeman thought I was confused!"

"Then why did the policemen tell me you were down in the High Street?" I tried not to sound aggressive, but didn't succeed.

"Did you take a note of their badge numbers? Was there a case number?" Ms Markham asked.

"No, of course not. Not necessary for a genuine mistake." Mother patted her visitor's knee again. "You pop along now and I promise I'll go and see Dr Benson and get this all sorted out."

"Well if you're sure?" Mrs Markham rose to her feet as my heart sank.

I followed her out to the hall as she struggled into her coat and retrieved her umbrella.

"Please believe me," I whined, "this is the most lucid she has been since I arrived yesterday and she is a danger if left alone."

"She has you, and we encourage as many of our elderly to stay in their own homes for as long as possible. There is such a long waiting list for places, months and years sometimes. If she really is as bad as you say she is, then assisted living would not be safe. She would need to be placed in a specialised care home and there are even fewer vacancies there."

"At least, could you please check on her records and find out the results of the tests she had at the hospital and make a decision based on that?"

"That will need her written consent, unless you hold a power of attorney? Do you?"

The thought of Mother signing over control of her affairs to me almost made me laugh out loud.

"No."

"Then I'm sorry but there's not a lot I can do. We cannot force her to go in for more tests if she doesn't want to. I will keep it all on file of course." Ms Markham gave me a kindly pat on the arm and before I could say another word she was through the door and halfway down the front path. At the gate, she paused and gave me a small wave before striding off down the street.

"Close that door, you're letting in all the cold air!"

I stood by the lounge door and watched Mother. Was she really suffering any form of dementia? How could I tell? I remembered that privacy rules were almost draconian now in England, and she would never sign anything over to me. Had her behaviour in front of Ms Elaine Markham been a flash of normal behaviour and example of one of the 'good' spells?

Suddenly Mother stood up and shrieked, an animal shriek that bounced off the walls and echoed from one side of the house to the other. Then she collapsed back into her chair and began rocking back and forwards. She keened like a child, wrapping her arms tightly around her body as she moved, her feet in her tattered slippers tapping up and down in rhythm with her cries.

I stood frozen, unsure what to do. Did she know I was watching her? Was this an act she was putting on to torment me? How could she be so lucid and charming one minute and like a wounded animal the next?

I crossed the carpet and gathered up the cups and plates and carried the tray back into the kitchen. As I filled the sink with hot water, I clutched the sponge so hard my knuckles turned white. I took several deep breaths. The bubbles fluoresced through the tears that were impossible to hold back, tears of frustration and misery. I took a deep breath. I was not going to break down, have a panic attack, or even feel sorry for myself.

I grabbed the first plate so hard it snapped in two. Another black mark. I swept it into the rubbish bin, and pushed it down out of sight. I thought it unlikely Mother would investigate, and if she did then I would stand up for myself. I would be assertive, as per Dr Cromptom's advice. I was tired of being as floppy as the dish cloth I was using.

I left the kitchen clean and tidy, the sides sparkling, the floor swept and mopped, and ventured back into the living room. Mother had fallen fast asleep in her chair, so I slid onto the couch and curled up with a book.

I picked it up and put it down several times, finding it almost impossible to concentrate. Tomorrow I'd go and see the neighbour who had contacted me, and explain what had happened so far. If the state, in all its wisdom, would not allow me to organise anything for my mother, and she was not going to cooperate, then there was no point in me being here. My hands were tied and I might as well leave. I wondered if Belinda had found her way home?

The evening passed without any further drama. I made a cup of cocoa and took Mother up to bed, ignoring her plaintive whines as I helped her into her nightclothes and tucked her in. All part of the cycle of life I mused; years ago she had done the same for me.

Wandering back downstairs I looked at the front door. There was no way I could see to prevent her from opening it again and going walkabout. Maybe if she did, it would prove to the Social Services she was incapable of being left alone and they could take over.

I went to bed early, even though I was convinced I wouldn't sleep. I persevered with the book, reading and re-reading the same page over and over again. It was after midnight when I turned the light off and snuggled down under the duvet. My hands tingled in the cold air and the edges of the window tinged with frost. The older generation were made of sterner stuff, and never thought to heat their bedrooms.

I was woken up in the early hours by a loud scream and leapt out of bed, landing in a heap on the floor. I grabbed my leg, strapped it on and, throwing my dressing gown round my shoulders, went out onto the landing. I fumbled for the light switch and saw a heap lying at the bottom of the stairs.

Mother was sprawled on the floor, one of her legs at an odd angle. She wasn't moving.

I raced down and felt for her pulse. It was weak, but she was still alive. I dialled 999 and asked for an ambulance and sat stroking her face, whispering soothing, meaningless phrases. Once or twice she moaned and even tried to get up but I told her to lie still.

When you are waiting for help, time stretches to eternity and back. The paramedics arrived within ten minutes but it felt more like ten hours. I scrambled to my feet to open the door. One lady and a man hurried to her side.

"I'll go get dressed. I didn't like to leave her."

"What happened?" the attendant, whose name badge said Sharon, asked me.

"I have no idea. Her scream woke me up."

As Sharon turned to open her bag, I scooted up the stairs and threw on pants and two layers of jerseys. By the time I got back downstairs they already had Mother on a stretcher and were about to carry her outside.

"Where will you take her? I'll follow in the car."

"St Andrews. Do you know it?"

"Yes." Of course I remembered. Growing up, we'd all been taken to outpatients to deal with the usual falls, broken bones, and on the one occasion my brother had stuffed a marble up his nose.

The ambulance doors slammed and it sped off down the street, blue lights flashing, but no siren; there was little need in the deserted streets.

The waiting room was deserted too. One old man perched on a plastic chair in the corner was snoring softly. I wondered how long he'd been there.

At last a body popped up behind the reception desk and called me over. She was efficient, not over-friendly and rattled off a list of information she required.

For a moment my mind went blank and without thinking I gave her my home address, then corrected myself as she needed patient information, not mine.

She questioned me closely as to how the accident had occurred. Had my mother tripped? Was I with her at the time? Did I see what happened?

No, no and no. Well I guess she tripped. No, the carpet wasn't frayed as far as I could tell. I'd not thought to look.

A shiver ran down my back as I wondered if they suspected foul play. Did they think I'd pushed her? My face went red, I began to stumble over my words. *Calm down Leah.*

"She has dementia. Yesterday she was found wandering in the High Street in her night clothes." My heart sank when I recalled her normal behaviour over tea with Ms Markham. Would anyone believe me?

It was several hours later when the doctor found me welded to the plastic chair that was threatening to become part of me. He sat down and I could feel him sizing me up. I felt guilty. I must have looked guilty.

He glanced down at his notes. "I understand Mrs Northam was found at the bottom of the stairs?"

"Yes. She must have got up at some time. The night before, she went walk about to the town centre in her nightclothes. The police brought her back."

"So, the police were involved? You have a case number?"

"No. I was on the phone to the Social Services at the time and I didn't think."

He nodded and wrote a note on the file balanced on his

knee. Like so many doctors these days, and Ms Markham too, he didn't look old enough to be out of primary school.

"We will have to report this accident of course."

The way he put the emphasis on the word accident sent shivers down my spine. "You don't think I pushed her, do you?" I said it without thinking.

"It's not for me to make any judgement. I can only assess her injuries."

I gulped. I'd not even asked what damage she had from the fall.

"How bad is it? How much…" my words trailed off.

"Not life threatening. She's got a few broken bones but we won't know more until after the tests."

"I see. So she'll be in hospital for a while?"

"That I can't say at this stage. We try to get patients home as soon as possible due to the shortage of beds. I'll know more later in the day." He rose to leave.

"Can I see her?" I stood up, surprised to see I was a head taller than him.

"For a moment, but she is heavily medicated."

I followed him through a doorway and into a short corridor and along a row of cubicles separated by plastic curtains. Mother was lying awake on a bed, her wild eyes reminded me of a rabbit caught in a car's headlights. As her eyes focused on me, she lifted one arm and pointed. "Tried to kill me, didn't you?" she screeched. "But this time you didn't succeed. I'm still alive. Disappointed?"

I took a step backwards and fled.

I stumbled into the waiting area and sank back onto a chair. I was trembling from head to toe. Would they believe her? Was it her word against mine? They'd know she was not sane. It was on her medical records, wasn't it?

The receptionist came out from her cubicle and approached me but I noticed she kept her distance.

"Please will you wait here?" Her voice was barely above a whisper as the new arrivals waiting for attention looked on. "The police will need to speak with you."

I could feel the tension in the room rise along with the curiosity level as the other occupants of A & E looked at me while pretending not to stare.

All I could do was nod, as I tried to make myself as invisible as possible. I'd left the house in such a rush I'd not even grabbed my handbag nor my phone.

The receptionist must have felt sorry for me because she suggested that if I liked to wait in the canteen, she'd let the officers know where I was.

I nodded and shuffled in the direction she was pointing.

I was the only person in the brightly lit room with its steel chairs and tables, except for a bored teenager behind the counter playing Candy Crush on her phone.

I searched in my coat pockets and found enough coins to buy myself a coffee. It was all I had with me apart from my car keys. I kept some emergency money in my car but was afraid to leave the building in case they thought I was trying to escape.

I must have dozed off for the next thing I remember was a policeman shaking my shoulder asking if I was Mrs Brand. I peered up at him as I rubbed my eyes.

"Yes."

"Just a few questions Mrs Brand." The policewoman next to him said.

I shivered. I must look guilty, I felt guilty, even though I'd done nothing wrong.

They were very polite, gentle even – nothing like you see on the television. To date I'd had very little contact with Her Majesty's law enforcement officers. The policewoman in particular was kind and kept her voice low as she asked me to give them my version of events.

I stumbled over the words. If I'd been in her position, I'd have immediately pronounced me guilty of attempted murder. I eyed the handcuffs attached to her belt and waited for her to snap them on my wrists.

A garbled voice sprang out of the black box perched on the shoulder of the young man and they both sprang to their feet. They checked my mother's address once more and told me to go home. I was to report to the station in the morning. Then they hurried out of the canteen and moments later I heard a police siren as they tore out of the parking lot.

I was past exhausted. I considered checking to see how Mother was but decided against it. I needed to sleep. I guessed I'd need my wits around me tomorrow.

As I turned the car into the driveway, I was surprised to see the front door wide open. Burglars, didn't they call it a home invasion in modern speak? That would be too much. Should I call the police? I choked back the laughter that bubbled up in the back of my throat. Hysterical giggles that caused me to rock back and forward in my seat.

Belinda raced out onto the top step, followed by a

pimply youth I'd never seen before, then marched over and opened my car door.

"Where have you been?" she demanded. "And where is your mother?"

"She fell down the stairs. She's in hospital." I clambered out. "And I'm going to bed," I added as I slammed the car door and made my way unsteadily into the house. It was as much as I could do to climb the stairs, fling off my outer clothes and crawl between the sheets.

If yesterday had been surreal, the following day was even more bizarre. At breakfast Belinda introduced me to her boyfriend Scott – if you could call "That's Scott" flung over her shoulder an introduction.

"Nice to meet you Scott," I lied, doing my best not to stare. Did all young men have rings dangling from every orifice, at least the ones I could see. His jeans were torn and frayed and screamed out for a visit to the laundromat, while his T-shirt was emblazoned with some picture sporting blood, swear words and a collection of skulls and human bones. His bleached hair was razed on either side leaving a mohawk tuft running from his forehead into a pony tail hanging down over his collar. I couldn't wait to see Mason's face when Belinda introduced him.

"Scott stayed over last night," Belinda's tone was confrontational. 'What are you going to do about it?' was the unspoken message.

I was past caring. I nodded as I made myself a coffee in the largest mug I could find. I turned to the pair of them.

"Were you here when my mother fell down the stairs?"

"Yes."

"No."

"What does that mean?"

"I was," Belinda repeated. "Scott arrived later."

I could tell she was lying. Why? "Where have you been? I was worried out of my mind." For a brief moment I thought I saw a flash of compassion flit across her face, but it didn't last.

"Scott arrived after," she pronounced each word slowly. "After it all happened."

"But I didn't see you!"

"Was asleep, wasn't I? In my room."

I didn't believe her. How had she got in without a key? I let it go as I slid two slices of bread into the toaster. Belinda had already raided the fridge and she and Scott were tucking into the cold meats and cheese I'd bought in for lunch.

"I've got to go to the station this morning."

"The police station?" Belinda's eyebrows shot up.

"Yes, the police station. Just routine after an accident. The hospital have to report it."

Belinda nodded.

"By the way, does your father know you're here?"

"Where else would I be? You dragged me up here."

"Belinda! You were missing for hours. I was worried sick about you."

"And I bet you squealed on me, didn't you?" Her face was thunderous.

"I had to! I thought you'd gone home. How would it look if…?"

"Yeah well, slept over with friends, didn't I? Guess you forgot I told you."

I sighed as I slathered far too much butter and marmalade on the toast. I had no option but to let it go. I'd still not worked out how much of a personal responsibility I should take for Belinda.

I was washing the breakfast dishes when the police knocked on the front door. They'd not waited for me to present myself at the station.

I preceded them into the lounge and perched on Mother's chair while they settled themselves on the sofa, different officers to the ones I'd met the night before.

"I must warn you Mrs Brand that you do not have to say anything. But it may harm your defence if you do not mention, when questioned, something which you later rely on in court. Anything you do say may be given in evidence."

I gasped. They suspected me of throwing Mother down the stairs.

The police lady added. "Mrs Brand, do you need a solicitor present? You are entitled to one. Normally we would conduct our questions down at the station but the builders are renovating at the moment."

I sat stunned. Didn't they only caution suspects after they charged them with a crime? That would be so ironic. I came north to help and now I was in more trouble than ever before.

"You think I pushed my mother down the stairs? That I tried to kill her?"

"Did you, Mrs Brand?"

"No! No of course not. I'd never be able to do a thing like that."

The policeman glanced at the file he was holding. "We have information that you and your mother do not get on. Is that true?"

"Uh, we've had our moments."

"Mrs Brand, can you tell us the reason you travelled up north from London. Was it to stay with your mother?"

I gave them the brief facts without going into any detail about the family conflicts. To my horror the police quoted from the report Ms Markham the Social worker had written, extolling how charming and delightful and alert my mother had been on her visit. How had they got hold of that? Wasn't all this protected under the draconian privacy laws? If the state refused to allow me see her medical and Social Service records so I could help her, how did the police get access? I stared in horror at the official notepaper the policewoman was clutching.

"Yes, she was very lucid during that brief visit, but I can assure you, my mother has dementia." One look at their faces and I realised they didn't believe a word I said.

"Are you going to arrest her?" The shrill voice came from the open doorway leading into the hall. Belinda stood there with her hands on her hips, looking at each of us in turn.

"I'm afraid we're not at liberty to discuss the case with…"

"She didn't do it." Belinda advanced into the room and plonked herself down on a chair.

"If you don't mind, this is a private…"

"You want the truth, don't you?" Not for a moment

was Belinda intimidated by our official visitors. "I was there. I saw it all, so you can take a statement from me."

The police people – or whatever's the latest pc label we should use – looked at each other.

"I saw what happened," Belinda continued.

I sat in stunned silence. She wasn't even in the house! Was she?

"I got up to go to the bathroom and I saw her mother," she pointed at me, "walk along the landing and at the top of the stairs she sort of swayed and then fell right down to the bottom. So there."

There was a long silence before the police constable said "And will you swear to this in court?"

"Yeah, but only if I have to."

There seemed little else to say, and a few minutes later they were scurrying down the front path and roaring off back to the station.

I was in a mild state of shock.

"This don't make us friends," Belinda announced as she slammed the front door behind them. "Last thing I want is the law sniffing round. I'm not about to tell people at school that my father married a murderer, who did in her own mother."

"But I didn't. I never."

"Well, so you say. But you owe me, right?" With that Belinda disappeared upstairs and I heard her giggling with Scott who thankfully had not made an appearance.

As I climbed into bed that night, the date clicked over on my phone. Tomorrow would be the first of May.

MAY

I am not going to bore you with all the technical details and the red tape that followed. The case against me was dropped, or at least I think it was. The police took copious statements and then left us alone. I'm aware how slowly the law moves, so at the back of my mind I continued to worry about it. They knew where to find me, so at any moment they might appear on the door step if they decided to prosecute.

I was bursting to ask Belinda why she'd lied to the police, but I just didn't have the courage to open that door. Maybe she had been in the house that night, I would never know for certain, but if she were, then why didn't she come and help when I was calling the ambulance? Did she just go back to bed, or was she trying to keep Scott out of sight? Either way, I never saw him again.

The hospital refused to release my mother until suitable accommodation could be found and, with the help of the lawyer who'd sold my house, I was able to navigate the maze of disposing of Mother's house and getting her settled into a private care home that cost the earth. I could only hope that the price I got for her property would be enough to last as long as she did and I left it in his capable hands to sort out the legal stuff.

Not for one minute did she let up in her condemnation of me, flinging out insults at every opportunity, but she'd exhibited sufficient manic behaviour, along with the test results, to convince the authorities she was not in a fit state to run her own life.

I'd returned to London and a very grumpy Mason, and Belinda was back in school and as far as we knew she was attending classes. I was sworn to secrecy regarding Scott, which was a bit of a relief to be honest, and he did not appear on our doorstep. I still didn't know if she met him up north or he'd followed her up there from London. I was relieved that Mason, tied up with his clients and his social life, never asked where she'd disappeared to after I reported her missing. Maybe he hadn't taken it in or he turned a blind eye. Either way the subject was never mentioned again.

I travelled north several times over the next weeks to sign papers and help Mother get settled in her new home, though she fought me every step of the way. By the end of May life returned to normal.

I buried my head in my studies and I was thrilled to discover that I still had the capacity to learn and I was really enjoying the course. They were kind enough to give me high marks for my first few assignments which boosted my self-confidence.

I spent many happy hours in the library but, although I escaped there to study, deep down I knew that the friendly chats I had with the librarian were the underlying magnet. He always had a ready smile. Any time he was not busy we would discuss all kinds of things and put the world to rights. We laughed about student days, when we talked late into the night planning how to make a difference and put the planet on the path to change and equality for all. We knew so little in those days when we were full of hope and inspiration.

I discovered his name was Bill Gates and we had a laugh over the difference between the billionaire and the librarian with the same name. I found I could relax in his company and, every time I drove home, I felt just that little bit more confident.

On the other hand, Mason soon eroded any good feelings I had about myself. He continued to niggle, criticise and, on occasion, shout at me. I was to blame for everything that went wrong in his life, whether it be work related, the conditions at home, or Belinda's failure to achieve top marks at school.

His daughter and I had called a truce of some kind. She was no more polite than before, but she led her own life and for the most part ignored me. I was sad about this but there was nothing I could do.

Andrea and I fell back into our comfortable friendship, though I found myself confiding in her less and less about my unhappy home life. I was beginning to sound like a stuck record, always complaining about one insult or battle after another. Even to my own ears I was sounding like a complaining bitch so, as the young say these days, I learned to 'suck it up' and said nothing.

I hugged the secret of my private studying close to my chest. The only person I'd confided in was Bill who gave me enough encouragement for a whole regiment of friends.

Life had settled down into a regular pattern.

And then it all started again.

The phone rang constantly with no one on the other end. Sometimes there was heavy breathing. I bought myself a whistle and blew it down the receiver a couple of times, but that didn't seem to deter the caller. I took to unplugging the phone whenever I was home alone. I had noticed that it never rang when either Mason or Belinda was in the house and it flashed briefly through my mind that one of them was to blame. No, now I was wandering into the realm of fantasy. It was just some joker who liked to scare women.

To add to my discomfort, at least twice a week something in the house was moved. On one occasion, two pictures on the walls changed places. I stared at the painting of a French pastoral scene that hung over the fireplace which had mysteriously swapped with an African print of an elephant in musth that Mason had brought home from a safari trip and hung in the hallway.

My hands shook slightly as I reached up and lifted them both down and returned them to their original places. I didn't have the courage to ask Mason if he had changed them over, and waited to see if he noticed I'd moved them again. He said nothing.

On another occasion I found all my winter clothes in the linen cupboard and the sheets and towels on the shelves in my dressing area. The contents of drawers in the kitchen, cubby holes in the writing desk, and crockery in the sideboard frequently rearranged themselves.

It's difficult to explain how this unbalanced me. I had

to be doing this without being aware. I was the only one in the house and, if anyone had broken in, they would have stolen my jewellery or taken the laptops and the money we had stashed away for emergencies.

Maybe the only way to solve this was to wire up the house and use one of those modern gadgets to record movement in the rooms?

I mentioned this to Andrea over lunch at our local favourite restaurant.

"You can't be serious, Leah!" she exclaimed. "I could understand it if you'd had a break in but who would bother to change things around. Are you absolutely sure you're not fiddling while day dreaming about something else?"

I was shocked. I'd been certain my best friend would support me.

"How will you explain this to Mason?" she continued. "He'll think you're spying on him and Belinda. It's a step too far, unless you want to destroy your marriage beyond repair."

"No, no of course I don't want that but…"

"What did the tests at the hospital show? The ones they did a few months ago?"

"I didn't follow up. Remember I had to rush north, and there was all that fuss over Belinda and school and, with one thing and another, I never did go back and see the doctor."

"That's your answer then. Make sure you're firing on all cylinders first and then maybe tell Mason about this creepy stuff. You haven't discussed it with him, have you?"

I shook my head and grabbed another cream slice. I

would have to watch my weight. I was comfort eating more than was good for me.

"And that's not good for you either," Andrea slapped my wrist gently.

"I know, but it helps."

"You know I care about you, Leah. It breaks my heart to see you slide down into this depression."

"I'm not that depressed, a bit sad really but…"

"I know depression when I see it, and being honest about your condition is the first step to healing. If you're having blank spells then you must get them diagnosed as soon as possible and there are loads of medications they can give you. We've come a long way from cold baths and electric shock treatment, and even lobotomies!" She laughed.

I didn't find that funny but forced myself to grin. Andrea was right. I'd make another appointment to see the doctor and insist on every test known to man.

When I walked into the surgery, Dr Morton raised his eyebrows. I apologised profusely – I was always doing that – for not following up on the appointments made, and haltingly tried to explain the crisis that had occurred since my last visit.

He squinted at me before he looked down at his notes and shuffled a few papers around. "You are right at the bottom of the list and it may be a few weeks until you're called in. I can't classify it as an emergency now."

"I understand," I mumbled.

He took my blood pressure and directed me to the bed

and poked and prodded me a few times while his nurse fussed around behind him.

Returning to his desk he scrawled a few notes, then tapped in further information on his desktop.

I rearranged my clothing and sat down in front of him.

"There's nothing more I can do for now, unless you'd like some pills to help you keep calm?"

I considered that for a split second and then declined. If I was unsure how my world was shifting around me when I was alert, the last thing I needed was my senses dulled. I shook my head.

"Well then Mrs Brand, the hospital will contact you for the dates of the tests I've ordered. If there's nothing else?"

I stood up to go. "Any idea how long…?"

He shrugged. "It may be a while. There are large backlogs, as you may have heard."

I left the surgery and, as I was driving towards home, I found myself turning into the parking area close to the library. At this point I was unwilling even to admit to myself I was seeking out my favourite librarian. I told myself the library offered a sanctuary, a haven of calm and peace where I could relax. It had nothing to do with Bill.

I selected a book from the shelves and settled down in one of the inviting arm chairs. I was far away trekking up the Amazon when I became aware of his presence.

"I was just going to make myself a cup of coffee," he said, his voice low and melodic. "Would you like one?"

"Yes please. That's really kind of you."

I watched him walk away, trying to guess his age. Not

much older than myself, still in good shape and kind. That's what made the difference, he was kind. I'd become so used to Mason snapping and snarling at me, and Belinda's indifference. Here, I felt appreciated.

The library was quiet and we chatted about books and the changes in reading habits. He asked how the studying was going, was encouraging and complimentary. He told me about his worries about the cuts in council funding and how it might affect the library and the job he loved.

It was hard to tear myself away and rush home to make supper. I left the car in the driveway. I would put it away later.

The house was empty when I walked in through the front door. You can usually tell, can't you? It has a kind of hollow, empty, neglected feeling. There were two empty coffee mugs on the kitchen counter that had not been there when I went out. Maybe Belinda popped back with a friend? As I picked them up to carry them to the sink, I noticed there were lipstick marks on one of them. Mason didn't allow Belinda to wear makeup to school; they'd had an almighty row about it only last month. Maybe her girlfriend had more lenient parents. For all I know about the modern youth, it might even be a boyfriend. I thought nothing more about it as I hurried to start chopping the vegetables.

Whoever was responsible for rearranging my household had done an excellent job this time. The saucepan drawer housed the plates and bowls, the tea towels were now in the cutlery drawer, the mugs and cups were in the fridge and I only found the frying pan by chance in the washing machine.

I slumped down onto a bar stool. Did I do this? It was bizarre. It must have taken quite some time to mess everything up like this. Should I ask Mason? Belinda? Why would either of them disrupt the kitchen? And, if I told them, it would only reinforce their opinion that I was mentally unbalanced. No, I'd have to work out a way to catch either one of them, or myself, up to mischief. I made up my mind to buy a couple of cameras and hide them as best I could.

I had to rush to put everything back in its rightful place and have the meal ready on time. Mason was usually grumpy when he got in from work and, if he couldn't sit down and eat the moment he walked through the door, he would sulk all evening.

The front door slammed announcing Belinda's return. I heard her thump up the stairs and then a few moments later more thumps as she came back down.

The next thing I heard was a loud scream.

"What's the matter?" I rushed into the lounge.

She whirled round to face me, red in the face, furious. "Where is it?"

"Where's what?"

"The telly. Where is it?"

I looked at the ring of dust showing where the television had been standing only that morning and my first instinct was to run and get a cloth and wipe it away. I blinked, but it made no difference. The television was not there.

"Have we been burgled?" Belinda rushed to the study

to check on her father's laptop and ran around frenetically opening cupboards and drawers to see if anything else was gone.

"No, it was all secure when I got back from the doctors."

"And they only took the telly? How soon can we get another one?"

"I don't know, Belinda." I sighed. "Your father will have to contact the insurance company and it will be up to them."

"We should call the police, right?"

A shiver ran down my back. I would prefer not to do that for very obvious reasons.

With Belinda right behind me I checked all the doors and windows but could see no sign of a forced entry.

"I'm going to get Dad to put in an alarm system. Bloody crime's going through the roof."

I smothered a giggle. Belinda sounded like an eighty-year old.

We were both startled by shouts from the garage. "What is going on in this house? Have you gone mad, Leah?"

"What now?" I spluttered as I ran through the laundry room.

Mason's car was half in and half out of the garage and the reason he couldn't drive it all the way in was the television on the floor in front of his bumper.

"What's that doing there?" Red-faced Mason was standing by the car.

"I have no idea. Belinda just noticed it was gone." I

walked forward to pick it up.

"I suppose you've been out again all day as usual, leaving this house wide open for any passing burglar."

"I only went to the surgery and then came straight home," I lied. Why did I do that? Why didn't I add I'd popped into the library? I wasn't going to change my story now.

"They must have been disturbed." Mason was examining the garage door looking for signs of damage.

"Yay, it's back. Dad, can you plug it in quickly, my programme is due – it's started already!" Belinda didn't seem to care why the television had been in the garage, only that it was reinstated as soon as possible.

I carried it back inside. From her reactions I didn't think Belinda would have moved it. Mason had been at work. There was no sign of a break in. The only person left was me!

I was going mad.

The next morning, I trawled the shopping centre looking for security cameras. I'd persuaded Andrea to come with me although she reminded me more than once that it would be far easier to buy one online.

I was praying that she wouldn't ask me what Mason thought about my intentions, and the last thing I needed was a delivery van parked outside when he came home. He'd find out what I'd ordered.

I had no idea there were so many different cameras on the market. Some recorded events for days, some only recorded through motion sensors, others had batteries which only lasted a few hours.

After much indecision, I chose four. Two I could stick high on the wall and conceal in some way, the others were free standing and resembled space-age ornaments. These I could place on shelves, one on the top of the kitchen cupboards.

Back home we acted like a couple of children as we played with various positions and tested the pictures that were streamed onto my phone. Andrea is even more technically challenged than I am and the purchase and setup took up the rest of the day – in between copious glasses of wine, swearing and giggling. Andrea had only just disappeared down the path before Mason turned into the driveway.

Mason and Andrea had never hit it off. He was very disparaging about her and she confided he was nothing but a bully and avoided him at every opportunity. I was not worried she would tell him I'd installed spyware in the hall, the kitchen, lounge and master bedroom, though I had sworn her to secrecy.

I threw a couple of pizzas into the oven, spread the mashed butter and garlic on a French loaf, and tossed salad ingredients into a bowl. Today at least, nothing had been uprooted from its normal place.

The rest of that month passed with no further strange incidents. The cameras recorded nothing, but then I found nothing lurking somewhere it didn't belong. I spent ages squinting at the footage that downloaded to my mobile, most of the short videos starred me, of course. Was I behaving strangely? Was I appearing to move robotically?

Were there blanked out times when I didn't remember where I was or what I was doing in the house? No to all of the above.

My studies progressed, far better than I expected, and I began to hope that I might even complete the course in record time.

Dr Cromptom's book lay undisturbed on my Kindle. Mason had been rather benign towards me lately so perhaps my new assertiveness had been effective? He paid little attention to me, but then the snide remarks and the criticisms were fewer.

Belinda was a wraith in the night, appearing at mealtimes, sitting in front of the television, until on her sixteenth birthday, her Father gave her a set of her own which he installed in her bedroom. After that I rarely saw her.

Most evenings Mason stayed in his study, or had meetings in town, so I pretty much had the place to myself. Strange, we identify loneliness with the aged and timid living on their own, but here I was in a house of three and yes, I was lonely.

I spent hours in the library, had numerous coffee mornings with Andrea, and studied the rest of the time I wasn't keeping the house running like clockwork.

I accepted my fate in a kind of dazed numbness, but the peace was not to last.

JUNE

The weeks flew by. I remember someone once said that the older you get the days pass faster. They're right. Most of the time I did my best to appear relaxed and happy, or at least calm.

The appointments came through from the hospital much sooner than I expected. They poked and prodded me, pushed me through noisy machines that thumped and banged. The earphones they gave me didn't appear to work and didn't muffle the noise at all.

When I climbed back into the car I felt as if I had been through a hurricane.

As I turned into the driveway and pressed the remote, nothing happened. What now? I climbed out and unlocked the up and over door and swung it out. The garage was full of black plastic bags.

I stared at them for several moments, to see if they moved. It was only a collection of familiar everyday objects but they were in the wrong place, and that made it scary. I half expected them to shuffle forwards and attack me like a crowd of angry aliens. Creeping forward I poked one with my foot. Nothing happened. I kicked it harder and it toppled over. My hands were shaking a little as I grabbed the nearest one and opened it.

It was full of clothes.

My clothes.

I rushed to open one bag after another and each one was crammed full of my jerseys, blouses, dresses, underwear, and even my shoes and handbags.

When I staggered into the house and raced upstairs to the bedroom, I saw that every drawer and shelf and cupboard had been emptied. Nothing of Mason's had been disturbed. His suits and shirts still hung on their hangers, his socks neatly arranged in rows and his underwear tidy and undisturbed. Only my clothes had been removed.

It took several trips from garage to house and up and down the stairs to drag all the bags back and unpack everything. Many of the blouses and dresses would need ironing. As I was putting things away, I remembered the security cameras. I was not responsible for this latest act of vandalism. I'd never do anything like this. Mad people didn't behave like this – did they? I'd left the house early this morning and I'd been at the hospital all day.

The cameras! It was time to find out who was threatening me.

When I first installed them, I would check the footage frequently, but when nothing was moved for days on end I'd relaxed and not bothered to look.

I perched on the edge of the bed and opened the app on my phone. All I could see was a grey background with sporadic white lines running across the screen.

I tapped in the numbers for the second camera and the results were the same. All grey, all blank. When I went to check the cameras, they were all gone! I couldn't have removed them myself, could I?

No. I'd bought them.

I'd put them in place.

I wanted them there.

Some primeval instinct would not have allowed me to dismantle them, I was sure of that, wasn't I?

Weaving my way between the black plastic bags on the bedroom floor I sank back on the bed. *Leah, you must be going mad. If either Mason or Belinda had found even one of the cameras, there would have been an almighty row. Accusations of my spying, sneering disbelief that anyone had broken in. I couldn't think of a single person in the world who would want to harm me, except perhaps my mother, and she was miles away and in no fit state to cause this mess. The only person responsible would be me. Therefore, it proved that Leah was mad.*

I fought back the tears as I shoved the bags into my dressing room and returned to put the car away in the now empty garage. I wouldn't mention this to anyone, not even Andrea though heaven knows I needed someone to talk to. I couldn't even confide in Bill. I liked him a lot but we'd only known each other a short time and I couldn't bear the thought of him turning his back on me, convinced I was insane.

It made matters worse that evening as both Mason and Belinda were in a good mood. Were they waiting for me to start whining about my disturbed wardrobe? If so, I was not going to give them the satisfaction.

My resolution lasted until the news came on. More death, destruction, fraud, another war breaking out. As the horrific scenes danced across the television I burst into tears, loud wracking sobs that shook me from head to toe.

Mason moved over and put his arm around me.

"What's the matter, Leah? I hate to see you so unhappy."

The love in his voice nearly caused me to have hysterics. When was the last time he'd shown me even the slightest kindness? "Has it all got too much for you?"

I stared at him hoping to learn if he knew exactly what had upset me. The unspoken message - plastic bags in the garage next to the green wheelie rubbish bins waiting for the dustmen – was crystal clear. I wasn't wanted here.

"You haven't been yourself for a long time. How about you see a counsellor?"

In normal circumstances I would have brushed aside such a ridiculous suggestion, but I paused. There was no one I could talk to. No one I could confide in. Maybe this wasn't such a bad idea. And, I would be seen to be cooperating.

I snuggled up to him and took his hand.

"If you think it would help?" I had yet to mention my hospital appointments to either of them, only to Andrea. With all this 'patient confidentiality' the NHS wouldn't tell my family. I was not going to admit I doubted my own sanity and was taking steps to find out for myself.

Mason rocked me gently, brushing his lips against my cheek.

"There's a good girl. Leave it all to me. I'll fix it. There's an excellent lady I've heard of and I'll set up an appointment. You're free at any time, right?"

Put like that it reminded me I had nothing else to do

any day of the week. I nodded and clung to him wishing this comforting husband would never revert to the angry, aggressive man I'd grown used to.

Mason dropped his arms and stood up. "That's settled. I'll phone you tomorrow and give you the time and date. I think she holds her clinic from home."

He walked out to his study, humming under his breath leaving me with mixed feelings. From as early as I can remember, I'd been taught that you sorted out your own problems. You didn't race off to some psychiatrist like they do in America. The British are made of sterner stuff, stiff upper lip and all that. Maybe, across the Atlantic they have the right idea. I was prepared to give it a try. I was falling apart bit by bit like a huge ball of wool unravelling and I wasn't sure how long I could hold it together.

True to his word Mason phoned me from the office the following morning. He'd made an appointment for two o'clock. "This is the address, and don't be late," he barked before disconnecting. The old Mason was back.

I raced around trying to decide what to wear. How should the average woman dress for a mental counselling session? I'd spent most of the morning ironing and throwing other garments into the wash. I felt violated. Some mysterious person had been riffling through my clothes. Now, they felt alien and not quite mine. Even to myself I sounded a little deranged.

Miss Cilla Prendergast lived in a smart part of town in a detached house with an immaculate garden and a large imposing iron knocker in the shape of a lion's head on the front door. A shiny brass engraved plaque invited patients to go around the side and through the small gate to the annex on the side of the house.

As I rang the bell I tried to stop shaking. My palms were sweaty and I felt beads of sweat tickling my scalp.

My first sight of Ms Prendergast was reassuring. She was about the same age as me, smartly dressed in classic fashion with matching skirt and blouse and sensible low-heeled sandals. I caught a whiff of a floral scent as she opened the door and welcomed me in.

She ushered me into a square-shaped hallway and through a door on the right. It was tastefully furnished with four chairs grouped round a coffee table and a cabinet over to one side holding a coffee maker and an array of drinks. The only other sign this was a workspace was the wooden filing cabinet in the corner under one of the pastel framed prints of the British countryside.

Ms Prendergast waved me to a chair and, picking up her iPad and a stylus, seated herself opposite me. Her voice was calm and reassuring as she asked me to describe how I was feeling.

For the first few moments I sat there frozen, and then it all came spilling out. I started at the accident, my long stay in hospital, then meeting Mason... here I hesitated, unsure how disloyal I might sound, but I ploughed on. I told her about my mother, my bad relationship with Belinda and how objects in the house moved around.

Once I started, I couldn't stop. I must have talked nonstop for over an hour and, when I finally fell silent, my mouth was dry while the tears continued to roll down my cheeks.

The counsellor did not interrupt me once. At one point she pushed a box of tissues across the table and sat back, making notes on her tablet. When I finally fell silent, she rose and fetched me a glass of water without saying a word.

The silence was uncomfortable and I rushed in to fill the gap. "Now you must really think me mad," I spluttered.

She brushed a stray lock of shiny, blonde hair off her face and smiled.

"No, of course not. A lot of your behaviour is quite normal. Most people would react just as you have. But what worries me..." she paused and nibbled the end of the stylus, "... are the hallucinations you are having now, possibly blackouts."

"But I don't think it's me. I've thought and thought, and I don't think I've moved things from place to place. I would have remembered. I know I would." I could hear my voice rising as I protested my innocence.

"I'm sure you're not aware of your actions, but let's not discuss that avenue any further right now. Let's wait until you have the results of the CAT scan and the MRI and take it from there, shall we?"

"And if they are normal? What then?"

"Let's cross that bridge when we come to it, shall we?"

I glanced at my watch, amazed to see I had been there for over two hours. How long a session had Mason booked? Wouldn't there be a queue of patients outside by now? I'd not heard the bell go once.

"I think," Ms Prendergast rose to her feet, "that is quite enough for today. Would you like to book again, say for Tuesday next week? Same time?" Her fingers tapped and slid across the device she clutched tightly.

"Yes, sure." I felt I had been dismissed like a naughty child at the end of detention. My initial warm feelings towards my new confidant had dissipated a little, yet at the same time she was a listening ear and it had been a relief to bring it all out into the open. I had talked myself to a standstill and, while I was a little puzzled as to why the counsellor had not followed up on anything that I told her, maybe she was saving that for next time.

Mason came home late from work, it was well after nine and his supper had dried out before I heard his key in the lock. For once, he did not snap at me but stated he'd already eaten and had further work to do in his study. As I heard the door click shut, I wondered why he'd not asked me how I'd got on with Ms Prendergast? Perhaps pressure of work had pushed it out of his mind.

I tidied up the kitchen and wandered back into the lounge. I suspected Belinda was up in her room but, unless she came to raid the kitchen, I rarely saw her now.

As I walked back into the breakfast room, I noticed my Kindle housing Dr Cromptom's book on the top of the high cabinet. I'd not given him a thought for weeks. Any spare time I had, time when I could concentrate and not worry about going mad, I'd spent on my assignments. That was the only part of my life that was going well. Strange,

I'd not told Ms Prendergast about home studying. I wondered why.

Nor had I mentioned installing security cameras to spy on my family. I didn't feel comfortable about that part. But I made up my mind to replace the cameras the next day and this time I would conceal them more carefully. I would also ask if they made a type that would alert me on my phone if they were moved or tampered with. It paid to be prepared for the worst. And I might not mention that to Ms Prendergast either. We all need some secrets, right? Just because she was my counsellor didn't mean I had to tell her everything.

The following morning a furious ringing of the doorbell had me hopping along the hall as fast as I could go. Andrea was standing on the doorstep grinning from ear to ear.

"It's me, bearing presents and surprises." She gave me a huge bear hug then left me to follow her into the kitchen where she was already sorting through the different coffee pods choosing a blend she liked. "This Java one I think." She handed me the plastic bubble. "Have I got news for you!"

I laughed. It was impossible not to. Andrea had that effect on people.

"Come on, spit it out. I can see you're dying to tell me."

She whipped an envelope out of her pocket and waved it like a Fourth of July flag. "Last month I entered a competition and today I found out I've won!"

"Come on Andrea, don't drag it out. Won what?"

"Okay, okay don't rush me. First, a chauffeur-driven limousine into the West End. Two nights at the Grand Intercontinental five-star hotel in a luxury suite and tickets to the Rory Beanicker concert with, wait for it, backstage passes! I am so excited."

"That's amazing. Tickets for his concert sold out in the first couple of hours and the last I heard they were going on the black market for triple the price."

"I know. But we'll be in there on VIP tickets."

"We?"

"You're coming with me."

"Oh, I don't know. Mason might not…"

"Bugger Mason. Who else would I take with me but my best friend? And, did you notice it was two nights away, that means…" Andrea paused for dramatic effect, "… we have a whole day in the West End to go shopping. And darling, am I going to hit the shops!"

My first thought was a shopping trip would eat into my study budget, but if Mason was prepared to sanction my trip, perhaps he might also throw in a little spending money. I could never tell which way Mason would react. Sometimes he would be caring and cooperative while at others he would suddenly fly off the handle and throw a hissy fit. It was the uncertainty that kept me off balance.

"I'll ask him tonight," I told Andrea.

"You'll tell him tonight. Come on Leah, stand up for yourself. Grow up girl. This is what you are going to say." Andrea put her coffee mug down and waved her arms theatrically. "Mason darling, just wanted to mention that Andrea and I will be up in London for two nights next week. Just a short shopping trip and the Rory Beanicker concert. I'll leave a couple of meals in the freezer, just pop them in the microwave."

"Um. I might be a little more tactful than that."

"Nonsense Leah. You must stand up for yourself." She moved to put her arm round my shoulder. "How many times do I have to remind you? Be a man, not a mouse." She giggled. "Make that a woman, not a mouse."

We both laughed. It sounded so simple when Andrea said it, but then she had no idea what it was like for me. One look at Mason's face when he was in a bad mood was enough to send me shrinking back into my shell. It's not as if he had ever hit me, or threatened me physically in any way or punished me by withholding money. Nothing like that. It was so difficult to explain, but it was the way he eroded my confidence, made me feel small, stupid and insignificant. He blamed me for anything that went wrong and had me questioning my own actions. OK, the silent treatment was the worst, but was any of that a reason to divorce? I could hardly expect him to support me if I tried to leave him. And then there was the question of money as well. I was too old and spoilt to live in a hostel, or rough it on the streets.

"Andrea to Leah. Come in Leah, are you there?"

"What? Oh sorry. It does sound exciting."

"Yup, I'm excited. I do like the chauffeured limo bit, don't you?"

We laughed again. From where we lived, it was less than an hour by train up to the West End of London and, if we wanted to, we could have gone there any day of the week, but the concert tickets and a luxury hotel? That was the icing on the cake.

"You've convinced me. I'll come. Even if Mason blows his top."

"Of course you will darling. I couldn't go without my best friend, now could I?" Andrea wiped away pretend tears. "Now it gives us a week to plan what we're going to wear. Do we need to hit the local boutiques first, do you think?"

To my surprise, Mason made very little fuss about the trip. He didn't like Andrea, not one little bit, said she was too pushy and not quite up to our standard. I have no idea why he thought that. She spoke perfectly well, dressed smartly and her house was every bit as expensive and well-appointed as ours, even more so. Maybe it was just her self-assurance and the fact she coped perfectly well on her own. He preferred his women to be shy, retiring and dependent on him.

I didn't announce my holiday break as a *fait accompli* as Andrea had suggested, but the moment I told him about her prize package he jumped right in and guessed she'd asked me to go. I admitted it and he simply told me to enjoy myself before disappearing into his study, briefcase under one arm.

I let go the breath I was holding and began to look forward to a couple of days away from the oppressive atmosphere in the house. The safe haven I had grown used to was now threatening and unwelcome.

Andrea could be overwhelming at times but I did enjoy her company. She gave me courage, made me laugh, and was larger than life. I felt safe when I was with her, more confident, happier, carefree.

We had a great couple of days. I didn't particularly enjoy the limo ride. Sitting sideways was a little unnerving, I'm used to facing forward while travelling and it was far too early in the morning, even for Andrea, to raid the mini bar and start swilling alcohol. We moaned there was no inbuilt coffee maker and laughed until the tears rolled down our cheeks.

The poor shop owners didn't know what hit them as we tried on one unsuitable outfit after another and generally behaved like middle-aged hooligans. Andrea was a bad influence on me, I know, but she was so much fun.

We both enjoyed the concert. It's not every day you get so close to one of the most famous crooners on the circuit. I have to admit the tour backstage was a little disappointing. The competition organiser collected us after the show and guided us through a labyrinth of dim, dusty corridors painted in a dismal green, and into a carpeted room crowded with people where we all hung around for over half an hour until the great man himself walked in. He barely nodded to the admiring crowd before he ducked out again, and that was the last we saw of him.

"Well, that was a bit of a downer," grumbled Andrea as we were propelled out of the stage door and into a dingy back alley. "I wasn't expecting to jump into bed with him, but a 'Hello, how are you?' would have been nice."

"He must get so fed up with all the sycophants all the time."

"Yes, well it's those same sycophants who give him

all his fame and cash. It does well for him to keep in with them. See how he feels if it gets out that he cares nothing for his fans." Andrea was obviously miffed.

I was too tired to debate it with her as I watched the buildings slip past in front of me like an old showreel. If I were honest, I felt a bit silly travelling around in a car this size. I wouldn't like to work out what our carbon footprint might be.

All too soon the prize outing was over and we were back home. I'd spent far less than I'd expected and squirrelled away a little more into my study account.

The moment the front door closed behind me, I crept around the house and checked cupboards, shelves, wardrobes and drawers to see if there was anything out of place. Nothing. Except for the dirty dishes piled in the sink – most likely Belinda's handiwork; her father would never leave crumbs on the side, or unwashed plates – everything was normal.

With the excitement of a break away from home, I'd not got around to replacing the surveillance cameras. Glancing around the bedroom as I unpacked my case I wondered if they were a waste of money. If I put new ones in place, I would probably be too scared to check my phone to watch me creating all the havoc. That would prove I was unstable. I told myself it was probably a waste of money.

I popped out to the local supermarket to grab a few essentials and ingredients for dinner and, turning into the driveway, I noticed a box in front of the garage door. It was an ordinary cardboard box, and I wondered why the courier had left it out here in full view, rather than tucked out of sight in the porch.

I picked it up and carried it through to the kitchen. There was no label on it, so I didn't feel guilty slicing through the tape and peeping inside. The moment I pulled back the flaps I reeled backwards with shock. The stench was overpowering. I fell back against the sink, my eyes watering and hands shaking as I fought to steady myself. I lunged forward and slammed the cardboard flaps back in place with one hand while I rifled in the drawer with the other for tape to close it again. But not before I'd caught sight of a mass of pink and red decaying flesh, most likely offal. I didn't have the courage to look closely at it or even touch it. It was some kind of putrefying meat, and strong faeces or similar but, whatever it was, it was beyond pungent.

I opened the back door and raced into the garden and placed the box out in the middle of the lawn. Mason could deal with that when he got home. I wasn't going near it again. For a brief moment I considered phoning the police but, after the episode with Mother falling down the stairs, I might be on a watch list of some sort. They kept records of people they arrested or suspected of murder, didn't they? Besides, they were overworked, and this was just an unpleasant prank, hardly life-threatening.

I emptied a whole can of air freshener, spraying in all directions but I could still smell it as I put the car away and brought in the shopping. Once again, I was shaking and I reversed my decision about the cameras. I would replace them and mentally added a couple of extra ones to the list, to fit outside the house as well as inside.

Mason was late home that night, one of those laws where if it could go wrong… He was none too pleased with my garbled description of the contents of the box and how horrible it was. Despite my pleas he brought it back in and placed it on the kitchen island.

"Please don't open it in here," I begged him, but he just gave me one of those looks.

I took several steps back, covering my nose with a tissue as he sliced open the lid with a knife and reached inside. He pulled out wads of crumpled brown paper and the missing blue bunny.

I gasped. No smell. No putrefying body parts. No threat.

Mason turned it over in his hands and gave it a good shake. "Is this," dripping with sarcasm, "is this what you were so afraid of?"

"No! It's not the same. It must be a different box. I swear the one I opened, the smell, it was…" I reached out and turned the box round, peering at every side. It looked the same. I could even see where I had opened it earlier but the contents… I was lost for words.

"Leah, you have to get a grip. This is becoming more than annoying. You have a serious problem. And…" he leaned in, his nose microns from mine, "it has got to stop. You do know what happens when people are irrational, don't you?"

I shrank back, mesmerised by the almost fanatical light in his eyes. I didn't even want to think what he meant by his threats. My sides turned to water and I spun away from him and thumped up the stairs. I threw myself on the bed and let my tears soak into the pillowcase.

The next couple of weeks went past in a kind of blur. I bought six more security cameras and hid them as best I could. I ripped an old stuffed teddy apart, one I was very fond of in childhood, and hollowed out the eye socket to replace with the lens. It looked a little out of place perched on the wardrobe, but then how often do people look up?

A second one I managed to wriggle inside a pottery cat. I'd always disliked it but Mason told me it had sentimental value. After watching a DIY programme on afternoon television, I managed to drill out a small hole in the stomach to accommodate the lens. Another excellent hiding place.

I love books, as you might have guessed, but I sacrificed one by cutting out a hollow in the pages and punching a small hole on the spine. It reminded me of my early teenage years when my friend Betsy and I had done something similar as a hiding place for the illicit cigarettes we bought at the corner shop. I put the book back on the bookcase in the lounge and stood back to admire my handiwork. It was impossible to notice anything out of the ordinary. Unless someone tore the house to shreds no one would even know they were on camera.

Now, all I had to do was wait.

Of course, the moment you prepare for any event, nothing happens and for several days not a single inanimate object moved from its appointed place. Instead of feeling reassured, I felt more depressed than ever.

They rang me from the surgery and gave me an

appointment to see the doctor. In answer to my feverish questions, the receptionist partly admitted that my test results were in.

As soon as I put the phone down, I picked it up to call Andrea.

"And what are you up to on this bright, sunny afternoon?" I could hear the laughter in her voice.

"My… my tests are in and Dr Morton wants to see me on Monday afternoon."

"That's good, isn't it?"

"I guess so, well, maybe. I don't know."

"Darling, you seem as right as rain to me. As sane and sensible as any almost forty-year old."

I groaned. "Don't remind me. I've only got another four days left in this decade."

"Ah, shame. What must it be like to be that old."

"Hang on!" I found myself laughing in spite of myself. "I'm only eighteen months older than you."

"Ah, but darling, a year and a half can be a lifetime. Just think, when I was born, you were already toddling around the house eating solid food and tormenting the cat. So, what exciting surprise have you got lined up for the big four-oh day?"

"Nothing, as far as I know."

"Mason will think of something. A trip to Paris…"

"Hardly. He's not that extravagant."

"He can easily afford it. You wait, he'll have a surprise for you, trust me."

Andrea was right. Mason did have a surprise, but it was not

what I expected. The night before my birthday, he came home late looking quite flustered and informed me that a case he was working on for his most important client had been brought forward. The court hearing was now scheduled for the following week and he was leaving in the morning to go down to Cornwall. The brief would take the weekend and he hoped to be back either Sunday or Monday night.

I opened my mouth to protest that he couldn't leave me, not on my birthday. Had he forgotten the date? Didn't he care? I squeezed my eyes tight and said nothing. What would be the point? One of the things that had attracted me to Mason was his drive and ambition. So many men are content to take what life hands them, but Mason went all out to make it happen. And look at the result; a beautiful house, an excellent standard of living, and I'd never had to count the pennies or check on the prices before I whipped out the credit card.

I made the right noises and went to rescue his dinner. He'd pack his own case, he always did, so there was nothing else to do but pretend this was just an ordinary Friday and I didn't mind in the slightest.

Bright and early next morning – Mason had departed at dawn – the phone rang downstairs. I crawled out of bed and, strapping on my leg, hurried down the stairs. It was either a crank call, the double glazing or conservatory people, or it was Andrea. No one else used a landline. I'd even suggested having it taken out; dinosaur technology I called it but, to my surprise, Belinda kicked up such a fuss, I let it drop.

"Happy Birthday to you, Happy Birthday to yeeeeeew. So, where's it to be then? Paris? Rome? A slap-up meal in town?"

"None of the above. He's gone."

"What do you mean he's gone?"

Did Andrea's voice sound strained?

"Gone, as in gone to Cornwall, I think. Client stuff."

There were several seconds of silence. "Oh, you poor darling. That settles it then. Tonight, you and me darling, we hit the town. Get your glad rags on and we'll go clubbing."

"Don't be ridiculous. At my age? I'm way past that. I couldn't stand all that row they play nowadays. And they don't dance. They wriggle and gyrate."

"Well it's good to know you've not completely lost your sense of humour. No, silly, I mean a grown-up sophisticated club for us fledgling wrinklies. So, I'll be round to pick you up at seven sharp. Posh gear, go have your hair and nails done. We are going to paint the town red."

Before I could turn her down, Andrea had rung off.

I slithered down onto the carpet and sighed. Which would be worse? Sitting here all alone on my fortieth birthday watching some inane programme on the box, or feeling a self-conscious fraud perched on a spindly stool in some darkened night club?

Belinda came bouncing down the stairs. "What are you doing down there?"

"Just thinking. Did you know it was my birthday today?"

She halted and swung round in the kitchen doorway. "Oh, no, Happy Birthday then." She walked on into the kitchen.

So, she hadn't remembered either, or decided to ignore it.

I scrambled to my feet and followed her. "I'm forty today." If I thought that would get me any sympathy I was mistaken.

"Fuck no. Wow! That's like old, really old. Hey do you remember the Second World War? We're doing that in ancient history."

"Believe it or not, no. I was born long after the war. Even my parents were born after the war."

"Bugger. Ah well, that's no good then is it?"

Belinda sloshed milk onto her plate of cereal and disappeared back upstairs leaving me to replace the muesli, sugar and milk back where they belonged. Maybe she should brush up on her maths instead of worrying about interviewing war veterans who must be fast approaching a hundred by now.

In the hope that Mason had planned a special treat, I had booked a hair appointment for this morning and, as I walked into the salon, I decided to have my nails done as well. To hell with it, I'd have a pedicure if they could fit me in and I'd pop into the boutique nearby and see if they had that dress in the window in my size. I deserved it, didn't I?

Two hours later, glancing at my reflection in a shop window and clutching the carrier bag containing my dream dress, I wondered what to do next. Of course, the library.

My oasis and place of refuge. I'd pop in just for an hour. Right now I couldn't face going back to the house with the mantlepiece bereft of a single birthday card, or to Belinda's sullen looks if she deigned to show herself for five minutes. She was probably out with her friends by now, though what excitement they got from hanging around the shopping mall I couldn't begin to fathom.

The moment I walked in through the doors Bill looked up and gave me the kindest smile. Why was it that, the moment anyone was nice to me, I wanted to burst into tears? Was that normal?

There was little time to chat with people coming in and out and a couple of rather obnoxious teenagers making crude comments about some old book they'd found on sex education. Despite that, I settled down into one of the cosy chairs and travelled back in time to Tudor England and the trials of Catherine of Aragon. And I thought I had problems!

I looked up to see Bill hovering close by with his coat on, ready to leave.

"Fancy a cup of coffee? It's my half day today and I always pop into Ann's Pantry on the way home. My treat."

I hesitated. *I'm married, but does that mean I should never have a coffee with a member of the opposite sex? Come on Leah, this is the twenty-first century, the century when we have a huge range of genders and half-genders and cross-genders to choose from.* I glanced at my watch. The afternoon stretched before me, empty and lonely, so what was the harm?

I smiled and gathered my things together. It was my

birthday – why not?

We sat and chatted over coffee and quiche with a salad. Bill was so easy to talk to and he made me laugh. I didn't tell him it was my birthday. I didn't want him to feel sorry for me, but I did admit to going out tonight to explain the hairdo and freshly painted nails. I hoped he wouldn't think I was a dilettante housewife who spent loads of money on dolling herself up. I still had problems with that. I'd been frugal all my life before I met Mason.

I also didn't mention Mason was away for the weekend in case it sounded like a come-on. It was obvious from the rings I wore that I was married. The conversation was about neutral subjects; music, films, books, the state of the nation and the political shenanigans over the EU. We had so much in common and similar views on most subjects. I believed that Bill respected what I had to say, and I felt more relaxed than I had been in weeks, even months and years. He made me think of myself as a person, not big and important, but someone whose thoughts and conversation mattered.

We were interrupted by the waitress who asked if we would like anything else. Her tone suggested that we would be wise to say no and, looking around, we were the only people left and the staff were itching to close up and go home.

Bill insisted on paying and, brushing my offer to one side, promised to let me settle the bill next time. So, there would be a next time? A wave of guilt washed over me, but I shrugged it aside. If both Mason and Belinda seldom made me feel good, why was I feeling guilty spending time with a man who behaved exactly the opposite?

We shook hands outside and wished each other a good evening and went our separate ways. If I was going to be ready for Andrea at seven, I had better hurry.

Andrea rang the doorbell precisely on time and the moment I let her in she pushed a huge box into my hands.

"I saw this and I thought it the sweetest thing. And it's the perfect gift for a young-at-heart forty-year old. A memory of your childhood. Go on, open it."

"Later? I love the anticipation and I feel so self-conscious when I receive…"

"Well you shouldn't. I want to see your face. Stop dithering and open it, woman! And yes, I will have a glass of white wine, since you're asking."

She followed me into the kitchen as I took a bottle from the fridge and grabbed a glass. Andrea didn't wait but whipped out the cork and poured out a generous glassful. "One for you too," she insisted, and filled a second glass.

"Not so much Andrea. I'm still on medication remember," I lied. It was the most tactful excuse I could think of. I had no intention of getting wasted. Being drunk does not appeal to me. I like to know what I'm doing and stay in control. A bit of a joke really, recent events had me spiralling out of control when I was stone cold sober. I took a tentative sip, before Andrea was urging me again to open the box.

There were two packages inside the fancy red box tied with a huge purple bow. The first contained a large bottle of my favourite perfume.

"Wow, that's brilliant, thank you!" I gave Andrea a big hug. "How did you know that's the one I like best?"

"Silly, you wear it all the time, so how could I not know? It's the other one you'll love." She pointed to the larger pile of tissue.

I unwrapped the paper slowly, savouring the moment, to see a stuffed, blue rabbit.

I froze.

"Isn't it just the cutest thing you've ever seen?" Andrea warbled. "The moment I saw it in the toy shop window I knew I had to get it for you. A girl can never have too many cuddly stuffed animals."

It was not the same as the one I'd found in my car, which had then disappeared from the garage. It was larger for one thing and, while the little version wasn't scary, I was not so sure about this one. Its large, black, spherical eyes held a hint of cruelty maybe? It reminded me of that horror film about Chucky the doll that came to life.

I gave myself a shake. *Pull yourself together Leah, it's a stuffed toy for heaven's sake. What's all this about it being menacing?*

I forced myself to smile. "Yes, it is cute. I'll keep it in the bedroom, on the bed."

"Best place for it. Something to cuddle when Mason is away overnight."

I'm not sure if Andrea noticed my startled reaction, she was busy on her phone calling an Uber cab.

The evening was not a great success. I think Andrea enjoyed herself and I worked hard pretending. The club was exactly as she described it, very upmarket, filled with mature couples, and the dance band played tunes from what the young now refer to as 'retro'. It still didn't feel quite right and I wondered if same sex couples who chose not to have a heterosexual partner ever felt like this when out in public. Perhaps the other patrons thought Andrea and I were an item, married even.

We had a couple of dances, when the music was lively, but I dashed back to our table when the smoochy, slow numbers were played. No way was I going to smooch around Andrea among dancers who were clinging to each other, melding their two bodies into one. My leg had begun to hurt, the straps chaffing, and my head began to pound. Every few minutes I glanced at my watch, willing the hands to rotate faster. If she noticed, Andrea said nothing. I think she was enjoying herself and, when the comedian came on stage, she laughed so hard she was forced to go and repair her make-up.

The moment she left the table, I was approached by an elderly bald-headed man, possibly old enough to be my grandfather, who asked me if I would like to dance. I smiled and shook my head. He persisted, but seeing Andrea return to the table, made himself scarce.

"Was that old codger making a play for you?"

"Hardly, he just asked me to dance."

"Don't blame you for refusing." She stared over to his table. "Looks as if he's worth a bob or two."

"Andrea, really! I'm a happily married woman."

"Are you?"

"Of course."

"Married maybe darling, but I'm not so convinced about the happily part. Ever considered leaving him?"

"Mason?"

"Who else?"

"No, of course not. Things might be a bit rocky at the moment, but it's just one of those lows every marriage has."

Andrea didn't look the slightest bit convinced.

"Well, it's your funeral, Leah. Only you can do what's right for you."

Her tone sent shivers down my spine. When we were children we'd joke and say 'someone just walked over my grave'. Then we'd giggle, but I didn't feel like giggling now. Fear – that was a good description of what was gnawing away at the back of my mind. For a fleeting moment I wished I was sitting here with Bill Gates. I realised that this afternoon was the first time in a long while that I'd felt safe.

At last, even Andrea had had enough and I breathed a sigh of relief when she got out her mobile to call for a taxi.

Now, I just had thirty-six more hours to wait until I found out if I was sane or insane.

JULY

I held myself rigid when I walked into Doctor Morton's consulting room and sat down. I took deep breaths in an attempt to stay calm.

He glanced at me, gave a quick smile and then consulted his notes. He frowned and scratched his head. I wanted to scream at him. Stop the torture, what do the results say?

"Mrs Brand..." *Get on with it.* "The majority of the tests are in, and I'm happy to tell you that they show no serious signs of dementia. But I would like to take a few further tests."

I breathed out. I wasn't out of the woods yet.

"There are signs of ageing, but that comes to us all."

I'm only forty I wanted to scream.

"But there is one result here I was not expecting."

"Uh, what, I mean…"

"I'm happy to tell you that you're pregnant."

"What!" I jumped up from the chair, and clutched the edge of his desk. "I can't be. No!" Visions of nappies, and sleepless nights and screaming tantrums flew round my head. What would Mason say? I could guess. He'd be furious. It would be all my fault of course.

"You don't look too pleased with the news." Dr

Morton sat back in his chair, tossing his pen from hand to hand.

"I… I don't know what to think. I'm forty, I'm too old to be a mother. My husband has two teenagers; no, his son is in his twenties. I'm not sure he'll be too thrilled." That was a lie. I knew he would be apoplectic. I ran the house the way he liked it, everything in its place, an oasis of peace and quiet as long as Belinda remembered to listen to her music through her headphones. A baby would throw all that out of the window. And what of the threats and the mysterious stalker? How would he react? Would the baby be in danger?

The silence dragged on. I sat there twisting the tassels on my scarf round and round my fingers.

Dr Morton leaned forward. "It's early days yet. There are options, so I suggest you discuss this with your husband and make decisions together. In the meantime, hop up on the bed and let me take a look at you."

I pulled the curtain aside and removed my blouse. "How pregnant am I?"

Dr Morton ran his hands over my tummy. He chuckled. "Oh, you're completely pregnant, and I'd say eight weeks maybe. I'll order an ultrasound scan and you'll have to make an appointment at the pre-natal clinic."

I wandered outside and lurched along the pavement to my car. I sat there, key in the ignition as I tried to gather my wits. I was still holding the sheaf of papers with further appointments for more tests. I thought they'd not left a stone unturned the first time.

It came back to me with blinding clarity, an early discussion with Mason, before we were married. 'I don't want children. I hope you understand that. I've two of my own, neat, one of each. I can't offer you that. I had a vasectomy after Belinda was born, so no chance I'm afraid. Are you okay with that?'

Yes, I had been, I still was. I was even older now, not as mobile as when I had my angels. I wasn't sure how I could cope. I looked down at my tummy not believing it could be true. Had Mason lied to me about having been fixed? I'd believed him, taken no contraception. Had whatever they did come undone in any way? How could I prove anything? Would he accuse me of having an affair? How could I prove I'd been faithful? I broke out in a cold sweat.

There was one thing I could do and, turning the key, I drove straight to the nearest chemist.

I arrived home with four boxes of different brands. I'd try them all, one after the other. There had to be some mistake. The tests had been mixed up somewhere. And if they had mis-labelled the pregnancy results did they have the right ones for my anti-madness ones too?

I abandoned the car in the driveway, my hands shaking as I tried to put the key in the front door. I was so distraught I didn't even notice that the blue bunny was sitting on the chair by the telephone, staring at me.

I rushed past it and up into our bathroom. I tried one test kit after the other and, one by one, they all indicated a pink line. I perched on the edge of the bath, and burst into tears. That's all I was doing every day, crying. When was the last time I felt free, relaxed and happy since the accident? Maybe those couple of hours having coffee with Bill.

I stood up and went back into the bedroom. The bed I'd made as usual this morning was now all rumpled. I pulled back the duvet, and saw that the sheets were half off and clumps of mud were smeared over them. No way had I done this.

Back downstairs I opened my bag to get my phone out. This time I was going to see who was disturbing the house.

It wasn't there.

I turned the bag upside down and shook everything out. Purse, hankies, lipstick, credit cards, wallet and hairbrush all tumbled onto the carpet, but no phone. I searched the pockets of the coat I had flung on the floor in my hurry to get to the bathroom. It wasn't there either. I went to check in the car, but that proved fruitless.

Back in the hall I phoned my number and listened. It rang at the other end and was abruptly turned off and it dropped into voice mail. Not my voice message, a distorted voice telling me that this number was no longer in service. I must have dialled the wrong number so I tried again. I punched in the numbers, one by one, verbalising them, only to hear the same electronic tone repeat what I had already heard.

If someone had picked up the phone and used the apps could they be spying on me here at home? What a horrendous thought. I needed to talk to the suppliers and ask them.

Belinda barrelled in through the front door. She stopped when she saw me slumped on the floor stuffing the contents back into my bag.

"What the heck…?"

"Lost my phone."

"Bummer. Need to take more care Leah, you'll be hacked. Bet you don't have the right privacy settings either. You old wrinklies not up to speed, are you?"

"Gee thanks, Belinda." But she didn't hear me, her bedroom door slammed shut before the words were out of my mouth.

As I turned to get up I came face to face with the blue rabbit. What was it doing downstairs? I'd left it propped against the pillows on the bed. Then I remembered the state of the sheets. I'd better sort that out before Mason got home. I was about to tell my husband I was expecting the child that, in theory, he was unable to father, and protest my innocence with the marital bed in the state it was? Was the rabbit left downstairs as a warning?

By the time Mason came home I was a nervous wreck. I'd pulled clean linen off the shelves, raced back down stairs and piled the dirty sheets into the washer, then crept out to the green wheelie bin in the garage and disposed of the incriminating pregnancy testing kits. I was still throwing a ready meal into the oven when he arrived home. I would wait to break the disastrous news after supper. He was often more mellow after dinner and a few glasses of wine.

For once Belinda condescended to join us, so I said nothing as the meal dragged on and on. Would it hurt if I waited a few more days? What if I booked a meal out and told him in a public place? Then he would have to keep his temper under control. Was that the coward's way out? I had a sneaking suspicion he would want me to get rid of it and I wasn't sure if I could do that. How ethical was it? I was a healthy female and… no, wait, was I? If I couldn't explain my behaviour to myself, how safe would I be caring for a helpless baby?

In the end I chickened out. Mason said barely two words to me, too busy reading a report next to his plate, and Belinda spent the entire time texting on her phone.

Belinda broke the silence to tell her father I had lost my phone.

He looked angry, then shrugged and told me to buy a new one fast. It was very inconvenient if he couldn't get hold of me. I told him I'd go first thing in the morning.

My skin crawled as I unstrapped my leg and slid between the sheets. Who else had been lying in my bed? Violation comes in many forms and whoever had been here was determined I should know, why else the mud and the pathetic attempts at remaking it? I watched Mason carefully, but saw no signs he was looking for my reaction. There was no way that Mason would get into bed with muddy boots, he was far too fastidious.

I couldn't sleep that night. I tossed and turned, one minute too hot, the next too cold. I couldn't get over the sense there were three of us in the bed.

I got up early and crept along the landing to the top of the stairs. I stopped. I was aware I was no longer alone. Some primeval instinct was telling me I was not the only one on the landing. My ears flared and I caught the sound of a gasp. Was this my silent tormentor? Was he here to rearrange more items, deliver more boxes of foul-smelling substances? I took a deep breath, prepared to scream, and then decided to cope with this myself. It's unlikely one shriek would wake Mason, he slept so soundly.

I took one step back, reached over, and snapped on the light. It's not what you're supposed to do is it? In the dark, you should have the advantage over a burglar, you know your house better than he does. I have no idea what made me do it, possibly the desperation to see who was making my life hell.

I swung round to see a young man around nineteen years old, his denim shirt hanging over his slit jeans, his hair all mussed and a pair of filthy running shoes in one hand.

The door he'd just left opened and Belinda peered out. When she saw me a look of horror passed over her face before it fell back into her usual sulky 'don't bother me' glare.

"Go," I whispered loudly to the youth who was swaying from one foot to the other.

He hesitated for a moment and then hot-footed it down the stairs and out of the front door, closing it quietly behind him.

"You'll tell!" Belinda spat at me.

I kept her waiting for almost a minute before replying. "No, but now we're even. You saw my mother fall and I didn't see anyone run down the stairs tonight."

She let her breath out slowly and visibly relaxed, but before she could disappear back into her room, I added "I hope you're taking sensible precautions. Not only the pill, which can let you down if you have a bout of diarrhoea, but also against STD's. Just a thought."

She flounced back out of sight but remembered to close her door quietly.

I changed my mind about going downstairs. The emotional exchange had me drained so I crept back to my bedroom and crawled in beside the snoring Mason.

I was frantically busy the next day as I went out to purchase a new mobile. The young lad in the shop was amazingly patient with his technically challenged customer. It had taken me months to learn how to use all the apps and put in all my contacts on my old phone. I discovered that most of the information I'd programmed into it was stored on some mysterious cloud somewhere. While I imagined clever satellites adding my activities to their memory banks somewhere in space, the young man – his name tag said Malcolm – told me it was really huge computer banks in large warehouses dotted around the countryside. So that's how our enemies could wipe us out, or at least our communications, they only had to locate them and lob in a couple of RPG's. I still had a lot of learn of course. The new phone also had features I'd never heard of and worked quite differently to my old smart model.

To my dismay, the only app that did not magically pop onto the new screen was the one for the hidden cameras. I asked Malcolm to download it for me and managed to type in my pin number, hoping he wasn't peering and memorising it.

I waved my credit card over the machine, rushed out into the nearest coffee shop, and pressed the playback button. Nothing. If it had recorded anything it was now blank, but maybe it wasn't talking to the cameras.

Back I traipsed to the camera shop, only to discover that to get the app to talk to the cameras was a one-off. It was a special safety feature, the helpful assistant explained. So, what was the answer? New cameras? The whole idea was ludicrous. People must lose their phones or upgrade them every day.

I looked round the shop but I couldn't see anyone who might be more knowledgeable. I didn't want to be rude and say I didn't believe him. I'd wait until I got home and google it.

Any woman who has been pregnant must remember those mood swings you suffer from in the early weeks. Apart from your boobs feeling tender, you burst into tears for no apparent reason. It was in this state that Andrea found me that afternoon. I'd spent a fruitless two hours on the Internet learning nothing about getting my new phone to talk to my spy cameras.

Andrea was just what I needed as she rocked me to and fro in her arms and muttered all the right words. She consoled me over the pregnancy and, to my surprise, was all in favour of a termination. "You can't possibly have this baby, Leah. What a bastard, getting you pregnant at your age. I could kill him with my bare hands!"

I had never seen her so angry.

"But Andrea, that would be like murder, killing my baby."

"Nonsense. It's not a real person yet. You're about seven, eight weeks, right? Well now it's not even a boy or a girl, and all this stuff about the sanctity of life, think of all those sperm that go to waste every day!"

I had to giggle at the thought.

"And they are full of life, swimming desperately as if their lives depended on it." She waggled her fingers to illustrate her point, making me laugh even more.

"The last thing you need is the extra burden of a baby at your age. Can you imagine? He or she is twenty and you'll be sixty-one and at that age, subjected to ear-splitting rap or similar, ouch! All your dreams of an exciting retirement travelling to exotic places out the window 'cos you'll need the money to pay varsity fees. Nooooo, my friend, wake up and smell the roses."

She did have a point, several in fact, but I was undecided.

"I'd need to tell Mason, It's a joint decision. It's his baby too."

"But didn't you tell me…?"

"I thought he'd been fixed, so I never took any precautions."

"Um. I'm not sure they make mistakes like that. Can it suddenly reverse itself without the guy noticing? You were a nurse, you should know."

"Hardly. It wasn't in the syllabus and in all my years in the hospital I never heard of it once."

"Well you'd better make up your mind soon, or it will be too late. I've been here ages and you've not put the coffee pot on yet. Move it girl."

Despite Andrea's words, as each new day dawned, I kept

putting off telling Mason I was pregnant. I could imagine Belinda's disgust that an ancient specimen like myself was in breeding mode, but I needed a lot of courage, Dutch or otherwise, before I faced his fury. I asked myself if I was unconsciously protecting the new life growing inside me but, if I'm honest, I wasn't sure I was in a fit state to be a good mother. Apart from my missing limb, I was a bundle of nerves and still not reassured I was even sane.

Ms Prendergast suggested upping the counselling sessions to three times a week, which Mason thought was an excellent idea. The only thing I was upping was Ms Prendergast's bank account.

I didn't think the sessions were helping. Instead of making me feel better about myself, she was at pains to point out my weaknesses. I was already well aware of these but, unlike Dr Cromptom who was upbeat and encouraging, she was almost accusing, piling on the misery heaped on me by Mason and even Belinda. She didn't say so in so many words, but her eyebrows would shoot up and she'd stare at me in disbelief when I mentioned the poltergeist activity in the house. She murmured something about being into the spirit world, asked me if I saw angels, and was I into certain semi-precious stones for protection?

No, no and no. Either I was having mini blackouts, or someone I'd come to think of as my stalker was deliberately driving me down the road to madness. Each time I closed her surgery door I felt more depressed than when I'd arrived.

Another day spent at the hospital, additional tests. I should have taken more interest in what they were doing, but I felt so listless I didn't really care. The nurses were all so young, jolly and friendly, and twittered on about the baby I wasn't sure I wanted. Heaven knows, the world is over-crowded as it is. In this modern day and age why was it taking all this time to decide if I was sane or not. It hadn't taken that long with Mother, but then she really was mad. Maybe I was sane and they simply couldn't find anything wrong with me. It was the one cheerful thought I had all day.

Mason was away on another of his trips up north and Belinda was sleeping over with a friend. I guessed Mason assumed it was a girlfriend. I wasn't so sure, but I wasn't going to waste any energy worrying about it. Now that would be a scenario; both of us pregnant at the same time! It would never happen. That would be a nightmare. I couldn't imagine that young lady thinking twice about a termination.

I'd just unwrapped a pizza to pop in the microwave when someone leaned on the front doorbell and kept a finger on it. That could only be Andrea. How did she always know when I needed her?

She bounced into the hall, wreathed in smiles.

"Go get changed, we're going out to dinner."

"But I just…"

She swept past me into the kitchen and grabbed the pizza, wrapped it back in its cellophane, and popped it into the fridge. "There, that's settled. Huh, plastic, mass produced pizza. Yeuk! How does a filet mignon au poivre a la sauce crème Courvoisier sound? With duchess potatoes, ratatouille, followed by melt in the mouth crème brûlée with seasonal wild fruits." She grinned.

"Okay, you got me. Give me five to get ready."

I rushed up the stairs thanking fate for one great girlfriend.

"Don't tell me you got freebies again," I said as I hopped into the passenger seat of her Lexus.

"You got it. Courtesy of a good friend of mine. It's the new steak house on the edge of town and I was lucky enough to be chosen to take a dear friend to be among their first customers. It's only been open a few days."

The car park was full and it was raining as usual. Andrea was thoughtful enough to drop me near the front door while she found a parking place. I huddled in the porch waiting for her.

The décor was very upmarket, soft lights and carpet that threatened to cover your knees. Not a place to bring a new baby and just the place where Mason would choose to dine. I dreaded telling him but put it firmly out of my mind for tonight.

The food was excellent and the atmosphere so relaxing I was in danger of nodding off. I'd not been sleeping much. The waiters were well trained, attentive and, against my better judgement, Andrea insisted I had a glass of white wine. Even that one drink hit me for six.

I glanced round the room when Andrea popped off to the ladies and when she returned to the table, she insisted I go as well. "It's amazing, like an Aladdin's cave. All crystal chandeliers and an enormous array of those little bottles of hand cream and sprays and… oh do go and look."

When Andrea made up her mind that she wanted me to do something, inevitably I ended up doing it. Yes, she was manipulative, or bossy, but in such a charming way it was so hard to say no. I laughed and agreed to go in a moment.

"No, now, I insist. You might forget. Go on, just to please me."

I unhooked my bag from the back of my chair and made my way across the restaurant. I could never decide if restaurants used subdued lighting to make the diners more glamorous or disguise the shortcomings of the food.

Andrea was right, the ladies was indeed a small masterpiece with fairy lights strung across the ceiling and those perfumed stick things in bottles and a long row of hand creams in different containers. I took my time, noting a few things I might just duplicate in my own bathroom at home.

As I walked back into the restaurant, I noticed two of the waiters carrying a dessert with one of those sparklers on top. Must be somebody's birthday. I paused curious to see where they were taking it. The table was tucked away in a small booth, a couple sitting close together, his hand in hers, gazing into each other's eyes. They looked up and smiled as the waiter placed the sizzling firework on the table. She looked up at him and clapped her hands and then leaned forward and kissed him. He turned and smiled at the waiter.

I froze.

Mason.

No, it couldn't be him, wasn't he in Scotland or

Cornwall or somewhere for a few days? I clutched the back of a vacant chair as tears filled my eyes. Oh Leah! Crying again. It will ruin my makeup. I swayed back and forward undecided. Part of me wanted to go and confront them while part of me just wanted to disappear down a hole in the floor. What should I do?

A waiter tapped me on the shoulder. "Are you all right Madam? Do you need to sit down?"

"What?" I stared at him, shook my head and made my way back to the table.

"What's the matter? You look as if you've seen a ghost."

"I have, or maybe a lookalike or a clone, or I need my eyes tested."

"Off to Spec Savers with you," Andrea chuckled. Then she noticed I wasn't laughing. "Leah, what's upset you? You're as white as a sheet."

I hesitated. It's not easy to tell even your best friend your husband was slobbering all over another woman whose birthday he was celebrating, when it was not so long ago that he'd ignored mine.

Andrea wasn't going to give up. "I've just ordered the coffees. So, tell. What's wrong?"

"Mason," I whispered. "He's sitting over there."

"Now don't be stupid and get worried. You're out having fun. You don't need to ask his permission to have dinner with me. You're an independent woman with your own life to lead. If he's still out working all hours then you don't have to sit at home warming his slippers."

"He's with a woman, and it didn't look like a business

meeting to me.”

“Of course it is. You can trust Mason, he’s upright and solid, if a bit boring. He’s not going to risk his standing in the community for a fling.”

“They looked far too cosy… and it’s her birthday.”

“There are plenty of women in high flying jobs. It’s nothing Leah. She’s probably a client he got off in court and they’re celebrating. When I got divorced the first time, my lawyer took me out for a slap-up meal. Mind, it’s the least he could do from the size of his bill.”

I wasn’t convinced. You can tell, can’t you? The body language, the looks, but then I only got a brief glimpse. Had I imagined it? Was it only a lookalike? It was possible in the dim lighting.

Andrea was still prattling on, but I wasn’t listening. I was too busy choking back the tears. This was the final straw. Everything in my life was crumbling around me and I felt like a train on a mountainside sliding backwards out of control.

“Leah.”

I snapped back into the present.

“Sit there, don’t move and I will go and investigate.”

“No, don’t. I don’t want to know.”

“Of course you do,” and, before I could reply, Andrea was on her feet and crossing the room to the tables closer to the restrooms. As she sat down again, she was shaking her head. I stared at her, afraid of what she was going to say. “They’ve gone. Or, there is no one remotely like Mason in this restaurant. You don’t think it was…” she paused, “… an optical illusion, do you?”

Oh no. Not more imaginary scenarios. I dabbed my eyes with a tissue and concentrated on the chocolate mousse the waiter placed in front of me. I'd pretend I'd not seen anything. It was only my overactive imagination. I picked up my spoon and changed the subject. This was the first time Andrea had mentioned she'd been married more than once, and maybe she was in the mood to spill a few secrets of her own.

By the time Andrea had dropped me off at the front gate and I'd assured her I was fine, I'd decided to put the whole incident out of my mind. It wasn't Mason in the restaurant, a simple case of mistaken identity. He was miles away in Scotland and he couldn't be in two places at once. He wouldn't be so stupid as to play away so close to home. As I turned the key in the lock and opened the front door, I could see that the stalker had been active again.

The blue rabbit was back in the chair next to the telephone, the furniture in the lounge had been rearranged, exposing dust patches on the carpet where I'd vacuumed around them not bothering to move them and clean underneath. I'd skimped a lot on housework, eager to spend more time studying.

Every cupboard in the kitchen had been emptied out and the contents neatly stacked on the island and the work surfaces. Whoever had done this, it had taken more than a few minutes.

I knew for certain it couldn't have been me. Andrea would have noticed. She'd been in the kitchen when she'd re-wrapped the pizza. I opened the fridge to check it was still there.

I wandered into the lounge and slumped onto the sofa and put my head in my hands. Who would hate me enough to do this to me? Belinda? No, we had a sort of truce, we didn't interfere in each other's lives. None of my relatives. I had no close friends and if Mason hated me that much he could easily divorce me. As a lawyer he would know the quickest and easiest way to do it. He didn't have to go to these lengths to get shot of me.

I was too tired to clear away tonight. I made myself a cup of hot chocolate and took it up to bed.

AUGUST

The calendar clicked into August and I'd not received notification for the ultrasound test. I still hadn't plucked up the courage to tell Mason of his impending fatherhood. He'd been attentive and loving towards me and I so enjoyed his attention and his hugs and kind words that I was terrified of breaking the spell. Yes, I know I'm a coward. *Just let me enjoy these few days of a happy, peaceful marriage*, I prayed. Once I've seen the baby on that screen in the hospital, I'll believe it's true. I'll have to tell him then. I still had time. I'd googled the parameters and an abortion was still legal up to twenty-four weeks.

The other good news was my mental tests from the hospital had found nothing basically wrong with me. I had the usual symptoms of a pregnant woman approaching middle age, but Dr Morton was smiling as he gave me the all clear. I questioned him about the hallucinations, the weird poltergeist activities and unexplained inanimate objects jumping from place to place, but he had no answer to that. He couldn't explain it, and suggested that maybe I should report the occurrences to the police and have them investigate. I wasn't about to explain why the police were the last people I wanted to involve. Was there a file somewhere on their computer systems naming me as a 'person of interest'? No, I didn't want to involve Her Majesty's Constabulary. I nodded and let the matter drop. It might be a good wriggle point if I did decide not to have this baby. I'd not be a fit mother, would I? Unstable, weird acting, unpredictable, highly excitable.

After that night out, nothing moved in the house for days. Of course, there was no footage of the perpetrator, I'd still not got around to replacing the cameras or getting some techie guy to re-instate the programme on my phone.

But I couldn't forget seeing Mason in that restaurant with that woman. And I hate to admit this but, in turn, I became a stalker. I didn't have the courage to accuse him, but I still needed to know.

I chose a day when he told me he would be home late, another evening meeting with clients, and I drove to a car park near to his office an hour before the end of business. It was impossible to see the front door to his offices. He rented a Georgian house close to the main shopping centre, so I was forced to leave the car and perch on one of those rare park benches. I pretended I was waiting for someone, reading from the Kindle in my hand, glancing up every couple of seconds.

He didn't appear. Maybe the meeting was in his office? I'd seen several of hSis staff leave around five o'clock, but not Mason.

I couldn't sit there for too long without people noticing, so in the end I was forced to drive home none the wiser.

I had a brainwave. I'd follow Mason to work in the morning and see where he parked his car. Then I would stake that out instead of his office. If he drove off somewhere, I'd follow and see what he was up to.

It looks so easy when you see it on the movies. The police and private eyes munch doughnuts and drink coffee and then trail the suspect. It's a lot harder in real life. The few times I attempted to follow Mason's car I either lost it in traffic, or he drove it to innocent places like the shopping mall or an office block and, on one occasion, I discovered he wasn't driving it at all. His secretary parked up, got out and delivered a large brown envelope before returning to the car park.

I wasn't sure Andrea was taking my fears seriously. To her it was one big mystery and she offered to follow him and report back. I turned her down. It was bad enough me behaving like a suspicious wife without embroiling my best friend in a conspiracy as well.

I gave up. I wasn't cut out to be a private eye. I'd just put the whole horrible incident out of my mind and push it well down into my subconscious.

The following day Mason arrived home, swept into the kitchen and nearly threw me off balance as he nuzzled my neck and told me to pack.

"Two tickets on tomorrow's morning flight to Paris." He was grinning from ear to ear.

I threw my arms around him and hugged him as hard as I could. Paris, the city of lovers. All my fears flew out of the window and I almost bounced upstairs after supper to begin packing.

The fear flooded back as I couldn't find most of my

summer clothes. The outfits I'd been mentally packing were nowhere in any of the drawers or on the shelves. I decided not to mention this to Mason and break the spell. I'd just have to do the best I could with my older and 'between season' clothes, and maybe pick up a couple of outfits in Paris. Now that did sound like a good idea.

"How many days?" I called over the bannisters.

"Just a week, sweetheart. Can't leave the practice for too long, even at this time of the year."

Seven days is not long, but better than nothing. I rang to cancel Ms Prendergast, but I only got her voice mail. I left a cheery message to say I was off to Paris with my husband and, when I returned, I'd consider if I needed any further appointments.

Everything went smoothly. I was a little dismayed to see Mason carry his briefcase onto the plane and, after the obligatory drinks – of course you have to pay now, even on the high cost flights – he dragged it out of the overhead locker and shuffled through his paperwork. I would not even comment on it. Nothing was going to spoil the next few days. The inevitable storm when we returned home was pushed to the back of my mind.

For two days we did the usual touristy things. It wasn't our first trip to Paris and thankfully we had both explored Notre Dame before; to see the now blackened ruins was heart breaking.

We sauntered alongside the right bank of the Seine, wandered through the galleries in the Louvre, and took the train for a day out at Versailles. The sky stayed blue, the weather balmy, and life was just perfect. I couldn't remember the last time I'd felt this happy and carefree.

On day three, things began to unravel. I'd ignored the few times that Mason had buried himself in paperwork in the hotel bedroom, but I was taken aback when he announced that he had a meeting for lunch, so could I occupy myself for a few hours?

Why did life always kick me in the teeth the moment I relaxed?

"Sure. I'll wander up to Montmartre and watch the painters."

Mason nodded and gave me a quick peck on the cheek before settling down at the table scribbling further notes.

I decided to take the Metro and then the Montmartrobus to the basilica, then wander around the main square and watch the artists in action before taking the cable car back down.

By the time I reached the Basilica de Sacre Coeur I was already hot and tired. I should have guessed that the crowds would be horrendous. I shuffled forward in a long line as we waited to get inside. I guessed there was a hold-up at the ticket office, but no, it was free. As I passed inside the building, I picked up a leaflet to learn that the basilica was dedicated to the sacred heart of Jesus and built as a national penance for the defeat of France in the Franco-Prussian War. They've had a perpetual adoration of the Holy Eucharist since 1885. It also stated it was the second most visited monument in Paris and built at the highest point in the city.

There were ushers on both sides of the aisles, reminding people to be quiet, no talking was allowed inside. They frowned at a family with small children who had no intention of keeping quiet. In despair, they fought against the crowd and pushed their way back outside against the flow of the slow-moving tourists.

As I swung round to look ahead, I froze. Wasn't that Mason in front? And the woman with him? Wasn't she the same one he'd been having dinner with? I tried to push my way towards them. This time I would confront them.

My efforts were fruitless. The line ahead of me simply refused to let me through. The ushers frowned and one even held on to my arm to prevent me from getting ahead. When I turned to protest and try to explain in my very limited French, he shook his head and put his fingers to his lips.

I could barely contain my frustration as I was carried along between two couples who slowed to look at every last pillar and motif and, by the time I finally reached the exit door, Mason – if it were Mason – and his lady friend were nowhere to be seen.

I raced round the exterior of the church as fast as I could hobble, my leg painful, which often happened at times of extreme stress, but the crowds were too dense.

I hoped they'd gone to wait for the cable car that takes people back to the city, but the queue stretched along the road and I couldn't see them anywhere. I'd not even noticed what she was wearing, only glimpsed them above the shoulder line.

I hobbled back to the front of the basilica on the lower road and looked out over Paris. The view was spectacular but the buildings were blurred through my tears. I moved over to the side of the steps and sat on the grass and took out my mobile. I needed to talk to the only friend I had. I tapped in Andrea's number, startled for a moment when I heard another phone with the same ring tone as hers chirp from somewhere behind me. I turned to look but was then distracted as she answered.

"Hiya Sweetie. Are you having a great time? Please tell me you are."

"Andrea, where are you?"

"Where do you think I am? Stuck here in Kingston, in the damp and the rain and the grey skies. Not in the glorious, lovers' paradise of Paris." There was a pause. "Why are you asking me that? Where the hell do you think I am?"

I gave myself a mental shake and brushed the tears from my eyes. "I don't know, silly, I guess. There was a phone that rang with the same tune as yours at the exact same moment…" I trailed off.

"Get a grip Leah, there must be thousands of phones with the same tones. Are things not going too well? Darling please tell me they are."

I gulped hearing her voice, her concern threatened to bring on more tears. "I thought it was them. I saw them."

"Saw who? And by the way, where is Mason?"

"Mason, I thought I saw Mason with that woman again."

"Oh darling, you must be imagining things. Why isn't Mason with you? Aren't you holding hands and sightseeing and all that stuff?"

"He said he had a business meeting and he'd be busy

this afternoon. So, I decided… Andrea, it doesn't matter. Forget I phoned. You're right, I was seeing things. I'll go grab a large brandy and we'll chat when I get home. Take care." I pressed the disconnect button. I half expected Andrea to call me back but the phone in my hand remained silent.

I rose to my feet and looked down the steps to the circular balustrade at the bottom. No, maybe not. I remembered from long ago there are almost three hundred of them. I'd go back on the road and queue for the cable car.

I glanced once more at the spectacular view, even in my nervous condition I could appreciate the beauty of my favourite city spread out before me.

It was the last thing I remembered as something, or someone, bumped me from behind and I went flying down the steps.

I came to in a hospital bed and opened my eyes to see Mason bending over me.

"My love, what happened?"

I struggled to sit up but the sheets were wrapped so tightly I wriggled like a worm and couldn't get free.

"Take it easy. You had a terrible fall, at Montmartre? Do you remember? What do you remember?" He peered at me anxiously.

"I was pushed, someone pushed me. I didn't fall." My mouth was dry and the words came out all jumbled.

Mason leaned over and poured me a glass of water and put his hand behind my head to help me sip through the straw. "Take it easy. You need to rest. They want to keep you in for a couple of days, run a few tests and make sure it's safe for you to fly home."

I struggled to sit up. "Mason, I was pushed. Someone tried to kill me. I was pushed down the steps."

"Hush now. No one wants to hurt you. Perhaps someone bumped you a little, but who would deliberately push you down the steps? It's that over active imagination again."

We were interrupted by the arrival of a doctor. He gave me a small smile and addressed us in English. "Madame Brand, I am so, so sorry about the baby. We tried all we could but it was a spontaneous evacuation. Very early days. I'm sure you and your husband will have many more young ones."

There was an uncomfortable silence. I kept my eyes fixed firmly on the bed sheets, I dared not look at Mason, but I could feel the tension radiating off him in waves.

The doctor prattled on explaining if the tests were positive I would be able to travel back to England in a couple of days. He must have sensed there was something wrong, as he mumbled a bit more and then made a rapid exit from my bedside.

Since I was in a ward with five other patients, it wasn't possible for Mason to make a fuss, but he looked furious.

"And when were you going to tell me about this… this baby? I did hear correctly? You were pregnant?"

My heart sank. Would Mason believe I'd been unfaithful? Or that a vasectomy could reverse itself without him being aware of it? That just couldn't happen, could it?

I turned away from him. I did not want to talk about it. I was not going to plead my case. I heard the chair legs scraping as he got up to leave, and the soles of his shoes squeaking on the highly polished floor as he walked out of the ward. I lay back defeated. I'd get nowhere with Mason. Andrea wouldn't believe me either. I was on my own.

They kept me in the hospital for two more days. Their testing was very thorough and once again I felt like a living pin cushion, although this time, as they shunted me through the CAT scan, I was treated to the melodious sounds of Charles Aznavour through the headphones. So very French.

Mason popped in once or twice but he didn't stay long. I had no idea what he was rushing off to do, or where he was going, but you can sense when people are just itching to leave. I lay there with pictures floating past my eyes. I could see him and her in restaurants, an evening dinner cruise on the Seine, making full use of our hotel room. I felt he was just waiting until we returned home to take me to task, while most likely he was cavorting round Paris with his mistress.

I am going mad Leah, I told myself, *if I'm not already mad.*

Once they discharged me, Mason decided to cut off the last day of our holiday and return home immediately. He'd not consulted me and he had already bought the tickets. I said nothing. I was still a little shaky, and popping painkillers several times a day. There was not a lot wrong with me apart from horrendous bruising, and I was very unsteady on my feet. I had mixed feelings about losing the baby. In one way it was a relief; I was too old, I didn't have the energy to cope with a bawling new-born and then later with an active toddler. On the other hand I felt so sad that I had lost the one human who might have given me unconditional love, another human to share the joys and sorrows of everyday life. Now I was getting carried away in a fantasy world.

We landed at Heathrow in the middle of a torrential downpour. Andrea was right about the weather. I looked up at the solid block of grey sky and my spirits sank. It was such a contrast from the bright blue sky above the clouds we'd flown through only moments before.

Mason collected the car and drove us straight home. Being me, I'd stocked up the freezer before we left and there was no need to even stop for essentials, unless Belinda had cleaned us out. I suspected she had not slept in the house alone.

I hadn't finished unpacking before Mason shouted up the stairs that he was going to the office. He advised me to take it easy and have a lie down. His voice was laced with sarcasm. I sighed. Back a day early, was there any real need to go to work? I'd hoped he'd stay with me, maybe even wait on me with cups of tea, get supper for a change. I wanted to have a sensible chat, face the elephant in the room together. We needed to talk. I had to explain. What was I thinking?

A few minutes later Andrea was on the phone.

"Saw your car in the drive. Back safe and sound?"

"In one piece, but covered in bruises." I sank down onto the bed, my head on the pillow.

"Oh my god, what happened? Bruises, what do you mean bruises?"

"Those big blue and yellow patches you get on your body when you fall down two hundred and seventy steps."

"You what?" her screech went right through me. "Are you there on your own?"

"Yes, why?"

"I'm coming over. You poor baby."

I didn't feel like seeing Andrea just then. To start with I'd have to get off the bed and downstairs to open the door for her. I wanted to close my eyes and rest for a few minutes.

As usual, Andrea barrelled into my hallway like an express train on steroids. She flung her arms around me, then stepped back when I winced.

"Oh, I'm sooooo sorry, I didn't think. Where does it hurt?"

"Just about all over. But there was nothing broken. I don't remember what happened"

"So tell me what you do remember." Andrea propelled me onto one of the stools and raided the coffee pods before selecting one and turning on the machine.

"I phoned you." I tried not to sound bitter.

"Yes, I know you did darling, but you were not making sense. You said Mason was with another woman, the same one from the restaurant? And then you thought I was there as well? In Paris? Could you see me? And why wasn't Mason with you?"

She sat beside me and took my hand. "Leah darling, you're not making a lot of sense lately. Are you sure you're all right?"

"Now you think I'm mentally deranged as well? Mad?" I whipped my hand away and moved round to the other side of the island. "I'm already having therapy, or had you forgotten? And it's not doing me any bloody good at all. The woman just sits there and makes it obvious she thinks I am mad."

Andrea busied herself making the coffee. "Leah, we all know we're not that unique, there must be dozens of people who look similar to us. I accept that. But to see two look-alikes together miles from home, well that takes a lot of believing."

I sighed. Had I been mistaken?

Andrea continued. "And why on earth did you think I was stalking you in Paris as well? At the same time?"

"It was your mobile phone ring."

"Must be a million people using the same tunes. Get a grip, Leah." She paused, a coffee mug in each hand. "The baby. Your baby. I'd forgotten. Is it…?"

"Gone."

"Oh." She put the mugs on the table. For several moments neither of us said anything.

"How do you feel about that?"

"I don't know, Andrea. I'm numb in mind and body. I don't feel life is real. I'm walking around in a fog." I wasn't going to mention even to my best friend that the baby would have been born of what amounted to rape on that night Mason took me so forcefully.

"Did they give you pills in Paris?"

"Yes, but…" I didn't want to mention that my out of body experiences had been coming and going all this year.

I was dismayed that Andrea didn't believe me. Was I the only one who thought I was sane? I was scared.

Andrea walked round and gave me a hug. "Darling, cheer up. It's just a bad time for you. You need to relax, chill out and ignore all the bad stuff."

"There is so much of it. It all seems bad."

"How did Mason react to you being pregnant?"

"We've not discussed it."

"What, not at all? You can't be serious."

"I hadn't got around to telling him about it, and then the doctor just happened to mention it in the hospital."

"As a result of the fall?"

"Yes. I think he called it a spontaneous evacuation or something similar."

"Oh god, Leah. I don't know what to say. Except I'm here for you."

"I'm glad someone is," and to my horror I burst into tears.

"You've always got me." Andrea rocked me in her arms. It was so comforting but, as she let go of me and turned away, I glanced up and saw her reflection in the window from the wall mirror in the breakfast room and her expression didn't match her words. I could have sworn I saw her smile. Another hallucination?

I continued to drag myself through each day. I visited Ms Prendergast three times a week but, every time I left, I felt worse than when I'd rung her doorbell. She gave me no encouragement, suggested no coping strategies, and I felt like an insect spread out on a dissecting board as I watched her wield a knife above me. How can someone be so exhausting just sitting there and making the odd deprecating comments? She wrung me out like a sponge.

As promised, I booked an appointment to see Dr Morton. He gave me his condolences about my miscarriage but said it was probably for the best, and then lectured me on taking adequate precautions in the future. I asked him how possible it was for a vasectomy to spontaneously reverse and he gave me a very strange look.

"It has been known to happen, but it's very, very rare. I believe it happens in one in four thousand cases and only in the case of poor surgery."

"Would the man be aware of this?"

"Doubtful, unless he made a woman pregnant."

"Do you know if Mason…"

"Your husband is not my patient Mrs Brand, and even if he were, I would not be at liberty to discuss his medical history without his written consent."

"Even to his wife," I muttered. I'd had it with these privacy rules and regulations. He refilled my prescription and I left his surgery none the wiser. I was to go back when the latest batch of tests were in.

The only time I relaxed and felt the least bit happy was when I went to the library and I found an excuse to pop in there most days. Sometimes I worked on my next assignment, sometimes I sat and read and Bill found lots of spare moments to stroll over for brief chats. I found his presence calm and soothing. For a short time, I forgot the poltergeist activity: the loss of my baby, the suspicions about my husband and his mistress, Belinda's appalling behaviour, and the fact that Mason and I had barely exchanged a civil word to each other since the holiday. He had refused to discuss the baby at all, but his face said it all. He did not accuse me of infidelity but the disgust on his face sent shivers down my spine. There was no intimacy between us at all.

Once a week, on his half-day, Bill and I would wander over to our favourite café close to the library and have coffee and cholesterol-inducing cakes. If I felt guilty about this on the first or second visits, I squashed those thoughts deep down and enjoyed his company. I might be a married woman but it was all innocent, two friends enjoying each other's conversations. There were no smouldering looks, no hand holding, no playing footsie under the table. Bill was the perfect gentleman and we laughed and chatted about books and plays, politics and the state of the world. Nothing could be more innocent.

I can't remember what opened the doors, metaphorically that is, but one day it all came out. I'd never discussed such secrets before. We'd been talking about our childhood. Like me, Bill had a horrendous relationship with his widowed mother, and it all spilled out from there. Once I started, I couldn't stop.

I paused, horrified at how I had been so open about the traumas in my life and fixed my gaze on my coffee cup, not daring to look up. Why, oh why had I chosen to destroy a beautiful, platonic friendship. I was filled with loathing and self-pity. At first, I didn't catch Bill's words.

"What?"

"I said Leah, that seldom have I met a more stable, down to earth, sensible woman."

"You don't think I'm mad then?"

He put his head back and laughed. "Not for one moment. I'm no expert mind you, but from the way you talk and the way you behave, I believe you are perfectly sane."

I let out the breath I'd been holding, allowing the tension to drain out of me.

"I think that deserves an extra doughnut, don't you?" He gestured to the waitress.

"I feel privileged you have shared your fears with me," he said, as she went off to fetch the order. "I'm not sure what I can do to help, but I'll have a good think and see if I can come up with anything." He rummaged in his pocket and bringing out a pen and notebook he wrote his phone number on it. He passed it across. "If you need me, any time, any day, call. Promise?"

I could only nod. His kindness made me want to burst into tears again.

Fate chose that moment for the woman I was convinced was having an affair with Mason, to walk past the café. She glanced in the window, paused for a moment, stared hard and then walked briskly away.

This time I had seen her clearly. It must be her. Why had she paused? And stared. If I'd not been sitting with Bill I would have jumped up and followed her. I wondered if Mason would mention it to me.

A wave of guilt swept over me. Today I had crossed the line and I wasn't sure there was any way back.

* * *

In the event Mason said nothing about my coffee shop date, though I hesitate to call it that. I'd been worrying for nothing, but soon I had other concerns to send me closer to the edge

.

SEPTEMBER

September started off quietly. Belinda departed for the new year at school in a huff. She muttered about wanting to backpack around Europe. She was too old for all this school nonsense with its rules and regulations and boring, immature people and the overbearing staff. I pretended not to hear. There was nothing I could do about it. With that attitude I thought it unlikely she would do well in any of her exams or achieve high marks for her coursework.

Her father was so intent on her taking a law degree and then joining his company to carry on the dynasty. I was convinced that didn't appeal to her in the slightest and, once or twice, I asked her what her dream career would be. She brushed me off on each occasion, thumping her way up the stairs and slamming her bedroom door shut. I refused to let myself get upset about it. I had enough to worry about as the house, or rather the objects in the house, took on a life of their own again.

The first problem was the water supply. After everyone had left one morning, I went to do the breakfast dishes but there was no water. I waited for an hour or so, thinking the water company was making repairs nearby, although they usually informed us in advance. I decided there was a burst pipe somewhere.

I looked out of the front gate but could see no activity. After an hour or so I phoned Andrea who was just on her way out. She had water. That didn't prove anything, she could be on a different network.

I phoned the water company in the afternoon, but they informed me there were no problems and suggested I checked the stop cocks inside and outside the house. When I tried to tell the impatient young girl on the other end of the line I had already done that, I realised she had hung up on me. I sighed and went to check them all again. Maybe I was wrong, but I can never remember which way they should turn for on and off. Since I'd not touched them it wouldn't really make a difference, would it? I twisted them in the opposite direction and tried every combination I could think of, from the stop cock outside the kitchen door to the ones underneath each sink. I had no luck.

Mason was not too thrilled when he arrived home from work to find no meal ready, no washing done, and the sink full of dirty dishes. He hardly gave me a moment to explain before he pushed past me in the kitchen and turned on the tap. The water gushed out.

I protested that only ten minutes ago there was no water, but he gave me such a look I cringed and turned away to prepare his supper.

This happened three days in a row. From the moment Mason left for work, the taps were dry. The moment he returned in the evening the water flowed like Niagara Falls. I was at my wits end. My husband made it quite clear he simply didn't believe me. He insinuated my dementia was getting worse and he was tired of wasting money on my counselling sessions with Ms Prendergast. He couldn't understand this as she had been highly recommended and had achieved amazing results with all her other patients. I had my doubts about that. How could she possibly prove it?

Three times a week I was still dragging myself over to her place, but each time I came away feeling worse than when I entered her pristine consulting room. I was so tempted to stop the visits but I knew what Mason's reaction would be. I wanted to be cooperative, so he couldn't accuse me of being difficult. I noticed I was becoming more and more timid, always fretting I would upset him in some way, only to have a torrent of abuse pour over me like a hailstorm. Whoever said that words don't hurt didn't know what they were talking about.

During the day I regained some of my equilibrium, especially if I took time to meet up with Andrea, or visit the library for a chat with Bill. I found I was popping there most days, even counting the hours until I could wander down.

The last test results came back and, according to Dr Morton, I was perfectly healthy. There was no explanation for my hallucinations, as he called them. He offered me tranquilisers and, despite my reluctance, insisted I try them for a couple of weeks.

I did, but they made me feel fuzzy. I found it difficult to concentrate and, after six days of walking around in a fog, with Mason becoming more and more irritable and angry, I gave up on them.

I was on my own and, bit by bit, I could feel my

confidence leaking out of me and I could not fix that with a new stopcock.

As the weeks flew by, even Andrea was beginning to lose patience. Not that she said anything, but I could read her body language and it was less than sympathetic.

"Look Leah, I've completely run out of suggestions," she said one afternoon. "You've tried the medical route. You even came with me to yoga a couple of times and that didn't help." She was right. I'd burst into tears in the middle of the session disturbing the whole class.

I considered a retreat; maybe a week in a quiet, rural area would set me right, but Mason was not in favour. It was obvious that his comforts came first and he was not prepared to cook and look after himself while I floated on a cloud with a group of latent over-aged hippies – well, that was his take on it.

So the only comfort I found was in the library. Even if Bill was busy and couldn't stop to chat for long, the atmosphere was peaceful, no pressure, and he even managed to make me laugh. I didn't mention my problems or the strange occurrences to him again. He subtly broached the subject once but I ignored his question. I switched off that side of my life the moment I walked through the doors and threaded my way through the bookcases.

There was another problem with the water supply. This time the supply was uninterrupted, but during the day I could only get cold water. I pointed this out to Mason and he held his fingers under the flow. "What's wrong with it? It's hot. Ouch!" He pulled his hand away.

I tested it but it was cold, it wasn't burning me. I stared at him. "It's cold," I repeated, "you must feel the same. It is cold."

He snarled and walked away. "Leah, face it, there is something radically wrong with you. Something in your brain is twisted. You've lost it."

I clutched the edge of the sink. How far had I descended into madness? I turned on the tap and let it run for several minutes. It was still cold. How could he say it was hot? Nerve receptors in your hands had nothing to do with being mad, I was sure of that.

"I'm going to call a plumber in the morning. See what he says. Maybe the thermostat on the tank has gone, or we might need a new tank."

"Bloody waste of money." Mason shouted from the hallway. "Don't you think you're enough of a financial burden on me as it is, without these fantasies of yours?" The study door slammed and stopped the conversation dead.

In the event, the plumber was business-like, raced in, found nothing wrong in the ten minutes he was in the house and departed leaving me with an astronomical bill.

The water ran hot for a couple of days and then ran cold for several more. I almost got used to taking freezing showers to keep clean. Then suddenly the water began flowing again, it went back to the way it had always behaved. It ran hot from the hot tap and cold from the cold tap.

I felt reality slip a bit further away.

I'd given up on my university course, it was as much

as I could do to get through each day; cleaning, cooking, shopping, washing, and planning the ordinary day-to-day tasks to keep the house ticking over. But there was something every day to unnerve me.

My clothes continued to rearrange themselves, never Mason's, only mine. I took photos of them most mornings and again after they had migrated. This proved they had been interfered with, but not who moved them. Could it be me? I was beginning to convince myself I was guilty. No one else was here. No one had a key to the house and no one had broken in.

I checked out the hidden cameras, but not once had I achieved any success. I even went back three times to the shop to complain. On one occasion the assistant, who was particularly helpful and sympathetic, took the one camera apart to show me there were no batteries inside. I felt so stupid, I slunk out of the shop and across the mall to stock up on more batteries. Sure enough, not one of the cameras was operational, no wonder all I could get on my phone was a grey screen with white fuzzy lines running across it. I even tested the new power sources before I put them in; I'd bought the long-life kind, you know, the ones with the pink bunnies that go on forever?

And that reminds me, the blue bunny in my house had a life of its own. Each time I left the house it moved. At first, I shoved it away in a cupboard, but next day it was sitting on the sofa in the lounge. I locked it in the garden shed, but somehow it found its way out and was sitting waiting for me in the hall next to the telephone. I tried putting it in the green wheelie bin an hour before the dust cart arrived to take away all the rubbish. Later that day I found it in my chair facing the television. I don't think it was the same rabbit; it didn't have wet tea bags all over its fur.

I thought I was being very clever, by taking it out with me one day. I popped it in a large plastic bag and deliberately left it behind in the post office. The lady behind me in the queue came running out and galloped along the street before grabbing my arm and pushing the bag into my hand. She was puffing and panting from the effort, her permed grey head nodding in anticipation of doing her good deed for the day. I could only thank her profusely and pretend I would have been devastated at the loss.

I changed direction and made for the library. It was blissfully quiet and I sank into an arm chair and closed my eyes. I'd hide the rabbit in here, right at the back, maybe even high up on one of the shelves. I saw no one watching me as I crept round the free-standing stacks before stuffing the bag into a space between the farthest shelf and the wall.

When I arrived home, I was elated to see no bunny. Yes, I know that's appalling grammar, but the absence of the stuffed animal I had come to loathe was such a relief.

I was bunny-free for almost a whole day until the doorbell rang. Even an everyday sound like that had me jumping with nerves. I sidled up to the peep hole and to my amazement Bill was standing on the doorstep.

I flung the door open and had a hard time not to fling myself as well. My voice wobbled.

"Hello, this is a surprise."

"Hi." He looked a little nervous. "See, I was just passing and one of the cleaners found this."

To my dismay it was the bag and the bunny.

"But how did you…?"

"There was a receipt in the bottom with your name on it and, of course, we have addresses for all the library members so it was easy." He smiled again.

"Come in, the least I can do is offer you a drink." I didn't think before I made the offer. I didn't consider the possible consequences. I was just so pleased to see a friendly face.

He followed me into the kitchen and perched on a stool while I rummaged in the fridge for the cold drink he'd asked for.

I had one of those lightbulb moments. "Don't you know some child who would love that rabbit? Uh, where had I left it?" I prayed the finder had not commented on the fact it was stuffed well out of sight and I'd not mentioned the stuffed toy that was freaking me out most days when I'd spilled my heart out to Bill in the coffee shop.

"No, sorry. Both my children are living abroad now as I told you."

"Yes, but maybe a neighbour?"

Before he could answer the front door banged and Belinda came barrelling into the kitchen. She stopped and stared at Bill.

"And who are you?" Without waiting for a reply, she turned and opened the fridge door.

"Belinda," I gasped. "That is so rude. This is Bill Gates from the local library and he was just returning something I'd left behind." The moment the words were out of my mouth I could have kicked myself. What was I doing explaining my visitors to a teenager who didn't even let me in to clean her bedroom? That was the way I so often reacted now, on the defensive, explaining my every action. Tomorrow I was going to get a grip and dive back into Dr Cromptom's tome on self-esteem. It gave me more coping skills than Ms Prendergast ever offered.

Belinda was not the least bit cowed. "I'm not sure Daddy would approve of you entertaining gentlemen friends in his house while he's out at work." That said, she went off into the lounge and turned on the television. I noticed she kept the sound much lower than usual and would be eavesdropping.

I rolled my eyes and Bill smiled again and whispered "teenagers." We both burst out laughing but the atmosphere had changed and Bill quickly downed the rest of his drink and made his excuses. Before leaving he popped his head round the door and said goodbye to Belinda who pretended not to hear him.

That evening at supper the moment Belinda plonked herself down at the table I told Mason that Bill from the library had dropped by. I hoped it would prove I had nothing to hide.

"Here? You mean he came around here? What for?"

"Just dropping off a parcel I'd left in the library." I spoke slowly, determined that my voice would give nothing away. I felt very nervous, but I wasn't about to let Belinda think she could use this as leverage against me. Right now, we were equal. I didn't squeal on her having her boyfriend staying overnight and she didn't recant her evidence about witnessing my mother's accident to the police.

"I don't approve." Mason reminded me of a two-year old about to have a temper tantrum. I was expecting him to start stamping his feet on the floor.

"It's the twenty-first century Mason. Men and women mix every day at work, in the pub, have the occasional coffee together, and chat while commuting. It's perfectly normal."

"Outside the house yes, not privately, not alone."

"Belinda was here." I glared at her daring her to say we'd been alone before she got home from school.

"So, tell me, what was this important parcel you'd left behind?"

Was Mason angling to catch me out in a lie?

"The bag over there." I pointed to where Bill had left it on one of the kitchen stools.

Mason stood up and walked over and pulled out the stuffed toy. "This?" His eyebrows shot up.

"Uh, yes."

"Do tell me why you bought a stuffed, blue rabbit when you already have one? Or is this the one Andrea gave you?"

For several seconds I froze, not sure what to say. I hadn't bought it and Mason and Belinda must have seen it around the house.

"It's the ugliest rabbit I've ever seen. Everyone knows rabbits are not blue," was her only contribution.

"They're collecting toys for the orphans at Christmas."

It was the first thing I could think of.

"Bit bloody early – in September?" Mason didn't sound convinced but, to my relief, he let it drop.

Why was I not surprised when the rabbit appeared back in his more usual place sitting next to the telephone? The telephone that never rang these days. The moment I was on my own, I unplugged it from the wall. Occasionally I forgot to reconnect it again in the evenings, but both Mason and Belinda were so welded to their mobile phones that they didn't notice we were no longer being bothered by the double glazing, conservatory, life insurance, fibre optic people, and all the other cold callers who'd all stopped phoning us.

One disaster followed another.

The next evening Mason strode into the kitchen and waved my mobile phone under my nose.

"And what is the meaning of this!" He screamed at me.

I had no idea what he meant but took the phone and looked at the screen. There was a text message.

I miss you every moment I'm not with you. Can't wait for us to be together again. All my love, Bill – followed by a row of smiley faces blowing kisses.

I nearly laughed out loud. I couldn't imagine Bill sending me a message like that.

"I have no idea. It's the first I've seen it."

"Obviously, or you would have deleted it, I'm sure." He snatched the phone back and scrolled up. "Oh look! Lots more." He read them out in a false voice. *"Darling, last night was the best ever. We must do it again and very soon. You're not to worry your head about the price of the best hotel, my time with you is worth every penny.*"

To me it sounded like something a teenager would write and I credited even Belinda with more sophistication.

I pulled my shoulders back and went back to loading the dishwasher.

"Mason, you can think what you like but I'm not having an affair, not even close. Those texts are as puzzling to me as they are to you. I have no idea how they got on there or who sent them." I straightened up and turned to face him. "You can believe me or not. I'm past caring. Just like you didn't believe me about the parcel, or the cold water or the water not working. I can't explain any of it. Or even that bloody rabbit that you pretend not to see." I slumped back against the side and noticed Mason jump back in alarm as I picked up the carving knife to put in the dishwasher. His eyes shone with fear and he took a step backwards.

"And no, I'm not going to attack you, however mad you think I am."

He hesitated, not taking his eyes off the knife as I dropped it into the rack at the back of the machine. He leaned forward and put his elbows on the island, head in his hands. "What am I supposed to think, Leah? Your behaviour this year has been beyond bizarre. You are not the woman I married. Not the woman I fell in love with."

What was Mason telling me? He didn't love me anymore? That he thought I was mad? I felt my whole body go stiff, I was unable to move. I stared at him. I didn't know what to say.

Belinda chose that moment to walk in with her dirty glass and rinse it under the tap. That was a first. When did she last do anything remotely helpful in the house? She hovered waiting to see what we would say next.

Mason sighed, stood up, and marched off into his study. The door banged, a sure sign he was not to be disturbed. But maybe for once I should change that? I followed him in, closed the door firmly behind me and sat down opposite his desk.

"Mason, we need to talk."

"I'm not convinced that would get us anywhere. If you've come in here to persuade me that you're not playing on the side, you're wasting my time."

"I can see you've already made up your mind. The most I've ever done is offer Bill a drink for going out of his way to return my parcel."

Mason looked up from the papers he was reading. "Oh, I don't think that's quite accurate is it Leah? Aren't you going to tell me about your cosy little cups of coffee in Ann's Pantry?"

I gasped. Who had told him about that? It was all so innocent, I kept telling myself that. Of course it was innocent, we'd done nothing wrong. "Are you having me followed?"

He leaned towards me over his desk and almost leered as he answered. "Why? Should I? What would I find out?"

"Nothing, nothing at all, so if you are looking for a reason to… to dump me, it won't be infidelity. I've been faithful to you from the day we met. Look Mason, please can't we just discuss what's happening like two rational people? I don't understand what is going on."

"Well how the bloody hell am I supposed to know if you don't? You're the one who's acting like a mad woman. Seeing things that aren't there? Making up fantastic stories."

"But I'm not, Mason. Everything I'm telling you is true."

"That your clothes jump around when you're not looking? The hot water feels cold? It only turns on when I come home? That a perfectly normal parcel contains detritus? A ticking cat under the bed. And this rabbit thing? Well that's the best of all. Does he chat to you when I'm at work? Have long conversations, do you?"

I'd heard enough. Instead of helping and talking and trying to find a solution, all Mason was prepared to do was mock me and blame me.

I stumbled out of the study and up the stairs and cried my eyes out on the bed. I didn't care if Belinda heard me or not. At some point I fell asleep.

To get me through the next couple of weeks I gulped down the pills that Dr Morton had given me, by the bucketful. I was walking around in a fog but I managed to get through each day – just. It was like walking around in my own personal cloud, the rest of the world kept at bay through a pale white mist.

Andrea dragged me up to the West End to see a show. She was convinced that would cheer me up. I think the play was quite good, but when one of the characters came on stage I stood up and cried out. Andrea dragged me back down into my seat.

"What the f's the matter with you?"

"It's her, can't you see it's her!"

"Who, what are you talking about?"

The people sitting near were shushing and glaring at us.

"That woman who just came on. She's my counsellor."

"Nonsense, it's just a lookalike," Andrea hissed. "We all have a doppelgänger, or whatever it's called. She's famous. She was in Coronation Street last year on the telly."

"I never watch that."

"I can't believe you've not seen her, they interview her all the time. Anyway, shush! Let's enjoy the play."

The moment the curtain came down I grabbed Andrea's arm and hustled her out of the theatre and along the street.

"What the fuck are you doing Leah? Where are we going?"

"The stage door. I want to see her close up and personal."

"You're mad."

"Maybe I am. But I want to find out for sure."

After the bright lights of the Strand, the side alley nearest the theatre was dark, dangerous and grungy. I almost fell over a homeless tramp curled up next to a row of stinking wheelie bins, and a sudden movement in the shadows scared me witless. What was I doing? I clamped my hand more firmly on Andrea's arm and headed towards the dim lights at the end of the alley. Were all alleys in London this long? I thought we'd never get through.

At last we turned the corner at the end into the road parallel to the Strand. It wasn't wide, but at least there were a few lights. I peered at each doorway hoping to see one marked, but it was the couple of Uber taxis hovering at the kerb that told me we were in the right place.

Had it been a rock show or a rapper on stage I'm sure there would have been a crowd of groupies hovering, but this was a serious play most likely to appeal to the middle aged. We were long past the fan brigade as Andrea and I hovered next to the doorway.

"Oh, come on Leah, this is a total waste of time. I feel such a fool." Andrea attempted to pull me away. "I'm sure the cast don't hang around."

Nothing was going to make me move. I had to find out for myself.

The main star walked out accompanied by a very distinguished gentleman. "Hello darlings," she gushed. "Like an autograph?"

"No thanks," Andrea replied rudely. "We're waiting for Melissa Stuart."

The great star gasped, looked daggers at us, and then swept past. I saw her escort's lips twitch as he looked over his shoulder. "She's coming now," he said.

Sure enough, a minute later, Melissa Stuart appeared or, as I knew her, Ms Cilla Prendergast.

"Miss Prendergast," I said stepping forward and blocking her path.

The look on her face told me I was right. "Leah?" It came out low and breathless before she suddenly pushed me out of the way. "That's not my name," she snarled.

"Now if you don't mind, I want to get home."

"And where would that be?" I sidestepped to stop her passing me but she put out a hand and shoved me away. If Andrea hadn't caught me, I would have ended up in the gutter.

The doorman appeared. "Having trouble Miss?"

"No, thank you Bert. I can handle it."

Before anyone could say another word, Melissa Stuart jumped into the waiting taxi which sped off down the road.

"It's her. I know it's her. The voice, the manner, the way she walks."

Andrea wasn't listening; too busy on her phone calling for a cab. "It will be here in two minutes," she announced, then looked at me and waved and smiled at Bert who was still hovering in the stage doorway. More cast members left and milled around waiting for a ride.

My best friend had planned to take me out for a meal after the show but she'd changed her mind as she gave our home address to the driver. She spoke quietly. "Leah, you have to get a grip. You can't go around accosting celebrities and making a nuisance of yourself."

"But didn't you see? She recognised me. She called me Leah, isn't that proof?"

"She called you by name?"

"Didn't you hear her? She said Leah."

"No, sorry I didn't."

I let out the breath I was holding. With no back up from Andrea, I would never be able to prove anything.

Over the next few days I googled everything I could find

about Melissa Stuart. I discovered where she went to school, where she trained, all the shows and television series she'd been in. Still a minor star, she was one of those performers I called a working actress. You might not remember her name but she was constantly in work. Of course, the Internet sites I explored didn't give her address or contact details and her agent wasn't likely to hand those out either.

I decided to stalk her.

I'm sure by now you're also convinced I'd lost it. This was not the rational behaviour of a middle-aged, middle-class woman. In my defence I can only say that I was trying to prove, if only to myself, that I still had a grip on reality.

I began by sitting in my car near to her surgery after one of our sessions waiting for her to leave. On each occasion only minutes after I left, she walked round from the back of the house, spent a moment in the front porch, and then climbed into a waiting taxi.

As I mentioned before, it looks easy following people when you see it on the movies. It's not. The first three times I lost her in the traffic, on two other occasions I couldn't find parking close enough to her practice to see her leave. It was over a week later that I got lucky and managed to stay behind the taxi all the way to where I thought she lived. Two days later I hovered near her house and saw her return, so I was convinced this was her address. I noted the street name and number and then went to the nearest library and asked to see the electoral role for that area. I gave them a story about wanting to check I was on the list giving my name as M Stuart at her address.

The helpful assistant perused the names and shook her head.

Looking over her shoulder I saw only one name for the house, Mary Smith. So I was wrong. I thanked the librarian and wandered back to my car. All those hours for nothing. It was a dead end.

While driving home I remembered something, and I couldn't wait to log on. Yes, her parents were listed as Rhone and Tom Smith. No wonder she'd changed her name. I delved into a few more sites and confirmed she was also Melissa Stuart. The next step was to follow her from her house to the theatre. This would not be as easy, since Mason and Belinda would be back home and expecting a meal. I could get away with being out a couple of evenings but not several days on end. I also noticed in the paper that the play was only running until the end of the month. That left me six days.

The fates were kind to me on my first attempt. I'd left plated salads in the kitchen, with a note to say I was out with no explanation of what time I would be home – I didn't feel the slightest bit guilty.

I followed a taxi down her narrow suburban street and was thrilled to see her walk out of the house and hop in. She didn't even glance in my direction. I nosed in right behind the cab and stuck to it like chewing gum.

As it headed down the Strand and turned into a side street, I wanted to clap my hands and shriek with delight. It stopped right outside the stage door and Ms Cilla Prendergast aka Melissa Stuart got out and disappeared from view.

My so-called counsellor was an actress. She was playing a part. Now I was not surprised that she was no help to me at all. I slowed down and pulled into an area by the park. Who would pay her to act that way? It had to be Mason. But why? What would he have to gain from it? The thought that she might have a twin sister never entered my head, well only for a moment, but then she'd known my name, hadn't she? I'd caught her off guard.

I couldn't wait to tell Andrea and called for her to come and have coffee the next morning.

She made all the right noises, but I could tell she didn't really believe me. Her body language did not match her words. She came and sat next to me on the sofa and patted my hands.

"Leah, darling, you are having such a shitty time. Tell me how I can help you, darling."

"No one can help me." I was well on the way to a full-blown pity party. Would nothing go right? I'd even steered clear of the library for days, worried that Mason might have me followed. I dared not give him any cause for accusations I was having an affair. Yes, I knew that grounds for a divorce only required you to say it had broken down, you didn't even have to commit adultery, but the thought of living on my own again scared the life out of me. Strange I should say that, living in his house was already scaring the life out of me.

"I just want to get away," I sobbed on Andrea's shoulder making her blouse all wet. "Get away from all the weird things, just live a normal life." I sat up. "Do you believe in magic Andrea? Things like poltergeists and stuff?"

"Leah! Get a grip. You've watched too many Hobbit films."

"I don't need you to laugh. I'm serious. Things are happening in this house I don't understand. Objects don't move by themselves. Sounds don't come out of nowhere. It's happening every day and it's driving me mad."

"I don't think you're mad, darling. But maybe you do need to get away for a break. A change of scene, somewhere new and fresh. Don't you have an old friend or relative you could stay with for a few days. Give you a chance to relax, put your feet up, swig a few gin and tonics and forget all this strange nonsense."

Andrea made me smile. The answer to all life's ills was another gin and tonic, or any other alcohol, come to that. The image of James's Aunt Deidre popped into my head. True, I had not seen her since the funeral, but I remembered her warmth and we'd kept in touch by email on a regular basis. She had also been very supportive when I mentioned getting married to Mason, and given me her full blessing.

"Aunt Deidre. She lives in Weston-super-Mare and her flat overlooks the sea, well, mud flats most of the time. I'm sure she'd love to have me, if she's not travelling. After Paris, I'm not too keen on leaving England right now."

"I don't blame you. You don't need any extra angst. Come, let's phone Aunt Deidre right away and I'll help you pack."

"Whoa, not so fast Andrea." She was making me feel panicked. "What about cooking for Mason and Belinda, the meals, and the house. I can't just leave."

"Don't be such a wuss. Of course you can. You went up north to sort out your mother didn't you, at a moment's notice? So, what's the difference?"

"That was for my mum."

"Exactly, and this time it's for you. That's your problem, Leah. You always put other people first, it's time you put yourself first."

She was right. Isn't that what Dr Cromptom had been telling me and the rest of the world. Basically me, me, me before anyone else, but that didn't seem right. It was not the way I was brought up. But then I was the one left behind to sort out Mother while Daphne and Martin followed their dreams. Maybe it was time I looked after myself.

The rest of that day Andrea fussed over me like a broody hen. She contacted Aunt Deidre, she pulled my suitcase down from the loft and helped me pack, and she made a list and phoned Sainsbury's to deliver enough food to feed Mason and Belinda for a month. I had descended into a mindless lethargy, unable to think coherently. I sat on the bed as Andrea rushed round gathering skirts, trousers, shoes and underwear and packing them all beautifully into the case, smoothing out the wrinkles by rolling them into tight little sausages.

She handed me my tablets and a glass of water and stood over me while I swallowed them. Rolling my spare charging cables before tucking them neatly into a side pocket, she re-confirmed my train ticket, her mobile phone balanced between her shoulder and her ear.

"Don't you worry about a thing. I can always pop in

and check Belinda and Mason are doing okay."

I knew Belinda wouldn't mind that, but I wasn't too sure about Mason. He didn't like anything about Andrea and, normally, they avoided each other like the plague. But I was past caring right then.

I was swept along in a frenzy of activity and before I knew what was happening, I was in a taxi on the way to Paddington station. Even a certain bear from Peru had more control over his life than I had then. I lay back, closed my eyes and drifted off. I was rudely woken by the driver shaking my arm to tell me we'd arrived.

Andrea had thought of everything. She'd tipped the Uber man extra and given him strict instructions to get me onto the correct platform and then onto the train. I was barely aware of his solicitous behaviour until I was safely settled in my seat, and given instructions to get out at the last stop.

It was dark by the time the train pulled into Temple Meads Station in Bristol. I was still in a trance as I pulled my case off the rack and wandered along the platform towards the exit in a daze.

"Leah, Leah, I'm over here!"

It took me a moment to realise Aunt Deidre was calling my name. The next moment, she had wrapped her arms around me in a bear hug and claimed my case. She guided me towards an elderly Ford of indeterminate model and bundled me into the passenger seat. I was aware of the look of horror on her face when she first saw me. I had let myself go. I'd not been to the hairdresser in weeks, not used make up, and paid little attention to what I was wearing. I was a walking ghost, tottering along as if I were ninety.

She chattered about this and that as she drove the twenty-odd miles to her flat in Weston-super-Mare, helped me inside, and bustled off to prepare a cup of hot chocolate. She acted like the loving mother I'd never had as she helped me unpack my night clothes and tucked me into bed.

"No need for talking tonight," she said. "We'll have plenty of time over the next few days. You need sleep, Leah. Come down in the morning when you are ready, there's no rush."

As she closed the door, I could hear the late-night weatherman on the television announce the weather conditions for the first day of October

OCTOBER

I have no idea how long I slept, but it was past lunchtime when my need for the bathroom woke me. The sun was shining brightly, reflecting over the sea, and the traffic hum along the promenade was curiously soothing.

I fumbled my way along to the bathroom, surprised to see how modern it was and that Aunt Deidre must be one of the few people in England to have a bidet next to the toilet. She had laid out bright, fluffy, dark turquoise towels for me and the warm water from the shower was refreshing.

Wrapping the terry towelling bathrobe round me I breathed in the lavender from the softener and felt better than I had in weeks.

As I walked back to the bedroom, Aunt Deidre popped her head round the sitting room door.

"Hungry?"

"Yes, I'm starving. Thank you."

"Continental or full English?" She didn't waste words.

"Just continental please."

"Ready in five."

I pulled on my tracksuit and ran a comb through my hair. I still couldn't think too clearly, but I was beginning to relax, just a little.

Aunt Deidre was one of those comfortable people. She made no judgement. She was calm and her genuine love of life oozed from every pore. Of medium height, her figure was rotund, wrapped in what I guess you would call flower power filmy dresses of the type popular with the hippies in the sixties. She wore flat sensible shoes or sandals with socks. I remembered my Mother at the funeral criticising her in a much too loud voice. Mother's opinion of anyone not wearing black to such a solemn occasion was that they should be strung up at the very least. She moaned that no wonder James had been such a loser; it showed in his family. If I had not been so distraught with grief that day, I might have hit her. Not that that was possible from the confines of the wheelchair loaned by the hospital staff who had very reluctantly allowed me out just for the service. I boiled inside, hearing my mother's vitriolic words. My beloved late husband had not been a loser. All those years studying medicine and everyone said what a brilliant doctor he was.

Today, Aunt Deidre's flowing skirt and multi-coloured top was reassuring and comforting.

"Sit down dear."

The croissants were warm and fresh, the butter soft, and she had laid out a selection of cheeses, ham and various fruits, jams and preserves.

"Were you expecting visitors or do you always have a fabulous breakfast like this?"

"I've been expecting you for weeks now."

"But..." Oh no! Just when all I wanted was normality with no surprises or upsets.

Aunt Deidre laughed at the look on my face. "Don't panic, love. I'm what they call a little fey. Nothing dangerous and nothing to alarm you. Now, when you've had enough, I want to hear everything. Your aura is all out of kilter and we need to know what's been upsetting you."

I wasn't too sure that I wanted to talk about it all. It was all so surreal. I'd sound as mad as I was feeling. I ran my fingers through my hair and was dismayed to see strands entwined in my fingers.

"You are not at all well, my dear." Aunt Deidre reached out and took the hair from my hand. She stared at it and then cleared the table before settling herself comfortably in a chair opposite me next to the fire.

It was warm and cosy in her sitting room, the comfortable chairs with their chintz covers, the framed Constable prints on the walls and the glistening silver ornaments on the shelves.

"Start at the beginning," she said.

"It must have been January, when we got home after the New Year's Eve party…"

"No, I mean right at the beginning, from the day you first met Mason. Start there."

"Wait, I've not taken my pills."

"Let's not take them just yet. Try and clear your head." She picked up the containers I'd brought to the breakfast table and peered at the labels before unscrewing the tops.

My insides curled up and I felt my stomach clench. I'd been looking forward to taking my usual morning doses. I always felt more relaxed afterwards – was I becoming dependent on them? I sat for several moments trying to focus in on that first day in the supermarket when Mason had sent me flying.

I'm not sure how Aunt Deidre processed all the information as I stumbled through my story. My sentences were disjointed. I remembered facts in the wrong order. I got side-tracked and rambled on. I talked and talked and every now and again the old lady got up and listened from the kitchen as she replenished my tea, served the lunch, and later placed a plate of my favourite doughnuts on the table. I gasped, how did she know those were the ones I liked best, or was it just an amazing coincidence? She laughed when she saw my face.

"I did mention I was fey, didn't I?"

The next few days passed in a pleasant, relaxing atmosphere and, bit by bit, I found myself less anxious, less tired and the fog dissipated as I took fewer pills.

We went for refreshing walks along the sea front, had coffee in the side street cafés, and even went to a movie. We laughed as we clutched each other battling a fierce onshore wind as we scuttled back to the flat.

Every morning Deidre encouraged me to talk, she wanted every detail. She seldom interrupted me but waited until I had finished and then asked one or two pointed questions. I noticed that she scribbled the odd thing in the notebook she had in her lap, but I thought little of it at the time.

At first, I felt stupid talking about cutlery the wrong way around, the noises, the antics with the water. I'm not sure I mentioned all that to you earlier, did I? I'd begun to hear noises in the house too. It sounded like a cheap horror movie and unbelievable, but Aunt Deidre sat and listened, only nodding every now and again. When I paused, she sat quietly, deep in thought. Her calm manner and lack of judgement encouraged me to reveal every detail. It was embarrassing to admit I had stalked my counsellor, and she only looked surprised when I explained how I'd proved she was an actress. I added in my defence that she had never done me the slightest good, despite the number of times I'd bared my soul in her sparse and clinical surgery.

It was so easy to pour my heart out to Aunt Deidre. I still held back with Andrea as I suspected she was getting fed up with me, and the only other person I felt comfortable with was Bill, and I didn't want him to think me mad, so I wasn't honest with him either.

"Tell me more about this blue rabbit." Aunt Deidre cut into my thoughts.

"I think I've told you everything. It's an ordinary stuffed toy, though I fantasise it has a vicious stare; the big black eyes are not friendly. And there must be a whole family of them, at least two – no three, since I threw one out and the one I flung out of my car in the garage got oil on it and the last one I saw sitting in the hall was clean. I don't think it could have been washed."

"No, those toys are never the same, the fur goes funny. I remember once staying with my sister and she'd just washed James' bear and he cried when she pinned him up on the washing line to dry. He was convinced it would hurt his best friend."

I smiled. Whatever else happened in my life I had those few years of pure happiness with James and our babies to look back on. No money to spare but oh so much love.

Slowly but surely, I began to relax and live again. I'd taken fewer and fewer pills since I arrived, but drank the various herbal teas my aunt-in-law was so fond of. I wanted to stay there forever but I was a married woman; I had responsibilities to my husband and to his daughter. This break was pure self-indulgence. I loved being this close to the sea and, should I ever be on my own again, I promised myself I would find somewhere, however small, where I could walk to the beach and watch the waves wash to and fro. The movement of the water reminded me how small my problems were in the greater scheme of things and, somehow, put things into perspective.

October was drawing to a close and I knew I could not delay my departure much longer. That sense of duty, drilled into me from birth by a demanding, petulant and cruel mother, was screaming at me to do the right thing.

I think Aunt Deidre was sad to see me go but, before we got in the car to drive to Bristol, she sat me down and pushed a glass of sherry into my hands. I looked at her in surprise.

"Call that Dutch courage, or Portuguese if you like." She swept her flowing scarf over her shoulder. "I want you to listen carefully, Leah."

I nodded.

"I've considered everything you've told me. I've watched you relax and blossom over the last three weeks and I want you to repeat three times 'I am not mad. I am perfectly sane'."

I chuckled.

"No, take this seriously. Do as I say. Repeat that three times out loud, to me."

I felt a bit silly but did as she asked. "I am not mad. I am perfectly sane."

"That is going to be your mantra from now on. Each time you feel unhinged you are to repeat that over and over, take deep breaths and believe in yourself. I loved James as if he were my own, and I loved that he chose to marry you. You're a good person, Leah, never let anyone tell you otherwise."

She reached into one of her voluminous pockets from among the folds in her wide skirt and handed me a chain with a black stone pendant.

"Black tourmaline. Wear this around your neck at all times."

I took it, feeling guilty as I had no belief whatsoever in crystals and how they could influence your life. That was all mumbo jumbo to my mind. But to please Aunt Deidre, I took the chain and fastened it around my neck. Strange that she believed in such powers since she'd been in charge of a large pharmaceutical laboratory in her younger days.

"I fear for you returning. I want you to take care, promise me?"

I nodded.

"There is a perfectly rational explanation for everything you have experienced. No magic, no poltergeist. It's man-made, Leah. Someone is out to hurt you. We just need to work out who and why."

"The who can only be Mason and or Belinda. But I have no idea why. That's the puzzle. Mason could get rid of me easily enough if he wanted to. People divorce every day of the week, some as often as they have hot dinners."

"With what we know it doesn't make sense. But we'll get to the bottom of it."

I was comforted by the way she said 'we'. I had no idea what she could do from a hundred and fifty miles away, but I promised her I would keep in touch every day, either by WhatsApp or via email. For an elderly lady she'd kept very up to date with modern technology.

As I reluctantly boarded the train, looking back to smile and wave goodbye, I felt my heart begin to sink. October had been a wonderful month in a sane and relaxing atmosphere. I'd become confident and capable and free from worries. As the train pulled out, I began to repeat my mantra over and over. 'I am not mad. I am perfectly sane.'

Could I maintain my equilibrium once I was back home? I prayed that I could.

NOVEMBER

If October was paradise, November was a nightmare. I had only been back in the house for a day when I began to feel nervous again. I reached for my pill box and only just stopped myself in time. I'd promised Aunt Deidre no more medication. She was convinced it dulled the brain and I needed to keep my wits about me.

As I let myself into the house around lunchtime, the walls seemed to close in around me. I'd not told Mason I was coming home and I was pleased to see there wasn't a blue rabbit sitting next to the telephone.

Room by room I explored the house. Nothing was out of place. In fact, the whole place was spick and span and I'd not been expecting that. I gave myself a good shake. I would put new batteries in the cameras, check the app was working on my phone and solve the mystery.

We'd discussed various ways I could do a little detective work. My aunt-in-law was a voracious reader of spy novels and came up with all kinds of suggestions.

I muttered as I walked around the house, making plans and committing them to memory, which was working surprisingly well.

I'd only been home for an hour or so when the doorbell rang. It was Andrea and she greeted me ecstatically, thrilled to have me back, and then commented on how much weight I'd put on.

"It's from self-indulgent treats but I feel better for it. And look, my hair isn't falling out. I feel great, and thank you for suggesting I take a break. It was the very best thing I could have done."

"You are taking your pills regularly, aren't you?" She was right behind me as I went into the kitchen to put the coffee maker on.

"Of course," I lied. "Just like the doctor ordered."

"That's all right then. So, when are we going shopping? Oh, what's that around your neck?" She reached out to finger the pendant.

"Black tourmaline, I think. Saw it in a second-hand shop and couldn't resist it." I'd told two lies in a matter of moments, what was I thinking?

I threw the empty pods in the rubbish bin and looked for the sugar. "So what news while I've been away?"

Andrea draped herself over the kitchen island. "Nothing much. Nothing ever happens around here. Oh yes, one thing. With all these council cuts they are closing the local library. Going to combine it with Croydon library I think."

I paused, one hand holding the fridge door open, the other wrapped around the carton of milk. My heart sank.

"It's probably a good thing," Andrea prattled on. "Guess libraries are pretty much obsolete today. No one uses all those old fusty reference books anymore, so much easier to google what you want to know. And it takes microseconds to download any book you want to read almost free. Soon, there will be very few shops left too. I think it's all so exciting."

My last refuge was gone. Leah, that's so selfish. What would happen to Bill? That was far more important. Would they give him a job over in Croydon? I would so miss our chats and the one place I could go for peace and quiet where nothing supernatural happened.

It was one thing to bump into each other in the library, quite another to arrange to meet up for coffee or lunch, even in a public place. That would constitute a date and close to committing adultery however innocent it was. Did you have to complete the sex act before they labelled you as an adulteress I wondered. One of those burning at the stake punishments?

"Leah, come back to earth!" Her voice cut into my thoughts and dragged me into the present. "You used to go to the library a lot, didn't you?"

"Uh, yes. Nice comfy chairs and a break away from the house. Did they say when they were closing?"

"Not the exact date, but I think it will be before the end of the year."

I tried hard not to let my feelings show as I faced the weeks ahead without a friendly face to talk to. Hey, what was I thinking? I had Andrea, no one could ask for a better girlfriend.

The front door opened and slammed shut and Belinda came into view.

"Oh, so you're back then?" She stood and glared at me.

"Yes, as you can see. So sorry," I snapped.

"Yeah. Bummer. The good times couldn't last forever."

Belinda pushed past me and headed for the fridge, slinging her school bag onto the counter and Andrea only just managed to save her coffee mug from being swept onto the floor.

"Bloody hell Belinda, that's crossing the line and you know it."

"You, don't have to live with her." Belinda pointed at me. "Always crying, always whining. She's no fun at all."

"She's not having an easy time." Andrea defended me.

"No one's having an easy time. At least she doesn't have to drag off to an effing school that sucks. Why can't they just leave me alone to do what I want?"

"That's totally unfair. It's your father who's pushing you to stay. You need to talk to him. Leah doesn't have a say in what you can and can't do."

"Yeah well. As they keep telling us, life ain't fair."

She banged about in the kitchen, piling a plate with biscuits, crisps and energy bars; all products that I rarely ordered from the supermarket in my effort to provide

Andrea rolled her eyes as Belinda thumped her way up the stairs before unlocking her bedroom door and slamming it behind her.

"Teenagers, who'd have them?" I sighed.

"They're not all as bad as her, Leah. She's been through a lot. Try to be patient."

"After two and a half years my patience is wearing thin."

Over the next few days I went steadily downhill. From

feeling confident, and almost cheerful, on my return at the beginning of the month, slowly but surely, I lost my grip on reality.

Household objects began to change places with alarming speed. The lights went on and off all by themselves. One moment I'd be sitting watching television and it would turn off and I was left sitting in the dark. Even the washing machine started up all on its own.

And the noises returned. Whistling. No tunes, just sudden mindless one-note shrieks that pierced my ears. Then there were the crashes and bangs, always in the next room, never in the one I was in at the time. Once or twice I heard voices, indistinct words, but full of menace.

Several times I called for Andrea to come and witness the disturbances, but not once did it happen when she was there. The moment she rang the doorbell, the sounds, flashing lights, whistling, appliances turning on and off; they all stopped. The only things I could point to were the re-arranged pictures, clothes, kitchen utensils and ornaments that had waltzed from one position to another. I grew tired of putting everything away. If I left things where they landed, then Mason would complain and ask me why I kept moving things. On a few occasions, when I'd been out, even the furniture was moved. One time the sofa had been turned around and had its back hard up against the television.

On another occasion the easy chairs were placed out on the lawn and it rained. As I dragged them back indoors, struggling to get them up the step into the kitchen, I knew I could never dry them out before Mason and Belinda came home. They were soaked through.

The disturbances went on day after day. The app connecting with the security cameras disappeared off my phone and when I tried to re-load it, they refused. I'd tried to reinstate it so many times, forgetting the password, or letting my fingers press the adjoining key, a warning displayed that for security reasons the app was closing down.

In a few short weeks I became a wreck. I fought against taking the tranquilisers as they just made me feel fuzzy and I needed every last shred of sense to concentrate on getting through each day.

I hid away in the house. I didn't want to face Bill at the library. He would see by the state of my hair, my sloppy clothes, the effort I couldn't make to put on any makeup, that I was falling apart.

I was ashamed, scared, and I even pushed Andrea away. Eventually she stopped calling round to see how I was. She had failed to cheer me up, or use shock tactics to shake me out of it and pull myself together.

I spent hours curled up on the sofa, tears falling into my coffee, with my hands over my ears to shut out the screams, whistles, thundering and banging which became louder and louder each day.

The evenings gave me some respite as, the moment anyone else came in the front door, an immediate peace descended. When she was home, Belinda took every opportunity to let me know she didn't want me there, and Mason eroded my self-confidence even further by nagging me, telling me off, complaining, and generally running me down. He was furious when he discovered I'd unplugged the phone. What if he missed hearing from an important client who was calling out of hours? I didn't have the energy to remind him that he, like his daughter, was welded to his mobile twenty-four seven.

I wasn't keeping up too well with the day to day running of the house either. I forgot to put the green wheelie bins out for collection and the rubbish was overflowing onto the garage floor. Several times I forgot to order in the food and I'd not prepared the evening meals. The dust accumulated on every surface and the carpet was sprinkled with fluff and needed a damn good clean.

A limp piece of lettuce had more backbone than I did and I finally accepted that I had indeed gone mad.

Mason surprised me by coming home in the middle of the day. He grunted when he saw me curled up in a foetal position on the couch and marched upstairs without saying a word.

He came back down a while later carrying my weekend suitcase and, for a fleeting moment, I thought he might have booked a surprise trip away, that he was going to be kind and loving like when he first met me.

"Come." He held his hand out and tugged on my arm.

"I can't go out like this," I mumbled. I'd not combed my hair, or even showered that day.

"No one's going to look at you," he barked, and tugged harder.

I scrambled to my feet and allowed him to pull me out into the hall and through the front door. To my surprise there was a man I didn't know sitting in the front passenger seat, who nodded to me as Mason pushed me firmly into the car and slammed the door. A bolt of fear shot down my spine, an almost primeval sense that something bad was going to happen.

"Let me out!" I tugged on the door handle, desperate to run back into the house.

"Calm down, Leah," for once Mason's voice was kind and caring, "No one's going to hurt you, we're just going for a little drive."

"Nooooo, I don't want to go anywhere. Let me out! I want to go home." I don't remember ever having a panic attack before, but I think I was having one now. I couldn't breathe. My mouth was open desperately trying to pull air into my lungs. All around me the scenery undulated. The sweat was pouring off me while, at the same time, I was shaking. I was desperate to move. Get out of the car. Run. But the doors wouldn't open.

I could hear Mason's voice telling me to calm down. Cut it out. Relax. No one was going to hurt me. He spoke quietly to the man next to him in the front but his voice was so low I couldn't make out the words.

Afterwards I wanted to kick myself for not taking note of where they were taking me. I was dimly aware that the housing became less dense and the buildings few and far between. The sun streaming through the windscreen was blinding me so much that later, I thought we'd travelled west.

At one point I gave up and curled myself into a ball on the back seat, with the tears pouring down my face. I don't remember ever feeling this afraid before, not even when I lost my leg. Why was Mason doing this? Where was he taking me?

At last the car stopped and I looked up to see a large ornamental wrought iron gate set between a pair of imposing stone pillars. The passenger got out, spoke into an intercom box mounted on the side and, as he got back into the car, the gates slowly swung open. I could see a long drive ahead, bordered by neatly cut lawns and an avenue of trees. Several bends later Mason brought the car to a stop before a large imposing mansion.

A lady in a white coat was waiting on the steps and came forward to greet us. She shook hands with our passenger and then stepped forward to greet Mason. I watched, trying to figure out what was going on.

And then it dawned on me. This was some kind of residential home. Was it for the mentally insane? Was Mason about to check me in? I fought down my rising panic. No. He couldn't. He wouldn't. I wasn't mad. I was as sane as the next person. I did hear the voices. Stuff did move around. The music turned on and off. None of it was a figment of my imagination. Why would no one believe me?

The nurse, or was she a doctor, came around to the back door of the car and opened it.

"Hello Leah, welcome to The Grange. We are so pleased to see you. Do you want to come inside for a nice cup of tea?" She spoke to me in the way that carers and medical staff do to the elderly or small children, as if they are half-wits. I wanted to shout at her.

She turned to listen to something Mason said and

asked me again. "Ah, a cup of coffee, would that be nicer?"

I was torn between shouting at her or ignoring her. I did not want to go inside. I did not want any of her coffee. I just wanted to go home. If Mason didn't want me in the house then I would leave. He didn't need to lock me away. Why was he doing this?

Miss White Coat was tired of waiting for a response so she reached in and tried to pull me out of the car by my arm.

I fought back, pushing her away, sliding over to the far side of the car, I even tried to kick her. I was acting in a manner I thought I would never behave.

As I backed up against the opposite door it was flung open and I fell out into the arms of two white-coated, heavy-set guys. They grabbed me on either side and walked me up the stairs and into the large tiled hallway.

A wide, imposing staircase led to the next floor and on either side there were doorways and a corridor disappearing towards the back of the house.

Miss White Coat kept pace with us, keeping up a nonstop flood of words which I'm sure was aimed at calming me down. Odd phrases like 'lovely rest', 'getting better', 'fresh country air', floated into my conscious mind, but none of them fooled me for a moment. How can you cure a person who isn't mad?

I was propelled towards a lift by both minders and the lady jailor and we were whisked up two floors. When the doors opened, they pushed me to the left and into a room on the right.

"Wait here for a while and I'll be back," Miss White Coat told me. "Take a nap and then we can have a little chat later." She indicated the bed against the far wall and, before I could answer her, they had all left and closed the door behind them.

The first thing I did was to look for a door handle but there wasn't one. This was a prison. I rushed over to the window and was horrified to see there were bars on it. I opened it as far as it would go, but not even a small child could have slipped out.

The room was at the front of the house and I could see White Coat, Mason and our passenger next to the car. They were deep in discussion. I was tempted to scream at them, beg for help, but the last shred of dignity stopped me.

The tears poured down my cheeks as I slumped down on the bed, my chest heaving, shoulders shaking, and my nose streaming.

I must have fallen asleep, for the next thing I remember was being shaken awake and Miss White Coat was sitting next to me on the bed. I glanced up to see if she had left the door open, but no, it was firmly shut. I wondered how she would open it without a handle on the inside.

Her voice was gentle and reassuring as she patted my hand. "Leah, there is no reason to be afraid. No one is going to hurt you."

"I've not done anything wrong. Why are you keeping me a prisoner? I want to go home."

"Of course you're not a prisoner, Leah. And of course you've done nothing wrong. We know that."

"Then let me go home."

"We just want you to stay for a little while to have a rest

and sort out all these strange things that are happening to you. We'll have lots of time to chat and put things to rights."

"This is a mental hospital, isn't it?"

"Now why would you think that? My name is Dorothy Wells, and there are more staff members for you to make friends with and I'm sure you're going to enjoy your stay here. We have an indoor swimming pool, a fully equipped gym, a games room, and even other patients to make friends with."

Patients, she said patients. That told me everything I needed to know. I was a patient too. Had Mason committed me? Who had arranged for me to be brought here? It had to be Mason. I couldn't stop the tears from rolling down my cheeks. It felt as if I would never stop crying. Yet I was hollow inside, where were all the tears coming from?

Dr Wells stood up. "I'll leave you to go back to sleep, and later I'll send up a tray. You must be hungry, and thirsty too."

"I'm not tired," I whined, like a petulant child, but she just smiled, nodded, and made for the door.

I sat up, scared to be on my own yet wanting her to leave me alone. I couldn't think straight. There was something I needed to ask, but I couldn't remember what.

"Wait!"

She turned back from the door. "Yes?"

"Where am I? What is this place?"

"It's a rest home for those who are having problems coping. We are here to help you cope, so you can return home soon."

"How long will that be?"

She walked back to sit next to me on the bed and put her arm around my shoulders. "Leah, it's too soon to tell. I'm sure we'll make good progress very soon."

"How long?" I persisted.

She paused, and I sensed she was reluctant to commit herself. "Soon… very soon."

"How soon is soon? A couple of days, weeks, months?"

I felt her body stiffen. She didn't want to tell me, and she wasn't going to.

She walked over to the door. "Let's take it one day at a time, yes?"

Before I could say another word, the door swung inwards and she was gone. I'd wanted to know what had happened to the case Mason had packed for me. All I had were the clothes I stood up in. No handbag, no phone, not even a toothbrush. I fought down feelings of claustrophobia. I'd never suffered from that, but no one had locked me up before.

I prowled round the room, pushing against the walls, fiddling with the windows, drawing the curtains back and forth. I opened and closed the drawer on the small desk, investigated the empty wardrobe, and peered inside the bedside table but, apart from those and an arm chair, the room was bare. Not even a light switch on the wall. Would they control the lights too? Decide when I could see or be left in the dark? An alcove off on the other side held a toilet, shower and handbasin. One small towel was on the rail, just large enough to dry hands on.

If I wasn't mad now, then in a few days I would be.

There was nothing to do. No one to talk to. I knew what it must be like to be caged in a zoo, guilty at the times I'd observed the beasts and never given a thought to how they must feel.

My stomach rumbled, reminding me that I'd not had lunch and it must be late afternoon by now. To my horror I saw that someone had removed my watch. Had they done that while I'd been asleep? I felt violated.

I tried sleeping again, there was nothing else to do but, the moment I closed my eyes, images of my first home swam before them. Happier days, playing with my angels; Brandon and the toy duck he loved, Henrietta and her rag doll, tucking them into bed at night, singing a lullaby after the bed time story, James coming in to plump up the pillows and kiss them before we crept out to spend time on our own.

There was nothing wrong with my memory, it was as clear as if it was yesterday. I sat up, determined to trace back into my past, get my thoughts in order, and try to pinpoint when life had begun to go downhill.

It was after that New Year's party, and it was now November? Only eleven months...

I jumped to my feet. What was the date today? The fifteenth. I hurried into the bathroom and tore a little piece off the edge of the toilet paper and rolled it up into a tiny ball which I placed on the top of the dividing wall at the end of the shower. I thought it very unlikely they would clean up there very often. I would add another ball tomorrow, and the day after, and each day to keep track of time. I wasn't sure that would help very much, but it gave me a little bit of independence and, if they had any hidden cameras to observe me, I didn't think those would extend to the bathroom.

I'd read about prisoners pacing to and fro in their cells, and measured the steps in mine: four paces from side to side, five from the door to the window. My pacing was interrupted by the door opening and Bully Boy 1 appeared carrying a tray. Bully Boy 2 was right behind him, watching me. He was carrying my suitcase which he placed on the floor. The tray was left on my table and they walked out without saying a word.

I grabbed the large mug of coffee first, before I tore the cellophane off the plastic spoons and attacked the food ravenously. A tasty stew and mash, and a lemon flavoured sponge pudding covered in custard. It was hot and nourishing. They had also brought two bottles of designer water. There were two pills on the plate which I decided not to take. If I had to prove my sanity then I needed to be alert.

I suspected they had added some kind of sedative to the food or drink, because no sooner had I finished eating than I felt too lethargic even to look and see what Mason had packed for me. I staggered over to the bed and went out like a light.

The sun shining in my eyes woke me in the morning. I recognised the familiar feeling of being in a fog, and panic set in. I could refuse to take the pills, but I couldn't refuse to eat.

A hot shower and a change of clothes helped to clear my

head a little and I used up time by washing out my clothes in the wash hand basin and unpacking the contents of my suitcase. Mason had included all the essentials; spare underwear, two changes of clothing, and toiletries. I noticed he'd packed my hairbrush, but no makeup. It wasn't likely I'd need it in here. He must have been planning this for some time.

My heart ached. I'd grown used to his sniping, moaning and constant undermining my confidence, but now I wondered how much he disliked me. When had all that started? Not just this year. That behaviour had crept in not long after we married almost three years ago.

Despite the fuzzy state of my mind I remembered to place a paper roll on top of the shower wall, pleased with this small victory. With nothing else to do, I alternatively sat on the bed or paced the room fighting to get my thoughts in order. Did they intend to keep me drugged all the time? What purpose would that serve?

Without a watch I'm not sure what time Bully Boys 1 and 2 came for me in the morning and escorted me down in the lift and into a comfortable office.

Doctor Wells stood up to welcome me and guided me to an armchair placed opposite hers. She sat, fingers poised over the electronic tablet on her knee.

"Did you sleep well?"

You know how I slept, so why bother asking? I shrugged and pushed my foot back and forward, moving the pile on the carpet this way and that.

"Leah, let's try and concentrate, shall we? Tell me what you can remember of your childhood. What was your happiest moment?"

So, we were going down the Freud route, were we? I was finding it hard to think, to concentrate. I felt the anger begin to build and did my best to control it. Any violent behaviour on my part would only give them the excuse to drug me and I was aware that Bully Boy 1 was sitting quietly on a chair behind me.

I sat, twisting my fingers in my lap, head bent forward, shoulders hunched. I did not want to talk about the father I loved, the mother who did not love me, the precious Daphne, and the could-do-no-wrong Martin. They were both so far away and cared nothing of what might happen to me.

"I want to make a phone call."

"Who do you want to call, Leah?"

"I'm not sure that is any of your business. You can't keep me a prisoner here against my will."

"Of course you're not a prisoner. What makes you think that? Who do you think wants to hurt you?"

"Then I can leave?" I stood up and I sensed Bully Boy 1 behind me also get to his feet.

"Sit down Leah, and let's talk for a little while."

I hesitated, then sat.

"That's great. Now, your parents?"

"If I'm not a prisoner, I can leave, right? I can get up now and walk out of the front door and into town?"

"Of course you can, but in a few days, when you've had a chance to rest and feel better."

I knew then that she was lying to me. I knew I couldn't trust her. I couldn't trust anyone.

I suddenly made up my mind that I would cooperate, or make them believe I was cooperating. I'd eat sparingly in case they spiked my food again and spit out any tablets they gave me, if I could get away with that. The more pliable I was, the more reason they would have to let me go. It was unthinkable that a perfectly sane person could be kept in seclusion. Way back in history, wives and assorted family members were locked away if they were a nuisance, and conducted tours were given to the gawping public to come and see the lunatics. But this was the twenty-first century. We'd moved on from there, or had we?

My biggest worry was I couldn't think of anyone who would come looking for me. My mother certainly wouldn't, and she was suffering dementia for sure. Andrea might be my only hope, but Mason could so easily spin her a tale that would satisfy her. He was now free to play with his mistress and wouldn't have to sneak into dark corners in restaurants. He would also be saving lots of money paying Ms Prendergast aka Melissa Stuart the actress to play the part, badly, of a counsellor who undermined me further.

"Leah! Leah, can you hear me?" I was so deep into my thoughts that I had tuned out Dr Wells and not heard a word she said.

"What?"

"Leah, I was asking you about your parents. Like to tell me about them?"

And so I did. I spun a tale of a bright and happy childhood with two siblings I adored. I emphasised that we all kept in touch regularly, hoping she might take the hint that someone out in the world would be asking where I was if they'd not heard from me. I went further, lying that we all Skyped each other at least once a week. I was pleased to see a brief frown on Dr Wells' face. This was news to her. Of course it was, I'd made it up.

I was on a roll. I mentioned names of old school friends, pretending I had made contact again recently when I travelled north to settle my mother in. I amazed myself with each story I invented.

Dr Wells had heard enough. She'd been tapping away frenetically on her tablet.

"Now Leah, are you up to playing some games?"

She meant tests of course. I nodded and managed a smile.

She guided me out of the cosy office and into what looked like a classroom. There were three desks with benches attached, like we had at school, and a whiteboard mounted on one wall. I noticed immediately the bars on the windows in here, even though we were on the ground floor. Not straight up and down prison type bars but the ornamental kind you see on Spanish houses they called rejas. Decorative but also serving a useful function.

"Just call me Dorothy," she instructed, since she thought we were now getting on so well. Was I fooling her?

She waved me to a seat while she unlocked one of the cupboards and took out a pile of boxes.

For the rest of the morning I put simple jigsaws together, matched shapes, dragged rings along an electrified curved line, answered hypothetical questions, and explained what I made of pictures composed of blobs and shadows.

I couldn't guess what Dr White Coat was scoring as she filled in information on her tablet, but I did my best to act as rationally as I could. Even when I got tired, fighting to concentrate against the effects of the tranquilisers I was convinced they'd put in my food, I thought I'd scored high on the 'I am normal' stakes.

As she cleared the last pieces of equipment away and locked them back in the cupboard, she announced it was time for lunch.

We walked down a corridor, Bully Boy 1, who had not left us for one moment, only a few steps behind. A little way along, a door to the left was flung open and a woman raced out and made a beeline for Dr Wells. She was dressed in a shapeless gown with flip flops on her feet. Her hair was in disarray and her eyes were wild. She launched herself at the doctor, screeching at the top of her voice, arms extended aiming them at Dorothy's eyes.

I faltered and stopped as Bully Boy 1 pushed me to one side and rushed to restrain the woman. Two more white coated attendants arrived in hot pursuit and between them they managed to wrestle her to the floor, held her down none too gently, and plunged a hypodermic into her arm. She relaxed and lay still, spread-eagled, on the pale green tiles. Her gown was rucked up exposing a pair of dark green knickers, the kind my grandmother used to wear. She was a desperate, sorry sight. Was she mad when she was first admitted, or had being locked away unbalanced her mind? I took a deep breath. Compared to her I was sane, but would I change in the weeks ahead?

Would I be kept here forever?

Two of the attendants dragged the unfortunate woman away through the door she'd escaped from. I could only stand and stare, tears pricking my eyes, and I wrapped my arms tightly round my chest to stop me shaking. It was my first lesson in what happens if you don't cooperate.

Dr Wells and Bully Boy 1 guided me on down the corridor as if nothing had happened. She swiped an access card and led me into the dining room. At first glance it looked like millions of other canteens the world over, except there were as many white-coated minders as there were diners. Some people were sitting quietly eating at the tables, a few were queued up at the counter holding trays. The moment we entered a hush fell over the room as they all stared at me. Then the noise began again. A couple of inmates shrieked and whistled, two men came over and began to tug at my clothes before they were rudely dragged away by the staff. One woman sat holding a baby doll, crooning over it, another was trying to tear her hair out. Altogether there must have been thirty patients in the room, and only a couple of them appeared normal.

It was how I imagined Dante's inferno. I took several steps backwards, but Dr Wells grabbed my elbow.

"Calm down Leah, relax. Most patients will have their meds after lunch and then they will be much calmer."

I could feel the panic rising in me, I wanted to turn and run, but I had to play the game. It took every last reserve of will power I had, so I only nodded and followed her and picked up a tray. The noise died down a little as we waited our turn, the watchers at the sides alert to any possible attacks or examples of bad behaviour. I could see the inmates were wary of them. They dropped their eyes and turned their backs. Some ate nicely using the plastic spoons others shovelled the food in with their hands. A few threw the food around, cackling if they managed to hit another patient. At least one scuffle broke out before the protagonists were forcibly separated and the two were removed kicking and screaming from the room.

I also noticed that all the inmates were wearing the long shapeless, green, unisex robes and all had either flip flops or soft slippers on their feet.

Dorothy Wells was aware of my reaction and stayed close to me. When the server had dropped two sausages, a spoonful of baked beans, and a dollop of mashed potato onto my plate she led me to a table in the far corner.

There was one patient sitting there, a young girl in her early twenties with large grey eyes and short brown hair cut in a pageboy style. She smiled and held out her hand.

"Hi, I'm Charlotte," she greeted me.

"Uh, pleased to meet you. I'm Leah," I replied. I put my tray on the table and shook her hand. Dr Wells sat down beside me.

"I hope you and Charlotte can become great friends."

There it was, the hint that I would be here long term. I held back a shudder.

"What are you here for? What's wrong with you?"

"Now Charlotte, you know that's against the rules. We don't discuss conditions. We don't pry and ask personal questions."

Charlotte frowned and ate in silence for a few minutes

while I began my lunch. I decided it would be safe to eat since different patients would require different medication so it was unlikely they had added anything foreign to the food. I would also need to keep up my strength.

As they finished, one by one, the inmates returned their plates and spoons to the staff behind the counter, some being frogmarched by the men in white coats, and in single file they queued up for their medication. One or two tried to duck out of line, but no one escaped. It was a drill worthy of any army.

I watched them carefully. It would be difficult to avoid the liquid meds handed out in a cup, but much easier to avoid the pills. I could only hope that's what they offered me.

As we finished and returned our plates, Charlotte and I joined the end of the queue and waited with Dr Wells to shuffle up the line to the trolley. When it was my turn, to my relief, I was handed a tablet and a drink of water. I used my tongue to shove it up to the top of my cheek before I took the sip of water and then opened my mouth to show I had swallowed it. I was escorted back to my room.

I went into the bathroom immediately and disgorged the slightly soggy tablet and flushed it down the loo, before checking my little paper balls were still on the shower wall ledge.

While I'd been out, someone had come in and made my bed, dusted the table top, wiped up in the bathroom, and my suitcase was gone.

They left me alone for a few hours. I was so bored. Perhaps the tablet should have sent me to sleep? I lay on the bed, eyes closed, thinking. I'd always been busy, especially before my nerves began to unravel. I thought long and hard, and reasoned that I had heard noises; things did move around, it was not my imagination. Someone was out to tip me over the edge, but I had no idea who or why.

DECEMBER

The days passed with regular monotony. Each day was pretty much the same. Different doctors talked to me, asking endless questions. Sometimes they placed wires on my head and monitored my reactions while showing me pictures, or making suggestions. If I was mad, I didn't feel it, and I convinced myself that, from the test results, they could see it too. I was relieved to see they no longer administered shock treatments, lobotomies and cold baths. What they had hoped to gain by asking these endless questions I had no idea. They did not hurt me and I was careful to moderate my behaviour. I would give them no excuse to sedate me and I became an expert in disposing of the pills and tablets. I only hoped they dissolved in the plumbing system and didn't give me away by blocking the pipes.

Some days were better than others, but boredom was my biggest enemy. After pleading and begging, though I hated to do it, they eventually let me have a stack of books to read, and when I discovered the library, although very small, it helped a lot.

There were two especially low points. The first was the day they took my clothes away and handed me one of the sage green robes to wear. I almost lost it. It was the final signal that this was my new home.

I began to lose hope.

The second blow was Charlotte. When we'd first met, she'd chatted about her life and the children she'd left in her husband's care while she had a short rest. 'A bout of post-natal depression' she called it. She would only be here for a short while.

I can't remember now how I found out, but it was a shock to discover that she'd been committed by the courts for murdering her baby. Two days later she approached me, held out her hand and said "Hello, I'm Charlotte. You're new here aren't you? What's your name?"

The only positive improvement was that I no longer heard strange voices, the lights didn't go on and off, the water flowed from the taps, no music suddenly blasted screeching into my ear drums, and none of the few things I had in my small room moved around. Life had stabilised.

Every so often I asked if I could at least make one phone call. I was desperate for a connection with the outside world, even if it was only to discover if my mother was still alive and being cared for properly.

Each time they politely refused. The excuses varied from 'the doctor isn't around to give permission' to 'it's too early in your recuperation period. It might set your excellent progress back if you try to cope with the outside world too soon'.

I kept a careful check on the paper balls. When they were in danger of falling off, I rolled seven little ones together into a larger ball to mark a week. So far, I calculated I'd been locked up for almost six weeks. It doesn't sound long, but each day stretched to eternity.

They stopped giving me the tests and asking me to play games every day. I guess there was nothing further for them to learn.

The highlight of my week was the time I was allowed to spend in the indoor swimming pool. Even there it was difficult to relax. I was never alone. I didn't trust the other crazies not to try and drown me, even if they didn't mean to do it. Most of them were unpredictable and I was constantly on the alert. It wasn't possible to see what might set them off, suddenly and without warning. From sitting placidly they'd begin screaming or howling or crying or start a fight. If I had a book to read, I preferred to escape to my room and be on my own.

Every morning, when I woke up, I reminded myself I was not mad. It was my mantra. Wasn't it a sign of madness to think you were normal and sane? I didn't care. I felt sane, I acted normally and, as best I could, I avoided all the other patients. Maybe a few of them were sane when they arrived here but weeks, months, and years later, the asylum fulfilled its promise and turned them into lunatics.

Then something happened.

I was lying on my bed one afternoon when Dr Wells opened my door and told me I had a visitor. My first reaction was to jump to my feet and rush to the door, but it could only be Mason and I wasn't sure I wanted to see him. I didn't think for one moment he was coming to sign me out. It had taken him long enough to make the effort to see me. I'd preserve what scrap of dignity I had, though that wasn't easy in a pair of soft slippers and a shapeless sage green robe buttoned down the front.

I took a few moments to wash my face and hands and drag a comb through my hair and then I followed the doctor down the stairs to the main entrance. Seeing the front door wide open I hesitated. I longed to run out there, over the grass, free, away from the nightmare, away from the boredom.

Dorothy Wells read my mind as she took a firm grip on my arm and shouted for someone to close the door. She steered me into a tastefully furnished lounge, where a log fire was burning in the large open fireplace. The mantlepiece above it held a small vase filled with tiny purple flowers beside a variety of ornaments.

The room reminded me of a stately mansion, large pieces of comfortable furniture, sofas, armchairs and a table over to one side. I barely registered the absence of bars on the ceiling to floor windows framed by red velvet drapes.

As we walked further into the room a man sitting on the sofa close to the fire stood up. For a fleeting moment I thought it was Mason, but as he turned to look at me, I could see he was much younger. There was a strong resemblance. He was the same height and build with a bronzed face and the same blue eyes.

My steps faltered, was this another trick of my fragile memory?

He was not alone. A man of about forty also stood up to greet me. He had nondescript features and I was sure I had never seen him before. He nodded to me as Dr Wells steered me into a wing chair opposite the fire.

I probably looked as insane as they said I was as I just stared at them. I turned to look at the doctor.

"I… I don't know these people. Who are they?"

For a moment she looked stunned then turned and spoke sharply. "I was told…" she began.

"That I was next of kin, yes." The young man spoke up.

"Then I think there's been some mistake." Dorothy took my arm and made to haul me out of the chair. "If this is some kind of joke I'm not amused. Such tricks can set a patient's treatment back weeks."

Hearing that, I grew angry and loosened her grip on my arm. The treatment I was receiving was minimal. All they did was stuff me full of pills. "I want to hear what they have to say." My voice was firm and steady.

Dr Wells let go of me but remained standing behind my chair, leaning on the back. I noticed Bully Boy 1 was hovering just inside the closed door.

The younger man bent down to shake my hand. "Leah, we've not met before but my name is Leo."

For a moment my mind went blank. "Mason's son? But he's in Australia."

He put his head back and laughed. His eyes lacked the hard, angry look I'd seen so often in his father.

"Right now, I'm in a mansion in Oxfordshire and I've come to visit my stepmother."

I pulled away from him. What reason could there be for coming to see me? No one put a mental institution on their holiday itinerary.

"Did your father send you?" I held my breath waiting for his answer.

"My father doesn't know I'm here. He's not even in the country."

"Where…?"

"A lot of people would like to know the answer to that one."

A wave of anger swept over me. "So what are you doing here? Have you come to gloat at the mad stepmother locked away?"

For a moment he said nothing, then, perching on the sofa next to my chair, he took my hands in his. "Leah, I have come to take you home."

"I'm afraid that's not possible," Dr Wells butted in.

The other guest who'd said nothing until now cleared his throat. "We can discuss that."

"There is nothing to discuss. Leah is here for her own good. She is not fit to be out in society, for her own safety and theirs. I will not entertain the notion of her leaving."

The word leave had never sounded so good, but I doubted Dr Wells would cooperate. I remembered stories in books when they took the prisoner out of his cell, invited him to dine well, feel the warmth of the fire, and treated him like a guest before throwing him back into the stinking, rat infested prison.

I was nervous. The young man looked like Mason, said he was his son, but I didn't know either of the visitors and I was a little afraid of them. If my husband was capable of locking me away here, he was capable of setting me free – for what? Murder? Who would know what happened to me if they let me go?

I shivered.

Dr Wells leaned over me. "You don't want to leave, do you Leah? You don't know these men, do you?"

I sat numb and undecided. Of course, I wanted to leave although I knew they couldn't just allow me to walk out of the front door. There would be paperwork to sign, formalities to complete. What was this young man thinking? I was aware that many of Mason's clients were on the shady side. It would be so easy to ask a favour, have one grateful customer send his goons to whisk me off the face of the earth.

Maybe I was being overly dramatic, but my mind was running riot, the result of all those books I read?

Leo took his hands away, reached into his pocket and pulled out a small plastic folder, opened it, and pushed it into my hands.

"Have you seen any of these before?"

There were several photographs, each in its own cellophane sleeve. There was Mason and a younger Belinda and Leo on the beach. Another of them eating what looked like Big Macs at a McDonald's. A Christmas scene in the house I recognised, and several more, the latest about five years ago. They were all at a wedding, the three of them lined up in front of a country church, arms linked together and smiling at the camera.

I looked at him, reassured. But I still couldn't understand what he was doing here and why he had come to see me.

He chuckled at the look on my face. "Leah, I have

lots to explain. Lots to tell you."

"But how did you know I was…?" Who had sent word all the way to Australia, and why should he care anything about a stepmother he'd never even met? Not once had Mason or Belinda ever spoken about him, apart from briefly in the early days when I first met the family.

"Why should you…?" I had all the questions and no answers to any of them.

Leo looked at Doctor Wells. "You have no objection if we take a walk outside? I promise you I will not abduct my stepmother. I have a lot to tell her and it's not for, shall I say, general consumption."

"In other words, none of my business," snapped Dorothy Wells.

"Exactly." For a young man, he must only be in his mid-twenties, Leo had a presence and confidence way beyond his years.

The doctor walked over and whispered to Bully Boy and then turned and nodded.

Leo helped me to my feet and we walked slowly out of the lounge, across the front hall and out into the crisp December air. I gazed at the sun sending weak rays through the fluffy clouds and took in a deep breath. It was the first time I'd been out of doors for almost six weeks. Why they preferred to keep the inmates inside I had no idea. I imagined Bully Boy 1 and Bully Boy 2 chasing after uncooperative patients, trying to round them up like sheep to get them back indoors, and I wanted to laugh.

As we walked down the shallow front steps, one of the carers threw a warm coat over my shoulders and dropped the shoes I'd not seen for weeks at my feet. I leaned on Leo as I put them on.

He said nothing as he guided me along the gravel path, past a dry fountain to a bench. We sat.

"Warm enough?" If I closed my eyes, I could almost hear Mason, except was there a slight Aussie twang to Leo's words?

"It's a long story Leah, but I'll make it as brief as possible. After years in the outback I feel the cold English winters, but I don't intend to talk where that lot might be listening." He nodded towards the house and pulled his scarf around his neck.

I turned to see Dr Wells watching us from the window. I could feel her eyes boring into the back of my neck.

"You know I've been in Australia for several years. Dad and I had a huge row, we've never got on and Mother was already playing away and was seldom at home."

"Personality clash? Your father can be very domineering."

"No, I was used to that. He gave us all a hard time. When I found out the sort of people he was dealing with I wanted to distance myself from it all. I'm no saint, but taking money to get those crooks off and keep them out of jail, I couldn't condone that."

I wondered how Leo found out about the calibre of Mason's clientele, but now was not the time to ask.

"He's hurt a lot of people, Leah. He's a cruel man, what today I guess you'd call a narcissist. He only thinks of himself and has no empathy. I hated him for the way he treated my mother. I'll never, ever forgive him for that. Once we were a happy family, then he broke it up."

That wasn't the story as I understood it. I'd been told that Caro had run off and left Mason. But this was neither the time nor the place to delve further. I stayed on safer ground.

"What brought you back to England?"

"An aeroplane."

We both laughed. It felt strange to laugh again. Not much of a joke but enough to make me smile.

"You also have Deidre to thank," he said.

"Aunt Deidre!"

"Yes, she was worried about you and decided to do a little detective work. And Belinda was also a mine of information."

"Belinda!" Now I was shocked. I sat up and turned to look at him. "But Belinda and I, we have never…"

"She was afraid… but more about that later."

"How did Deidre find you?" Now I was intrigued, had all this been happening while I'd been locked away?

"Let's just stick to basics, Leah. We don't have much time. I'm here to tell you that I'll get you out, just as fast as I can. I've brought Jeff Hastings with me. He's a specialist in mental health and he'll start the ball rolling. We can't take you home today, but we're talking days rather than weeks."

It was all surreal. I pinched myself to make sure I was not dreaming. I was scared this was another trick. A way to prove I was mad. I'd stopped trusting anyone.

"Have you spoken to Andrea? Can she come and visit? I've missed her. She was the only one who listened to me."

"Maybe later." Leo appeared uncomfortable. He stood

up. "It's too cold to talk here. There is so much to tell, but it can wait. The important thing is we get you home."

I nodded and got up to follow him. I looked back over the pristine green lawn, tempted to race across the surface barefoot, feel the grass between my five toes, revel in the freedom to spread my arms, throw my head back and shriek with joy. I restrained myself and shuffled back towards the house. I dare not do any of that, they might take it as a sign of madness. Was I really going to get out of here? It's hard to hold onto reality when all around you people show signs of insanity.

I said goodbye to Leo and Dr Hastings, who'd been in deep discussion with Dorothy Wells. As I stood with her in the doorway and watched them drive away my eyes filled with tears. I felt both elated and very scared at the same time.

I looked at Dr Wells, trying to read her mind, but her face remained impassive, she was giving nothing away.

"Right, back to your room then, or would you prefer the dayroom?"

I shuddered. I had avoided mixing with the other patients as much possible. Not able to relax, never knowing who would start screaming next, or who would attack another patient or one of the carers. It was exhausting, constantly on guard for the slightest movement, watching to see if someone was coming close. It was hard to believe that in this modern day there were places like this.

As I lay back on my bed I went over and over the short conversation with Leo. Still so many unanswered questions, but he believed, and I guess Aunt Deidre did too, that I was not insane. The thought that Belinda liked me was also a puzzle; she had never shown any affection to me, and why did Leo deflect my question about Andrea?

The next few days dragged. I couldn't believe how slowly they passed. I tried to bury myself in a tattered copy of *War and Peace* I found in the library, but it was impossible to concentrate. Everyday images flashed before my eyes, scenes I'd given up hope of ever seeing again; shopping in the high street in the rain, browsing in the clothing stores before having coffee and cake in Ann's Pantry, so many little things we all take for granted until they are taken away from us. Most prisoners can count the days until the end of their incarceration. There, there were no guarantees.

At supper, Charlotte made a beeline for my table. "Hello, my name's Charlotte, who are you? You're new here aren't you?"

"No, I've been here for weeks and I told you my name is Leah."

She looked puzzled then prattled on. "I'm going home soon," she smiled brightly. "I have a little son. His father is looking after him for me, just till I get over this depression. They say it is common for women to feel down after giving birth, did you know that? But I'm much better now and ready to go home."

It took all my willpower not to scream 'Murderer. Forget it. You're never going home. Do you know what you did?' Instead I just nodded and smiled at her.

"Hello, my name is Charlotte what's yours?"

I switched off, hoping she wouldn't turn violent. So

far she'd been passive, but you could never tell. It might have been the look on my face that set her off, for all at once she stood up sending her chair flying, and lunged across the table aiming for my eyes. I leaned too far and I fell backwards as she came around the table to attack me.

For once I was grateful to Bully Boy 1 who raced over and pinned her arms to her sides. She kicked and screamed, fighting like a wild creature. It took three of them to subdue her and pin her splayed out on the floor. A third orderly came running over, hypodermic in one hand. Within moments Charlotte went limp and Bully Boy 1 flung her over one shoulder and carted her out of the canteen.

A staff member pulled me to my feet, my prosthesis at an odd angle where the strap had broken, and helped me back to my room. She took the leg, promising to have it back as quickly as possible. I hopped into my bathroom and threw up in the loo.

Several more days passed and still no word. I was beginning to despair. I could feel myself slipping from hope back into a deep depression.

Yet another day began and still no one came. That morning my hand slipped as I placed another toilet paper ball on the top of the wall and I knocked several of them flying. They fell on top of each other onto the floor of the shower. I scrabbled around, trying to retrieve them but I knocked the tap and the water poured down over me. It was impossible now to separate them and be sure how many there were. I had lost track of time. I burst into tears just as the door opened and Dr Wells stood in the archway to the bathroom watching me crawl, fully dressed, slopping around on the shower floor. More proof that I was insane, just as she suspected.

"They've come for you," was all she said before turning and walking out, leaving my door wide open.

I picked myself up and, peering round the frame, stared at the way out. Like a rabbit caught in the headlights I hesitated. Not once, in all the weeks I'd been here, had I been let out without an escort. It was even a little frightening.

I looked down at my dress, it was soaked through, you could see my underwear, I looked almost naked. I grabbed a towel off the rail and used it to cover as much of myself as possible.

I hobbled out into the hallway to find Dr Wells waiting for the lift.

"I need dry clothes. I can't go anywhere like this."
She sighed. "Wait there."

I sat on the bed and waited. Bully Boy 1 gave a perfunctory knock on the open door and plonked my suitcase down beside me. Without a word he turned and left, closing the door behind him.

I changed as quickly as I could and then realised that I couldn't get out. Bully Boy 1 had closed the door and I was trapped. I broke out in a sweat as I looked through the belongings I'd not seen in weeks.

Time dragged. No one came and I was getting close to panicking. I opened the window as far as it would go but there was no one to shout to. The garden was deserted.

I paced round and round the room, banging on the

door and calling out.

I have no idea how long it was before Dr Wells flung open the door and snapped. "What's taking so long?"

She must have known the answer when she saw the door was closed. I said nothing and, with my case in one hand, I pushed past her and walked to the lift.

"I still think it's a big mistake," she murmured as the lights flashed up on the indicator.

"I was sane when I was brought here and I'm sane now," I replied, "though this place is enough to change that."

"That's so unfair. Have we hurt you in any way, mistreated you? Been unkind?"

She had a point. It was the freedom they denied me and their refusal to admit I was healthy and depressed with good reason. I was one of the lucky ones. Someone out there cared enough to rescue me. I wondered how many were still incarcerated with no one to help them.

Leo and his sister were waiting in the lounge. As soon as she saw me, Belinda rushed over and gave me a bear hug nearly knocking both of us over. I gasped at the onslaught but recovered in time to hug her tightly.

Leo reached over and took my suitcase and together they escorted me outside. I was not even tempted to look back and thank the staff. I'd not even learned the Bully Boys' names and I had no affinity with Dr Wells either. I wanted to forget this place and everything about it.

The nightmare was over.

As we pulled up outside the house I looked to see if it was any different, but no, nothing had changed.

Belinda was treating me like an invalid helping me out of the car and up the front path. I let her, even if I was quite capable.

To my surprise the rooms were clean and tidy and Belinda led me to the armchair in the lounge, plumping up the cushions and helping me sit, before rushing off to make a cup of my favourite coffee.

Leo and I exchanged grins. "She's very keen to make amends," he whispered.

"I have so many questions I don't know where to start."

Belinda hurried in with the tray, she'd even found some of my favourite cakes. She fussed, handing me a plate, a fork and a serviette. I was tempted to ask if she should be in school, but I had no idea what day of the week it was or if she might even be off for the holidays.

"Okay, who's going to tell?" Belinda was eager to get started.

"Maybe you can tell Leah about the first months before all the weird stuff began."

"Sure." She settled herself comfortably on the sofa, nursing her coffee mug. "You probably didn't guess that Daddy never really loved you. He knew who you were before he even met you."

I nearly dropped my plate. Trust the youth to be blunt and honest.

"He met you in the supermarket, right?"

"Yes."

"He'd been stalking you for ages. Well, you know the stuff about how he got you to marry him and all."

"Uh, yes. I do remember that. I was keen on marrying him too, you know."

"Whatever. And he gave you a good time I guess, until he decided it was time for you to go mad."

"Are you sure Belinda? Where do you get all this from?"

"Come on Leah, get real, all that stuff moving around? I'm not blind you know. Then things getting worse and worse. And you were acting strange. I'm no dummy. Even I could see what was happening – well some of it anyway. Once Leo worked it all out, he explained how it was done."

Leo left the room and re-appeared carrying the dreaded blue rabbit. I gasped.

"Where did you find that?"

"This one? In the garage. There are several of them."

"I threw at least one away."

"What you were not aware of is that each one of them is wired."

"I'll get the scissors." Belinda jumped up and brought back the pair from the kitchen.

Leo slit the rabbit open to reveal a small box inside.

"What's that?"

"A voice activated device, like the Amazon Alexa or the Google Assistant. These have been modified though. They record conversations, the controller can listen in…"

"That was Daddy," Belinda butted in.

"Yes, and he could also programme them to send out voices, turn the water and the electricity on and off, play music and various noises, open and close the curtains and so on. Leah, there's the answer to your haunting, enough to drive you mad."

"Wait, that doesn't explain everything."

"All the stuff moved around? And like the armchairs in the garden?"

"Yes, all kinds of things changed places. Pictures, kitchen utensils, my clothes. The rabbit couldn't make those move."

"You're right, there was an accomplice."

"Who?"

For several seconds there was silence.

"I did it the first time. Daddy suggested it might be fun to play a joke on you so I re-arranged all your panties. But afterwards you looked so upset and I felt mean, so I said I wouldn't do it anymore."

"So who was the accomplice? No one else has a key to the house."

"Duh! We all know you keep a spare key outside, under the flower pot. The whole neighbourhood knows that, Leah."

How could I have forgotten something as simple as that? We'd even used it on New Year's Eve to let ourselves in.

"You still haven't told me…"

"It was Andrea."

"No!" I wanted to burst into tears. My best friend, my only friend? How could she?

"Leah, I know this must be a terrible shock. I'm so sorry." Leo stared at the carpet, refusing to meet my eyes.

"It is what it is, I guess." I stood up and began pacing the room, trying to get my thoughts in order. "So, I understand that Mason targeted me even before he met me.

He married me, then had me locked up as mad after messing with my mind."

"Yup, that about sums it up," said Belinda cheerfully.

"But why? Why would he do that?"

"I warned Dad before I walked out that he was dealing with the wrong sort of clients. They had him over a barrel. They paid him well but they were also blackmailing him. He needed money, a lot of money, so he could make a run for it."

I sat down again. This was a situation I'd never imagined. Mason in trouble? Mason, the pillar of the local community, in financial straits? Mason, a member of all the right clubs and societies?"

"But we were never short of money. He never questioned anything I bought, or told me to be careful. No, this doesn't make any sense. Why would he have me locked up? Why not just divorce me if he wanted to get rid of me? If I was a financial burden?"

"He married you for your money, Leah."

"Now I know this is all nonsense. I was broke when I met your father. I lived in a one bed flat and I could barely afford the rent. I couldn't get a job with only one leg. And I most certainly never pretended I had money."

"It's what you didn't know when you married him. One of Mason's clients was a broker who liaised with an insurance company. You were aware that your first husband had taken out a massive life insurance on himself to provide for you and the children?"

"No! No, I didn't know."

"And that's not all," Leo continued, "there was also a

hefty claim against the other driver's car. It was one of those with a manufacturing fault and they had to recall thousands of cars to be modified. The car company was ordered to pay huge damages in the event of a claim and, with the loss of three lives, the sum was large. Add those two together, Leah, and you are a very wealthy woman."

I gasped. "I had no idea! None. No, wait Leo, I would have known about this. They would have found me and paid up."

"Apparently they tried, but the court case dragged on and on and you had moved and, I think, changed your name?"

"Yes, but… My mother knew where I was."

"I can't tell you why, but she refused to say where you were and then she told them she didn't know who you were. Then she said she thought you had gone to join your sister in Canada. They followed up on that but got nowhere."

"Australia."

"What?"

"Daphne's in Australia. It's my brother Martin who is in Canada." I wondered if my mother had been deliberately unhelpful out of spite, or was it the result of her dementia. I'd never know for sure.

"So Leah, we're rich! I mean you're rich. What are you going to do with it all? Can we go on a cruise? Round the Mediterranean, I've always wanted to go on one of those, so cool, and can I bring a friend?"

"Hang on a moment Belinda. If I was Leah, I'm not sure I'd want anything to do with this family." Leo glared at her.

"Where is Mason? You said he's gone? Gone where?"

"We don't know. I did some snooping around and found out he'd purchased tickets for South America, for two."

I sat back down, head in my hands. "Why didn't Mason tell me I had money, or help me claim it? I would have shared it with him."

"If Dad came into a fortune, he would not have shared it with you. Trust me." Leo ran his hand through his short blond hair. "He was outwitted by his senior partner before you were married."

"What do you mean?" It all sounded so bizarre, I was beginning to question my own sanity again. "And what brought you back from Australia?"

"I told you about your Aunt Deidre. She began to look up the rest of Mason's family when you disappeared. You'd promised to keep in regular touch when you came back from Weston-super-Mare."

"And I didn't, no."

"So she travelled down here only to discover that Belinda had no idea where you were and that her father had also disappeared."

"And Leo had only just arrived," Belinda added. "Your aunt is real fun, we went shopping loads! Then Leo began to look for you and found you in that place."

"I'd not been in the house five minutes when I had Neil Soames on the line from Dad's firm. He didn't know where he was either. Told them he was going on a week's trip to see several clients but that was ten days earlier and he'd not phoned in once. Soames admitted to me that he's been unhappy for some time, several years in fact, about the calibre of clients being represented by the company. While everyone has the right to be represented in court, Dad was bending the law in more ways than one to get hardened criminal gang bosses off… wait just a moment."

Leo got up and walked across the hall into Mason's study returning with a folder which he handed to me.

"Do you remember this?"

I opened it and read the first page. "Yes, I think it's the document Neil had me sign before I married Mason. I remember being a little upset at the time as we don't usually have prenuptial contracts in England. If we divorce then all the goods are shared out." I thought back. I'd felt more than a little upset, I was insulted. "He explained to me that in the event of a break up I was not entitled to anything from Mason. I would only be entitled to what I had before the marriage."

"Exactly. But it works both ways."

"But I had nothing. Mason was the wealthy one."

"This is better than an Agatha Christie play!" Belinda enthused, then stopped as Leo frowned at her.

"Soames wasn't convinced you had any money but, like many lawyers, he was cautious. He also knew at the time you met Mason he was heavily into Andrea. In fact, Andrea was one of the reasons Mum left him. It's been going on for years."

"I had no idea." I sat back shocked. "But her house, the gardeners, the home cleaning service, she must be wealthy in her own right."

"Who do you think was paying for all that? True she did get a sum when her husband died in that plane crash, but it wasn't enough to support a lifestyle as good as she wanted."

I tried to clear my head as Belinda went off to make more coffee, drifting back to listen in case she missed anything.

"Wait, there are more questions."

"Fire away."

"I saw Mason with his girlfriend, and I was with Andrea at the time, so it couldn't…"

"It was all staged, Leah. A setup, a girl he hired for the evening, and I found receipts for an extra flight to Paris. Aunt Deidre told me of the torrid time you had there. You were convinced you saw both Andrea and the girlfriend there?"

"Yes, just before I was pushed down the steps at Montmartre and ended up in hospital and lost the baby."

"You were pregnant!" Belinda screeched from the kitchen. "Why didn't you tell me?"

I grinned at her. "We were not exactly on speaking terms, were we?"

"Uh no, guess not." She disappeared into the kitchen again.

"Is that everything?" Leo asked.

"Yes, I think so. No, wait, this counsellor. She was a fake?"

"I can't help you there. I've not been through all of Dad's paperwork yet, but I'll keep an eye open for any receipts. Why would she have been a fake?"

"Part of the elaborate plan to make me question my own sanity and push me further into madness."

I remembered it was Andrea who took me into London to see the play starring the same woman. How much money did I have now if they went to all this trouble to have me committed?

"It would have been easier in the long run for the pair of them to bump me off." I noticed it was getting dark and stood up to close the curtains.

"Worst thing they could have done, for two reasons. First there would have been police intervention and it's hard to get away with murder these days. But the main reason is the insurance monies would only be paid out to you, and then to your next of kin in the event you were sectioned permanently. In the terms of the policy, if you died, they would not pay out."

"I heard Dad grumbling on the phone the night you told him all the tests from the hospital were clear." Belinda popped her head around the corner again. "He sounded right pissed off. Say Leah, you're not preggers now are you?"

"No." I paused. "I don't understand why your father waited over two years before beginning to destroy me?"

"The dog."

"Dog?"

"Zeus." Leo leaned back in his chair. "Even before I walked out Dad was besotted with that dog. He'd never be free to skip off anywhere while the dog was alive."

I'd been right. It had all started the day the dog died.

As I turned to pull the last curtain, I saw movement outside our gate. No, please don't tell me I was imagining things again. Seeing shadows. I began to shake. The fog swirled around me and I froze as the shadow opened the gate and began to walk up the front path. The doorbell echoed in the hallway.

"I'll get it," Belinda raced to open it. "Yes, she's here. Come on in."

Belinda bounced into the lounge and behind her was Bill.

"I've missed you at the library. But I didn't want to leave without saying goodbye."

"Sit down please." I waved to a chair.

"If it's no trouble."

Once he'd settled down and I'd offered him a drink I introduced him to Mason's children before Belinda disappeared upstairs, and Leo went off into the study to continue sifting through his father's paperwork.

"You heard they're closing the library. It was the last day today."

"Yes, and I'm so sorry."

"Life moves on. My condolences on your husband."

"Pardon?"

"It hit the local papers. Local business man goes missing. I presumed he's had an accident of some kind?"

Now was not the time to fill in the details. I shrugged. "Maybe it's for the best. But what are you going to do?"

"They've offered me a position in Weston-super-Mare, to run one of the college libraries. I'm quite looking forward to it. Working with lots of young people."

My heart sank, but only for a moment. Weston, what a great idea! I was a woman of means and I couldn't stay in this house, it wasn't mine. If anything, it belonged to Leo and Belinda. But I could start afresh and, if Belinda wanted to, she could come too. She got on well with Aunt Deidre. The possibilities were endless.

I smiled at Bill. "I don't think we need to say goodbye just yet," I told him. "I'm looking forward to next year."

Belinda peered over the balcony and eavesdropped on the murmured voices from downstairs, and it was only the ring tone from her mobile that sent her into her bedroom, closing the door behind her. She frowned when she saw 'number withheld', but accepted the call. "Dad! Where are you? …. That phone number you left was for Leo! ... No! I could have coped on my own. … I'm sixteen, have you forgotten? … Yeah, she's home. I don't know, there's a guy here called Bill. They're slobbering all over each other. Please, please will you stay in touch? Where are you? … Yeah, I'll stay with Leah, she's not soooo bad … You will phone me? ... When are you coming back?... Tell me where you are, please? …" There was no reply as Mason cut the call and Belinda's tears fell onto the silent phone in her hand.

EPILOGUE

It was a year later when I walked into my favourite coffee shop in Weston and froze. It couldn't be? Was I hallucinating again? What was she doing here?

I walked over and stared at her.

"Andrea? I thought you were somewhere in South America?"

She looked puzzled. "Who told you that? Why would I go to South America?"

I sat down opposite her, my head spinning. "You and Mason…"

"What about Mason? What's he got to do with it?"

I waved to the waitress. She knew what I ordered most mornings. "You and Mason, running off together after locking me up so you could get your hands on my money."

She stared at me, tears appearing in the corner of her eyes. "Leah, I have absolutely no idea what you're talking about. Yes, Mason and I had a fling a long time ago, when he was still with Caro, but that was over before he even met you."

"But Leo said you were…" My mind was spinning.

"I never trusted Leo. He never got on with his father. He was always talking about going to Australia but he never went."

"He didn't go to Australia?"

Nothing made sense.

"Bit difficult since he was locked up at Her Majesty's pleasure."

"Prison!" I shrieked, startling the waitress as she put my coffee and doughnut on the table and raced back to the counter.

Andrea reached over and took my hand. "Leah darling, I don't know the full story. I can only tell you what I know."

"Then tell!" I poured six packets of sugar into my cup without noticing.

Andrea took a deep breath. "The facts as I know them. Mason married Caro, they had Leo and Belinda."

"Hardly news." I couldn't resist the sarcasm.

Andrea traced her fingers across the table cloth. She didn't look at me.

"Mason and I had a fling. One reason we split was Leo's behaviour. He did everything he could to protect his mother. He got in with a bad crowd and got sent down for a couple of years. Drugs mostly, and some robbery with violence or however they describe it in their official reports. But I also got fed up with Mason's bad temper, always criticising, pompous, bit of a narcissist, always putting me down."

I could relate to that. "But Leo, not in Australia?"

"No, here in England."

"And then?"

"Please, believe me Leah, Mason loved you. He probably still loves you. He would never hurt you. He's just a bully. Once he met you, I kept my distance. He didn't like me giving him the push, and I liked you. Heck, you were my best friend and I had no intentions of upsetting your marriage. Mason did tell me he had to disappear for a while, something to do with his dodgy clients."

"So that part was true."

"Who told you what? Leah, you're not making sense."

I sighed, trying to process what I'd believed for months. "I believed that Leo saved me from the mental home, when he came back from Australia. He told me that you and Mason had skipped to South America."

"He was always one for a good story. And you believed him?"

"Of course, why wouldn't I? Mason had gone; you had gone, and Belinda backed him up."

"I always hoped Belinda would stay on the straight. Most likely she believed Leo as well."

"Well she bunked school, and lost her virginity much earlier than I did."

"Darling, everyone loses their virginity earlier than you."

We both laughed and for a moment I saw the old Andrea and I realised how much I'd missed her.

"Where's Belinda now?"

"She's living with Bill and me here in Weston."

"And Leo?"

"I have no idea where he is. He may still be in his father's house for all I know."

"Be wary of him darling, he will have his reasons. Especially reasons for getting you out of that loony bin. He came around to see me after you were taken off, and warned me not to contact you in any way. I'm sure he was holed up in the empty house next door, it's still not sold.

"Okay, it was shit of me as a friend, but he's violent, and I'm a coward. I thought you'd be safe wherever it was they took you. So, I packed my bags and took a long break in Portugal. When I came back you and Belinda had moved and I had no idea where you were."

"Is it true that Mason was paying for your house and all your running costs?"

"Get real kid! That has to be another of Leo's fairy tales. I would never take a penny from him. I pay my own way. Always have."

"Where are you living now? This is one hell of a coincidence seeing you here in Weston." I was suspicious all over again, but then what Andrea said made sense. It would take a lot of technical knowhow to install those electronics and move heavy furniture about. If Mason was innocent, I couldn't even begin to imagine Andrea managing all that by herself.

Andrea looked embarrassed. She flicked crumbs around her plate with her cake fork. "I guess you could call it my conscience? I wanted to see you again. I knew you were friendly with that guy in the library…"

"Bill?"

"Yeah him. So I contacted the library services and came down to see if he knew where you were. I'm pleased you've hooked up with him, he'll treat you better than Mason ever would. I wanted to say I'm sorry I wasn't there for you. And, I wanted to warn you about Leo."

"If things go pear shaped again, I can get by and stay independent."

I reached across the table and squeezed Andrea's hand. "You're forgiven. Friends, we'll always be friends."

"I don't deserve your forgiveness but I'll take it. So tell me, what do you do for fun around here? I'm here for a few days so let's paint the town red."

I had to laugh. Andrea never changed. I refused to worry. I had Bill who made me deliriously happy, Belinda had mellowed, and Leo was hundreds of miles away.

I had my best friend bac k. The future looked bright.

XXX OOO XXX

ABOUT THE AUTHOR

Lucinda E Clarke has been a professional writer for almost 40 years, scripting for both radio and television. She's had numerous articles published in several national magazines, written mayoral speeches and advertisements. She currently writes a monthly column in a local publication in Spain. She once had her own newspaper column, until the newspaper closed down, but says this was not her fault!

Six of her books have been bestsellers in genre on Amazon on both sides of the Atlantic winning several medals and certificates. Lucinda has also received over 20 awards for scripting, directing, concept and producing, and had two educational text books traditionally published. Sadly, these did not make her the fortune she dreamed of to allow her to live in luxury.

Lucinda has also worked on radio – on one occasion with a bayonet at her throat – appeared on television, and met and interviewed some of the world's top leaders.

She set up and ran her own video production company, producing a variety of programmes, from advertisements to corporate and drama documentaries on a vast range of subjects.

In total she has lived in eight different countries, run the 'worst riding school in the world', and cleaned toilets to bring in the money.

When she handled her own divorce, Lucinda made legal history in South Africa.

Now, pretending to be retired, she gives occasional talks and lectures to special interest groups and finds retirement the most exhausting time of her life so far; but says there is still so much to see and do, she is worried she won't have time to fit it all in.

———————————————

© Lucinda E Clarke Spain 2019

TO MY READERS

If you have enjoyed this book, or even if you didn't like it, please take a few minutes to write a review. Reviews are very important to authors and I would certainly value your feedback. Thank you.

Why not sign up for Lucinda's newsletter for special offers, competitions, news on other authors and new releases. http://eepurl.com/cBu4Sf Subscribers get a free book and the exclusive serialized back stories to the Amie series.

Web page: lucindaeclarkeauthor.com
Facebook:
https://www.facebook.com/lucindaeclarke.author
Email: lucindaeclarke@gmail.com
Blog: http://lucindaeclarke.wordpress.com
Twitter: @LucindaEClarke
I love to hear from my readers.

Also by Lucinda E Clarke

Walking over Eggshells

The first autobiography which relates Lucinda's horrendous relationship with her mother and her travels to various countries.

The very Worst Riding School in the World (free)

Who in their right mind would open and run a riding school when they can't ride, are terrified of horses, with no idea of how to care for them and no insurance or capital. Add to that two of the four horses are not fit for the knacker's yard Yes, that would be me.

Truth, Lies and Propaganda

The first of two books explaining how Lucinda 'fell' into writing for a living – her dream since childhood. It began when she was fired from her teaching job, and crashed out in an audition at the South African Broadcasting Corporation. In a quirky turn of fate, she found herself writing a series on how to care for domestic livestock, she knew absolutely nothing about cows, goats and chickens. And it all continued from there.

* * *

More Truth, Lies and Propaganda

Tales of filming in deep rural Africa, meeting a ram with an identity crisis, a house that disappears, the forlorn bushmen and a video starring a very dead rat. You will never believe anything you watch on television ever again.

Amie - African Adventure

A novel set in Africa, which takes Amie from the comfort of her home in England to a small African country. Civil war breaks out and soon she is fighting for her life.

Amie and the Child of Africa

As Amie goes in search of the child she fostered before the civil war broke out, she encounters a terrorist organization with international connections. She is not alone, but one of her friends will betray her.

Amie Stolen Future

In one night, Amie loses everything, her home, her family, her possessions and her name. She has nowhere to turn, but she has no freedom for other people now control her life and if she does not obey them, they will not let her live.

Amie Cut for Life

A look and listen mission turns out to be more sinister as Amie is left to rescue four young girls who are destined for the sex slave trade with a horrifying twist.

Samantha (Amie backstory)

A light comedy as Amie's sister ventures overseas for the first time with her boyfriend Gerry – if it can go wrong, it goes wrong.

Ben (Amie backstory)

Ben's story of his passage into manhood and the beginning of the civil war in Togodo.

Unhappily Ever After

The real truth you've never been told before. In Fairyland, Cinderella is scheming to get a divorce with a good settlement from King Charming, and the other royal marriages are also in dire trouble. This year's ball is approaching, along with a political agitator hell bent on rousing the peasants into revolting against their royal masters.

Reviews

*That Lucinda E Clarke can write and write well is not in question. This memoir left me breathless at times. She writes of her adventures, misadventures and family relationships in an honest but entertaining manner. I wholeheartedly recommend this book, (**Walking over Eggshells**) buy it, delve in and lose a few days, well worth it.*

---

*This book was written with such consummate skill. I have enormous admiration for Lucinda E Clarke as an author. She not only knows how to write an edge-of-the-seat, well-constructed story that would make a brilliant movie – she does it using beautiful, spare, intelligent, and amazingly descriptive language. By the time I got to the end of 'Amie' I felt as though I'd been to Africa – seen it, touched it, smelled it, heard it... loved it and hated it. Everything that is the truth of the country is there in this book. Can I give it six stars please? It deserves it. (**Amie an African Adventure**)*

---

*Lucinda E. Clarke takes the reader on another fast-paced African adventure full of suspense and twists and turns. The characters are so well developed that I felt as if I was watching a movie while reading this wonderful book. Mrs. Clarke both entertains and educates the reader about the African experience. The story never lags and quickly pulls the reader in this new adventure. (**Amie and the Child of Africa**).*

What a great book! I have so enjoyed this and love the tongue-in-cheek, self-deprecating humour with which Lucinda Clarke relates her experiences. It's quite fascinating to read how she becomes involved in writing and broadcasting, and also really interesting to realise how much easier it was to get in touch with decision makers in the days before the digital onslaught. Either that or Lucinda is being overly modest and making it look simple! I loved the descriptions of her early experiences in

Libya - both funny and frightening. And of course, there are lots of memories for me here as I moved to South Africa in the early eighties and always listened to Springbok radio. The style is easy and fluid, and I have enjoyed every page, riveted by the quantity of writing she managed to do without any previous knowledge of the subjects. Amazing. For me, this is the best one of Lucinda's yet in terms of keeping me pasted to my Kindle! I've read two of her other books before, and I'll definitely be reading the sequel to this one! **(Truth, Lies and Propaganda)**

I picked this one up purely on the basis of how much I enjoyed reading the first book and I was not to be disappointed. Lucinda E Clarke is one of those writers who can tell a story effortlessly in a way that just carries you along with her adventures. I have to say she is fast becoming one of my favourite authors. The book revolves around a period of her life as she returns to work in Africa and she uses her natural writing ability to not just recount events but to entertain along the way. Her skill is not in telling extraordinary tales but in making often ordinary real life stories come to life and it is in the smaller details of each story that I often found myself most enthralled. I cannot recommend this book and indeed the previous one highly enough. If your next book purchase is from the pen of Lucinda E Clarke you will have made a wise decision indeed. A thoroughly deserved 5 stars out of 5 from me. **(More, truth Lies and Propaganda)**

The author's imagination and humour are combined to create a story that makes your smile or LOL from beginning to end. It is a rollicking pantomime of dry wit and well-described imagery that works exceptionally well. Highly recommended. **(Unhappily Ever After)**

An excerpt from …
Amie - African Adventure

They came for her soon after the first rays of the sun began to pour over the far distant hills, spilling down the slopes onto the earth below. At first the gentle beams warmed the air, but as the sun rose higher in the sky, it produced a scorching heat, which beat down on the land with relentless energy.

She heard them approach, their footsteps echoing loudly on the bare concrete floors. As the marching feet drew closer, she curled up as small as she could, and tried to breathe slowly to stop her heart racing. No, please, not again, she whispered to herself. She couldn't take much more. What did they want? Would they beat her again? What did they expect her to say?

There was nothing she could tell them she was keeping no secrets. She knew she couldn't take any more pain every little bit of her body ached. How many films had she seen where people were kicked or beaten up?

She'd never understood real pain, the real agony even a single punch could inflict on the body. Now all she wanted was to die, to escape the torture and slide away into oblivion.

The large fat one was the first to appear on the other side of the door. She knew he was important, because the gold braid, medals, ribbons and badges on his uniform told everyone he was a powerful man, a man it would be very dangerous to cross. He was accompanied by three other warders, also in uniform, but with fewer decorations.

They unlocked the old, rusty cell door and the skinny one walked over and dragged her to her feet. He pushed her away from him, swung her round and bound her wrists together behind her back, with a long strip of dirty cotton material. She winced as he pulled roughly on the cloth and then propelled her towards the door. The others stood back as they shoved her into the corridor and up the steps to the ground floor.

She thought they were going to turn left towards the room where they made her sit for hours and hours on a small chair. They'd shouted and screamed at her and got angry when she couldn't answer their questions. This made them angry so they hit her again.

She'd lost track of the time she'd been here was it a few days, or several weeks? As she drifted in and out of consciousness, she had lost all sense of reality. Her former life was a blur, and it was too late to mark the cell walls to record how long they'd kept her imprisoned.

This time, however, they didn't turn left. They turned right at the top of the steps and pulled her down a long corridor towards an opening at the far end. She could see the bright sunlight reflecting off the dirty white walls. For a brief moment, she had a sudden feeling of euphoria. They were going to let her go!

She could hear muffled sounds and shouts from the street outside. It was surreal there were people so close to the prison going about their everyday lives. On the other side of the wall, the early morning suppliers who brought produce in from the surrounding areas were haggling over prices with the market stallholders, shouting and arguing at the tops of their voices. Not one of them was aware of her, of her pain or despair. Even if they *had* known, they wouldn't give her a second thought. Why should they care? She didn't belong here. Only a few years ago she'd never heard of them or their country. The sounds drifting over the wall that were once so foreign had become commonplace, then forgotten, and now remembered. She was aware of the everyday bustle and noise of the market, goats bleating, chickens squawking, children screaming and the babble of voices. But all these sounds could have been a million miles away, for they were way beyond her reach.

Hope flared briefly. Her captors had realized she was innocent. They'd never accused her of anything sensible, and she still didn't know why she'd been arrested. She knew she'd done nothing wrong. Her thoughts ran wild, and she tried to convince herself the nightmare was over at last.

All the doors on either side of the corridor were closed, as they half carried, half dragged her towards the opening in the archway at the end. The closer they got, against all reason, her hopes just grew and grew. They were going to set her free. She was going home.

As they shoved her through the open doorway, she screwed up her eyes against the bright light, and when she opened them, it was to see they were in a bare courtyard, surrounded on three sides by high walls. As she looked around, she could see there was no other exit leading to the outside world.

Then she saw the stake in the ground on the far side, and brutally they dragged her towards it. She thought of trying to resist, but she was too weak, and there was too much pain. It was difficult to walk, so she concentrated on putting one foot in front of the other, determined not to give the soldiers or police or whoever they were, any satisfaction. She would show as much dignity as she could.

The skinny one pushed her against the post, took another long piece of sheeting from his pocket and tied it around her chest, fixing her firmly to the wood. She glanced down at the ground and was horrified to see large brown stains in the dust.

Not freedom; this was the end. She squeezed her eyes shut, determined not to let the tears run down her cheeks, but the sound of marching feet forced her to open them again. She saw four more men, all dressed in brown uniforms, with the all-too-familiar guns who had lined up on the other side of the courtyard opposite her. They were a rough-looking bunch, their uniforms were ill fitting and stained, and their boots were unpolished and covered in dust.

She was trembling all over. She didn't know whether to

keep her eyes open to see what was going on, or close them and pretend this was all a terrible dream. She was torn. Part of her wanted it all to end now, but still a part of her wanted to scream, 'let me live! Please, please let me live!'

The big fat man barked commands and she heard the sounds of guns being broken open as he walked to each of them handing out ammunition, then with the safety catches off, they shuffled into position.

To her horror, she felt a warm trickle of liquid running down the inside of her thighs. At this very last moment, she had lost both her control and her dignity. They had not even offered her a blindfold, so she closed her eyes again and tried to remember happier times, before the nightmare started. Briefly, she glanced up at the few fluffy white clouds floating high in the sky as the order to fire was given.

-/-/-/-/-

www.ingramcontent.com/pod-product-compliance
Lightning Source LLC
LaVergne TN
LVHW042352190726
843493LV00005B/979